❧ The Maharajah's Monkey ☙

Natasha Narayan was born in India but emigrated to England at the age of five. She has had many jobs in journalism including working as a war correspondent in Bosnia. Like Kit Salter, Natasha loves travelling and exploring new places. She hopes to get to see some of the far flung deserts and mountains of her heroine – even if it's by bus rather than camel and yak. She lives in Oxford.

A Kit Salter Adventure

The Maharajah's Monkey

Natasha Narayan

Quercus

First published in Great Britain in 2010 by

Quercus
21 Bloomsbury Square
London
WC1A 2NS

A CIP catalogue reference for this book is available
from the British Library

ISBN 978 1 84724 529 8

10 9 8 7 6 5 4 3 2

Designed and typeset by Rook Books, London
Printed and bound in Great Britain by Clays Ltd, St Ives plc

The Maharajah's Monkey

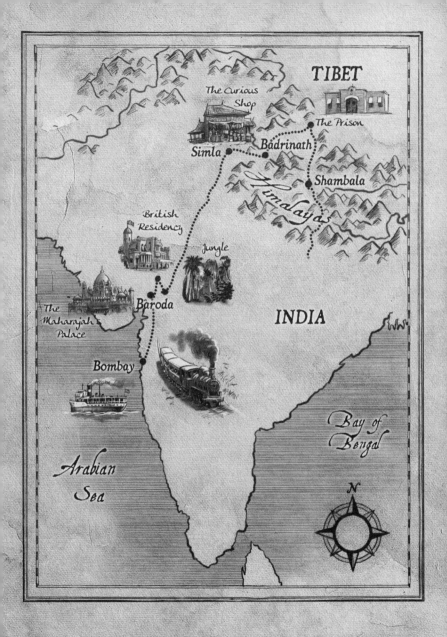

❦ Part One ❧

❧ Chapter One ❧

'Measles.'

'Tomatoes.'

'Radish.'

'"Your lips are rosier than any radish",' Waldo said, in a pompous voice. 'Hmm. Not bad at all. Go on, Kit. Put it in the letter.'

'A rotten radish,' Isaac added, grinning.

'Hush,' I hissed. 'Some of us are trying to concentrate.'

My friends clustered around, pelting me with suggestions, as I forged a love letter to my governess. I kept half an eye on the schoolroom door as I worked. This thrilling note was just the sort of thing a tall dark stranger might dash off, a figure from one of those romantic novels my governess devoured under her bedclothes. I could imagine him clasping Miss Minchin in his arms, while covering her upturned face in burning kisses. My governess would be wearing a trailing organdie gown and, for once in her life, a smile!

If only he existed.

If only I, Kit Salter, could bring the character I had dreamt up to life! He might even offer to marry my governess, freeing the four of us from endless lessons and even more endless nagging.

'Miss Celestina Minchin, your skin is whiter than a lily, your eyes are bluer than a periwinkle, your lips redder than a –'

My pen had come to a halt. Obviously Miss Minchin's lips were not redder than a radish, that was hardly romantic. I needed inspiration. How to describe them? To tell the truth, they weren't exactly lovely. Usually they were snapping at me or pursed in a grimace. Not the kind of lips to inspire love letters.

'If you don't like measles or tomatoes,' said Waldo, in a sulky voice, for he always loves to take charge. 'How about blood! The Minchin's lips glisten like a pool of fresh blood!'

'I'm not trying to give her nightmares,' I explained gently. 'It's meant to be a love letter. I know. I'll compare her lips to a rose.'

'Boring!' they chorused.

'Some roses are pink,' Isaac added. 'A kind of horrible peachy colour like a baby's bottom.'

Meanwhile my best friend Rachel sat apart from the rest of us, arms folded in disapproval. She glared at me, her brown eyes trying to pierce my conscience. I knew she disapproved of the joke, for you see, Rachel cares. She is always considerate of other people's feelings. But I ignored both her looks and my conscience. If I listened to that pair of killjoys I would never have any fun.

'We're running out of time, Isaac,' I urged. 'The Minchin will be here any minute.' Taking up my pen again I continued in the same dashing handwriting.

'Your lips are redder than the reddest rose. You are celestial indeed, Miss Celestina . . .'

'What does "celestial" mean?' Waldo interrupted, peering over my shoulder.

'Heavenly,' I snapped. 'It's a joke. A pun on her name, Celestina.'

'Not a very good one.'

I ignored him, for what does Waldo know about puns? Quickly I scrawled:

You shine brighter than the Morning Star. I would be in heaven at just one glance from your eyes. My dear lady, I implore you, meet me at the entrance to the Ashmolean Museum on the stroke of ten this morning and I will pluck up the courage to offer my heart.

Your secret and devoted admirer.
Sir X

PS No insult to your reputation is intended. You may bring a chaperone if it pleases you.

I had no fear that my governess, the Minchin, would recognise the handwriting. Forget embroidery and the piano, one of my finest accomplishments is the ability to disguise my hand. I have forged sick notes from my papa and grocery bills from our housekeeper. I thrust the note in the envelope and sealed it, hurriedly placing it on her desk and scurrying back to my place. Just in time, for I heard the sharp clack of my governess's heels on the steps outside as she swept in with a flurry of crinoline.

'Good morning, my little lambkins,' she greeted us, as if we were babes in the nursery. She paused and looked at me. 'Are you quite all right, Kathleen? You look uncommonly flushed this morning.'

I frowned, annoyed that, as usual, she called me Kathleen. My name is Kit, pure and simple, Kit Salter. No one else calls me by the girlish name of Kathleen, so why does she persist in it? Rachel could lecture all she liked. Quite frankly the Minchin deserved to be taken down a peg or two.

'I have a twinge of indigestion this morning, Miss Minchin,' I muttered.

She stared at me suspiciously. 'You haven't been *banting*, have you?'

'Certainly not,' I replied. 'Only nincompoops bant! Starving yourself just to be thin! Just to be able to fit into some silly old corset! Giving up puddings and chocolate cake and ices and caramels and –'

'And those delicious chocolate tiffins they sell at Bunter's cake shop,' Isaac added helpfully.

'And sherry trifle,' I continued. 'I just love sherry trifle and –'

'That's enough,' Minchin snapped, a hungry look in her eyes. 'I would have you know I bant myself; very occasionally, of course. Purely a question of health, you understand, I have no vain interest in being slim. If your digestion is really upset, may I recommend Beecham's Powders? They have certainly helped me. Now. To work.'

Clacking and whooshing around the schoolroom like a starving ghoul, the Minchin distributed our grammars and workbooks. It was only when she returned to her desk that she noticed the lavender envelope lying on her desk. Glancing up from my work, I watched her open it. As she read the message, she flushed, as the anonymous writer of her love note would put it, 'redder than the reddest rose'. The flush started in her cheeks and travelled down her neck, till in truth, she did look like a tomato. Or a measle. She half rose from her chair and then subsided down again. Her lips trembled. I looked at Waldo. His eyes were shining, as were Isaac's, but Rachel turned a troubled face towards me.

'Children, I find I have an urgent communication to

attend to,' the Minchin said, rising unsteadily from her seat. 'I have just this minute received a note from the . . . my . . . um . . . aunt.'

'Nothing serious I trust?' I said, in my most concerned voice.

'Not at all,' she replied, too quickly. 'Well – at least, one hopes not. She has a weak heart. One cannot be too careful. Pray continue with your work.'

With that the Minchin swept out. To my surprise she didn't go downstairs, but up, towards her bedroom.

'Send her our very best wishes!' Waldo called after her, before turning to us. 'That woman could lie for the Empire,' he said admiringly.

Well, it served the Minchin right. She always treated me as if I were a bad smell. Even worse was her habit of trying to mould me into a polite young lady, like a lump of common clay.

'The Minchin's gone up to her bedroom. She's seen through the trick,' I added.

'Hold your horses,' Waldo said, talking like the American cowboy he is at heart. 'She'll be back in the saddle.'

He was right. A little later we saw the Minchin tripping down the stairs, though she was far too preoccupied to notice us. My, what a transformation, though hardly for the better! Her hair was done up in a bun from which she'd teased little tendrils of hair to cascade down her scraggy and powdered cheeks. Two patches of what I suspected were beetroot juice stood out like spots of fever against the white cheekbones. Her frame was squeezed into the tightest corset possible, under a rose damask tea dress. She looked like a girl going to her first ball, until you noticed the set, almost desperate, gleam in her eyes.

'I don't think it's very kind to mock Miss Minchin like this,' Rachel said quietly, as we watched her clack unsteadily downstairs.

'Why ever not?' I demanded. Underneath my bluster, though, I was a little disturbed. It was only a joke and there had been such a glitter in the Minchin's eyes.

'Miss Minchin is nearly thirty years old.'

'Why should I care?'

'At her age she is unlikely ever to get married.'

'So what? *I* don't want to get married. Not *ever*. Aunt Hilda isn't married and she has a fabulous time.'

'Miss Minchin hasn't the money to go exploring, Kit.'

I was silent for a moment, as I realised that lack of money might mean taking on an unpleasant job. Like being a governess to me. Then I rallied. I simply could not give in to Rachel's preaching:

'Why does everyone talk of marriage as if it is the only thing a girl can do? It just means exchanging the orders of a father for those of a husband.'

'When did your father ever order you around?' Rachel asked, raising her eyebrows in mock astonishment. 'You're the only person who gives orders around here. Apart from your Aunt Hilda, of course.' But I'd had enough of Rachel. Ignoring her I called out to my real friends.

'Come on, Waldo and Isaac, let's go to the Randolph Hotel.'

'What for?' Waldo asked.

'Don't you remember? Aunt Hilda and Gaston Champlon are announcing their new trip. The formation of the first Anglo–French Exploration Partnership. They might be going to Africa or even Outer Mongolia. There's bound to be newspapermen and everything, a terrific fuss!'

The others followed me, Rachel dragging her heels as usual. Why was I lumbered with such a goody-two-shoes best friend? Rachel needs no lessons in kindness, but what had happened to her sense of fun? Can't a person have a joke now and then? Did she always have to look at me as if I were a particularly thoughtless slug? My mind was whirling with resentment against my friend as we thundered down the stairs, but I suddenly drew up short.

Two burly strangers were lounging outside the drawing room. The faces were burnt raw and they wore army uniforms. They brought a whiff of heat and dust into our home. Where could they have come from?

'Hello, miss,' one of the men greeted me.

'Who are you?'

'We're with the Memsahib,' he replied. I was puzzled for a moment, till I remembered memsahib was the name for the British ladies who helped rule our Empire in India.

I heard my father's voice through the door, calling out to me. I went in to the drawing room and there he was, Dr Theodore Salter, perched on the sofa in his oldest trousers and a moth-eaten jacket. Opposite him was a skinny lady, with prominent eyes and a neck like a camel. Clearly the Memsahib. I couldn't keep my eyes off her neck. When she talked, her Adam's apple rolled up and down like a restless cricket ball. Slumped next to the lady was an angelic boy, with shoulder-length hair – shining golden curls – framing a pale face.

'Who are those men outside?' I burst out as I rushed into the room.

'Our protectors!' the skinny lady replied, raising her eyes to heaven.

'Pardon?'

'Our lives are threatened. We are guarded by the Crown's soldiers day and night.'

'Kit,' my father put in. 'This is Mrs Spragg. She is recently returned from India with her son Edwin.'

'My husband is the Resident – that means Queen Victoria's personal representative, you know – in Baroda, India,' Mrs Spragg informed us. 'Poor dear Edwin suffers so much with the heat and the mosquitoes we've decided to educate him here in Oxford.'

My mind boggling, for I couldn't imagine why this woman needed to be guarded, I glanced at Edwin. He was sallow as a bowl of whey, in his velvet sailor suit and looked as if he had never been out in the sunshine in his life, never mind the heat of India. I *instantly* decided Edwin was a drip. I hoped he would not be joining us for lessons. Just our luck to be foisted with someone even less fun than Rachel.

'Darling Edwin is so advanced. Such a marvellous little prodigy. You know, Professor Salter, he learnt to read when he was just four years old!' Mrs Spragg said to my father.

Papa, who was probably reading Latin in the womb, didn't respond.

'As you can imagine, we all realised that we had someone really special on our hands.'

'Why?' asked Papa, who is sometimes very slow on the uptake. Without bothering to reply, Mrs Spragg, world authority on Edwin, went droning on.

'You never saw such a reader as Edwin. My, how he devours his books. He can read a whole book in an evening. Not childish amusements such as story books, any more. At the moment he's in the middle of that historian. What's his name? Thomas Carlyle. Such an elegant writer, Edwin always says!'

'Do you not find Carlyle a little emotional?' my father asked the boy, interested.

Darling Edwin mumbled a reply, which I could not hear.

'I must say I favour Gibbon,' my father went on. 'By the way, do you want a macaroon?'

Papa held out a tray of the treats. Cook makes them especially well, with plenty of sugar and soft, flaked coconut. Edwin reached out his hand greedily, but Mrs Spragg snatched the tray away.

'Edwin couldn't possibly,' she gasped. 'His digestion is so delicate, you understand. Just a little of the wrong thing leads to the unmentionables.'

'Why unmentionable?' Papa, who was being more than usually slow, asked the boy, who replied with relish:

'Looks like hot chocolate.'

'Pardon?'

'Diarrhoea.'

Mrs Spragg hurried on, talking loudly over their voices: 'Of course after all the trouble in India we couldn't leave

Edwin in that heathen country a moment longer. I won't stand for violence! His health is so delicate it would be –'

'What violence?' I interrupted, aware that my friends were hovering, restless to be away.

'Didn't you hear about it? The Maharajah of Baroda, that wicked man, he tried to poison my husband! He invited us all to the palace for tiffin. The bearers brought out the cakes and sherbet, a lovely spread. But the rotter had put arsenic, diamond dust and copper in my husband's lemon sherbet. A wicked concoction.'

'How dreadful,' I gasped.

'That isn't the worst of it. Poor dear Edwin took the cup laced with arsenic, he nearly died! He lay on the floor, foam coming out of his mouth!'

They didn't need arsenic to kill Edwin, I thought, glancing over at the pale boy on the sofa. A puff of wind would do it.

'What happened to him?' I asked.

'Edwin took weeks to recover and I fear still –'

'I don't mean Edwin,' I interrupted. This woman could talk of nothing but her son. 'The Maharajah, the poisoner – what was his name?'

'Malharrao? I'm convinced he is a madman. Well the British arrested him, of course. He was charged with attempted murder. He was brought to England by steamer to stand trial. But the horrifying thing is –' she stopped dramatically.

'Yes?' I prompted.

'On arrival at Liverpool, Malharrao was put in Walton Gaol.'

'A fearsome place,' my father said. 'Impossible to break out of.'

'But *he* did. He simply walked out of his cell – it was found by the warder with the door swinging open, empty!'

'Extraordinary,' I breathed. 'But how did he escape?'

'It is a complete mystery. But one thing is for sure –' she paused dramatically.

'What?' I asked.

'He must have had outside help.'

'Perhaps he was a lockpick,' I said. 'There are people like that – think of the great escapologist John Nevil Maskelyne.'

'Absolutely impossible,' Mrs Spragg insisted. 'No, there is the stench of corruption about this case! The gaol authorities found a single gold sovereign under his bunk. The gaolers must have been bribed. There is money at the back of this. *Someone* with money – someone who could pull strings wanted the Maharajah out of that gaol.' Mrs Spragg glanced around warily, as if even here there might be spies, listening. 'We've been warned that Malharrao might come after us. That is why we have to be so very careful with Edwin.'

Edwin shivered and Mrs Spragg moved protectively closer to him. I felt a rush of sympathy for Edwin and his mother – and chided myself for judging them so fast. It is one of my greatest faults – making judgements on people I hardly know. How frightening to be pursued by this mad Maharajah.

I wanted to hear more, for it was an intriguing tale but Isaac was tugging my arm. My friends were impatient, if we didn't go we might miss the fun at the Randolph. We said our goodbyes and were leaving when Rachel burst into screams. How she screamed! Such shrieking must have roused the whole house. I rushed over to her. She was clutching her neck, where I could see a large red mark, the kind a particularly vicious wasp or a snake might make.

A wasp? In February?

Something was glinting on the floor, I bent down and picked it up. A tiny thing, no bigger than the tip of a sewing needle. It shone in my palm and I stared at it uncomprehendingly. What on earth was it? A fragment broken from the housemaid's pins? A sting from a strange wasp? Was this the thing that had caused Rachel's wound?

'THIS WILL NOT DO.' Mrs Spragg sprang up from the sofa and raged at Rachel. 'You'll UPSET poor Edwin.

His nerves cannot stand hysterical behaviour.' She turned to my father. 'Professor Salter, unless you can control your pupils we cannot have Edwin join you.'

'As you wish,' Father said mildly.

I stared at the thing in my palm and in flash I understood. Tiny and deadly, it was the dart from some strange oriental blowpipe. Just as I realised this I caught Edwin's eye. He was smirking at me quite openly, as his mother raged at Rachel for scaring her poor delicate boy. Edwin must have picked up the blowpipe from India. Perhaps from one of the native bazaars. Mrs Spragg's angel had just attacked my best friend.

Sometimes you should trust your first impression. Here I was berating myself for being too hasty to judge people – when I was right to dislike Edwin. There was a wicked imp under that angelic exterior. Well, this time he had picked the wrong person to play tricks on. If we had not been late for Aunt Hilda's conference I would have taken my revenge there and then.

As we left I scowled at the boy. He caught my eye and a glance of perfect understanding flashed between us. We were at war! And this golden-haired poppet was thirsting for the battle. I'll pay you back for this, Edwin, I promised myself, just you wait and see.

ᔕ Chapter Two ᔕ

'I need my eyesight tested,' Waldo sniggered as we made our way through the throng at the Randolph Hotel. His eyes were fixed on my aunt and he was grinning away unpleasantly. 'I'm seeing things.'

'Spectacles would bring out the colour of your eyes,' I replied, in mock sympathy, knowing that my friend was far too vain to consider them.

'Your aunt. She looks almost . . . handsome!' he snickered. 'Like a man in fancy dress.'

I scanned Aunt Hilda, dominating her audience from the heights of a massive podium. At first glance she looked like her usual self, a cross between some sturdy heathen statue and a good old British bulldog. At second glance there was something odd. Was that a bow in her hair? This wasn't right. She was wearing a lilac gown with a pretty white lace collar. Too pretty! The lace frothed and tumbled over her dress in a waterfall of feminine frills. I would never wear such a collar. What on earth was my aunt doing in it? Where were her famous check waistcoats? Those pantaloons that confused small children into thinking she was a man?

My gruff, mannish aunt – the woman who had forced the fearsome Tartars of Omsk into giving up the jew-elled diadem by sheer willpower – was dressed like the Minchin. Like a flighty young lady dolled up to impress her beau. What on earth was going on?

Then a thought struck me. Champlon. The French explorer must have coaxed my aunt into dressing up like a Gallic poodle. There was definitely something Parisian in the cut of her lilac gown. Monsieur Gaston Champlon was a great dandy, with his waxed moustache, Malacca canes and embroidered sateen waistcoats. Now he'd turned my aunt into an advertisement for the fashions of the Champs Élysées. Why, together, Hilda Salter and Monsieur Gaston Champlon would make a most ridicu-lous pair of adventurers!

Ignoring Waldo, I settled myself on to a bench. Unfortunately, I knocked into a man in an awful tartan jacket, who scowled at me. Then Waldo stamped on my foot, making me wince in pain.

'Watch out, you clumsy oaf!' I snapped, turning on him.

'What have I done?' Waldo replied, good-humouredly, but I was still upset with his remarks about my aunt.

'You stood on my foot. I'm a girl not a Turkey carpet!'

'Oh, you're a girl, are you? I didn't realise.' His blue eyes tried to gaze into mine, but I looked away. 'If you're a girl,' Waldo went on, 'why don't you behave like one?'

'What, you mean preen and simper and drop my handkerchief,' I retorted. 'No thanks!'

'No one said anything about simpering. Just try and –'

'You'll never be satisfied till I ask your permission every time I want to sneeze!'

In our irritation both of us had raised our voices. I noticed the man in the tartan jacket, a perfect stranger, smirking at our tiff. The man winked at Waldo, as if to signal that girls will be girls. To my astonishment my so-called friend winked right back. This was too much. I turned round, presenting both the eavesdropper and Waldo, with my back. Pretending to be indifferent, I admired the room. I had never been to this new hotel before and was impressed by the gilt mouldings on the ceiling, the huge plate-glass windows, the chandeliers dripping with glittering crystals. The Randolph was certainly a very modern place, with wonderful views down St Giles of Oxford's ancient soot-coloured colleges. While I was musing thus, I noticed a man, a groom from the look of his coat, scurry up to Aunt Hilda. She pulled out her watch and consulted the time, then with increasing agitation looked down at notes in front of her. Something was wrong.

I shouldered my way through the crowd to my aunt. She was barking at the groom who'd brought her the message.

'Is everything all right?' I asked.

My aunt turned to me, distraught. 'It's a catastrophe, Kit.'

'What is?'

'The conference was meant to start half an hour ago. Well, I thought Gaston was merely delayed but Jinks here informs me that his horse has gone. There is no sign of him! He's vanished! You realise what this means?'

'He may have just been called away,' I tried to soothe.

'Poppycock. Monsieur Champlon has played the foulest trick on me.'

'You can't know that, Aunt Hilda.'

'It is as clear as daylight. Gaston Champlon has run out on me, the cowardly cur. I went along with everything, just to please him! He persuaded me into this foolish dress for starters.' Her hands plucked at the ruffles on her bodice. '*This* is how he repays my trust. This is . . . is too, too awful. For *me*, Hilda Salter, to be humiliated like this, now, in front of everyone.' Aunt Hilda was no longer bothering to keep her voice low and I saw some of the people in the front row were plainly listening. 'GASTON HAS JILTED ME.'

I wanted to point out to Aunt Hilda that she had

been about to form a new Anglo–French exploring team, not become Mrs Champlon. But one look at her face and wiser counsel prevailed. Leaning over the podium I reached out for her. I was surprised, and touched, to feel her hand quivering in mine. Suddenly she felt vulnerable.

'Please, remember your dignity, Aunt Hilda,' I murmured gently. 'People are staring. You don't want this to end up in the newspapers.'

It was the right thing to say. Her hand stiffened inside mine and a stubborn look came into her eyes: 'Certainly not!' she growled. 'I will let no man . . . No Frenchman humiliate me!'

'You must make an announcement,' I went on. 'Think of some excuse.'

She nodded, composing herself. I could see the effort in the lines of strain that stood out on her neck. I left her and hurriedly made my way back through the crowd. Pointedly I ignored my friends' surprised looks. Usually I would have included them in my plans, but today I felt like working alone. As I left the room my aunt had risen and was delivering a speech, hardly a tremble in her bassoon of a voice. With typical bravado she made no mention of the missing Champlon, but forged right into her glorious vision for exploring the Himalayas, the greatest unconquered mountain range in the world. Hilda Salter was going to venture to the roof of the world!

Mid-morning and Magdalen Street was relatively quiet. A few people gave me suspicious glances as I ran pell-mell past the golden stones of the new museum: the Ashmolean. I knew my father had organised rooms for Champlon in Jericho at Worcester College. It was a stroke of luck, for I was firm friends with the porter, a man named Simpson. I had fond memories of playing as an infant in the sunlit college grounds.

Simpson was dozing in the Porter's Lodge, almost hidden behind a haze of pipe smoke. When I rapped on the window he woke with a start.

'Bit early for a nap, isn't it?' I asked cheekily. Behind him the clock showed it was ten.

'You've forgotten your old friends, Miss Kit. What is it? A month since you came to see me? Too grand you are, now you're a fine young lady.'

'I'll never be a fine lady, Simpson,' I retorted. 'Even if I wanted to, it'd be impossible to forget you – the lectures you've given me! How is the gout?'

One of the drawbacks of a college porter's job is the amount of fine port and food he is allowed to consume. Simpson paid dearly for his rich diet in shaky knees and chronic indigestion. Indeed, I feared that the college would soon retire him.

'Me stomach hurts something dreadful. Feels like I've

a bunch of eels in there, it does.'

'You must come round to Park Town. Cook's herbal remedies can cure anything,' I replied and then, the courtesies over, got to the point. 'Simpson, I've come on an errand for Monsieur Champlon. I need to get into his rooms.'

'Right at the back of the college, up three flights of stairs. Me knees won't stand it.'

'Can I have the keys?'

'You're up to some sort of mischief, Miss Kit. I can see it in your eyes,' he grumbled, but nevertheless he trudged over to the key board and retrieved a set for me. I took the time to thank him though I was burning to be off. I could feel in my bones that there was some sort of mystery about Champlon's disappearance. Speed was of the essence.

My heart pounding, I raced up the dim and narrow stairwell to Champlon's rooms – 3B on the third landing. The key was a hefty brass affair, which looked as though it had been made in the Middle Ages. It was almost impossible to turn in the lock, and I was just about to give up when, with a rending groan, the levers clicked into position and the door creaked open to reveal a large study. The walls were panelled with ancient oak and on them hung a number of rugby cups and rowing trophies that I guessed must belong to the student occupant of the room. I could see no sign of Champlon. The room's usual inhabitant struck me as a hearty sort of person who played a lot of sport and didn't trouble himself too much with his lessons. Indeed there wasn't a single book in the study. Then I saw the open door to the bedroom.

Here there was plentiful evidence of the Frenchman in the rows and rows of dandified suits, the lines of polished shoes. There were remarkable quantities of eau de toilette, gold-plated razors, ebony hair- and shaving-brushes on the dressing table. One of the scent bottles was uncorked; I took a sniff and recoiled in disgust. It was sickly sweet, a combination of musk and jasmine which instantly called Champlon to mind. I knew the Frenchman carried a miniature silver bottle of this awful scent stuff around, I'd seen him take it out and dab some on his wrists. What looked like a brand-new full-length mirror had been hung up by the dressing table, probably so that Champlon could check that his attire was faultless. Everything was neatly hung up or lovingly folded and packed away. These were treasured possessions. I found it hard to believe that if the Frenchman had fled, he would have left his beloved things behind.

I sat down on the bed and studied the room, the conviction growing in me that Gaston Champlon hadn't, as my aunt believed, disappeared of his own free will. Something had happened to him. I was guessing it was something sinister, because he was just as excited as Aunt Hilda about their new venture. If their Himalayan expedition was a success, both Aunt Hilda and Champlon stood to make a fortune, not to mention write their names in the history books. There was no way Champlon would have just left Aunt Hilda in the lurch. However, this room was so perfect, so spotlessly clean and tidy it wasn't going to give me any clues.

Or was it?

I shivered in the chill breeze that was blowing through the window. How could I have not noticed before? On a freezing winter's day the window had been violently thrust upwards – and when I came closer it was clear that a pane of glass, now half-hidden by another glass pane, had been smashed. Blending in with the rich reds and browns of the Turkey rug below the window, a series of small muddy marks arrested my eyes. I bent down and examined them. They could have been bare footprints, but if so they were made by the smallest of children – no bigger than a five year old. The marks were curiously splayed out, with occasional indentations that must have been made by toenails. Remarkably long toenails.

The marks could, I guessed, have been made by a young thief, who had smashed the window to gain entrance to Champlon's bedroom. But what a nimble thief! How was it possible to have climbed three storeys up a sheer stone wall?

I leant out of the window. Down below I could make out the cultivated greenery of the college gardens, the glint of boats on the canal and the untamed spaces of Port Meadow beyond. What I had assumed was a sheer stone wall, was, in fact, old and crumbling. Plenty of places where an enterprising urchin might grab on to jutting stones. But what made it even more likely that someone had climbed up these walls was the rampant Virginia creeper. The gnarled roots of the flourishing shrub that covered the Worcester College's walls were thick enough to support the weight of a child, I was sure of it.

I was glad Rachel was not here. Not to mention my father and all the other people in my life, lining up to tell me how reckless I was. Biting my lip, I eased myself over the window sill. Moving with extreme caution I found a foothold in the creeper. Then a handhold and then, so carefully, down I went. You might think I had taken a foolish risk. Believe me, I knew what I was doing. I have always enjoyed climbing trees, but this time I was not scrumping for apples. If I lost my hold and fell, or the creeper broke, I would be dashed to pieces on the flag-stones eighty feet below.

Halfway down the creeper, I became convinced that

someone else had made this perilous descent, and very recently too. Fronds of the Virginia creeper were displaced and broken and many of her leaves flattened. Some twenty foot above the ground I saw something white poking out of the creeper's foliage, just past my hand. Straining, I reached out for it and retrieved the thing – a slip of cloth. It was only when I had safely reached the bottom that I examined the cloth. It was a handkerchief, a dainty piece, of the finest white linen. Embroidered in the corner was a monogram of curling letters: G C. Gaston Champlon.

I couldn't help crying out in triumph, causing a student in white cricket flannels who was strolling over the lawn with his nose in a book to look up in surprise. Luckily whatever he was reading was more interesting than a girl climbing the creeper, for he gave me but a glance. So, I thought, Gaston must have climbed down this creeper. Or, at the very least, someone who had stolen his handkerchief.

The slip of fabric clutched tightly in my hands, I fell down to the ground. The passage of human beings must have left *some* marks. Nothing, of course, in the flowerbeds under the walls except clods of earth and some withered, wintry stumps of plants. But on the frost-dusted lawn two sets of footprints were visible. The urchin's strange twig-like tracks and, following them, at a run by the look of the smudged marks, a set of adult prints. The feet were hurrying away from the college towards the edge of the garden and the canal.

In hot pursuit, I set out after them.

❧ Chapter Three ❧

Panting, I reached the canal and scanned the ground to the left and right. Nothing! I could have screamed in frustration. I knew they must have come this way. The footprints were perfectly clear. Yet as soon as the tracks reached the path they disappeared. To my right was the ancient stone of Worcester College and to my left the Eagle Ironworks and Lucy's factory, belching smoke. The pair of them could have gone either way – into town past the colleges, or to the industries of Jericho. There was simply no way to tell. For a moment I wished I hadn't set off on my mission in such a bad temper with my friends. If Rachel, Isaac and Waldo were here, we could split up into two teams, each of us trying to follow the tracks of the missing Frenchman.

I was a little downcast as I watched the sunlight sparkling on the canal. The banks were fresh with rag-wort and lilies, the ducks hibernating under reeds to keep warm through the chill of winter. Then my eye was arrested by a clump of vivid colour just before the bridge. It was a knot of working barges, moored by the canal side. Of course! These canals were arteries of trade, horse-drawn boats taking coals to the mills of Manchester and returning with all manner of pottery and goods. Some people are nervous of the bargees and call them filthy, thieving rascals, little better than Gypsies. The Minchin, for example, would always take a detour if she saw a canal boat coming. Well, I have always liked boat-people and have never listened to such talk. When I was younger, I used to play with a girl called Rose Nell Coxon, whose family lived on a horse-drawn coal barge. Every few weeks the barge used to come into Oxford and she would scurry up to Worcester College to see me. Of course the bargees were dirty, you would be too if you had to live on a thirty-foot boat, thick with coal dust and crammed with ten of your brothers and sisters. There was nowhere to wash on the barges except the canal, and nobody fancied a dip in those foul waters.

Rose Nell was as good a friend as I've ever had.

If I was not mistaken, a figure was watching me from the nearest barge. I hastened towards it and saw that it was a massive woman, wearing layers of thick smocks, her hair wrapped in a strip of dirty cloth. She had paused in her work, a steaming copper bowl of suds lay on the deck at her feet. Her eyes were suspicious, giving no indication that she would welcome a talk with me, but I persevered nonetheless.

'Hello,' I called out politely. 'I wonder if you might help me with something.'

''Pends what yer askin',' the woman replied, making no movement towards me. From where I stood on the bank I had to shout to make myself heard.

'I'm looking for someone. A man with a large moustache, a dapper little fellow.'

Something glinted in the woman's eyes and involuntarily she glanced to the side. She knew something, I could have sworn it.

'I mean you no harm,' I said, trying to speak softly and respectfully. 'Please, help me. I am a friend of the Coxons.'

The woman's face softened. Abandoning her washing she came towards me and I could see that she moved with a limp.

'Tragedy what 'appened to Pete,' she muttered.

I nodded, sympathetically. Rose's father had an accident at work – he was killed by a swinging iron wheel and the whole family had left the boats to live somewhere up north.

'I was a particular friend of Rose,' I said. 'Have you any word of her?'

The woman shook her head and all the while I had

the feeling she was examining me, seeing if I would pass her test. I must have done so, for she said, 'I feel half naked I do, just let me go inside and get decent. Me name's Peg, by the by.'

With these words, Peg turned her back to me and limped towards the cabin, entering her home by a small painted door, which she had to stoop to get through. I was surprised that Peg felt she had to change her clothes to talk to me. In a minute she reappeared and all became clear. Her worn smocks and grubby headscarf remained the same, but she was hoisting her skirts and I could see that her left leg was made of wood.

'Peg Leg, that's what they call me,' Peg said grinning. 'Got the finest left leg on the ole canals, I do. Anyway, dear, what's it you wanted to know?'

I described Champlon in detail, trying to curb my impatience, for I couldn't help feeling that time was passing. When I came to a stop, Peg looked at me in silence for a minute, a speculative glint in her eye:

'Whassit you want, I wonder?' she asked, finally.

'I just need to find the Frenchman,' I replied. 'He's a friend of my aunt's and he has disappeared and left her in the lurch.'

'Jilted 'er, has he? That's what you get from trusting yer heart to one of 'em Frogs.'

'You've got it wrong,' I protested, but Peg Leg was

already continuing:

'I don't hold with foreigners, I don't. Give me decent English folk any day.'

Of course I should have held my tongue but the silliness of Peg's comments annoyed me. I mean you can't chose not to *hold* with everyone outside England. Like it or not they simply *exist*.

'I'll wager you don't know any foreigners,' I protested.

''Course I do,' she replied indignantly. 'Gorn up and down these canals, I 'ave. I'm a woman of the world. Come to that they even 'ave 'em in Oxford – an Indian in that barge yonder. A real sight 'e was.'

'An Indian?' I asked, wondering, because it sounded most unlikely to have an Indian on the canal.

'Great strapping fellow 'e was, always wore a bit of yellow cloth wound round his 'ead. Looked like a big tea cosy it did.'

'It's called a turban,' I replied. 'I believe Indians wear them to protect their head from the sun. It is burning hot in the deserts of India.'

'Well it's not 'ot 'ere,' Peg remarked, casting her eyes to the heavens. A grey light was coming down from the sky on to the bright boats. It looked to rain or snow. A land of sunshine seemed very far away. 'A right nincompoop he looked, goin' round like a giant teapot.'

All this talk of Indians was very interesting but it was a distraction from my search for Champlon. I had to focus, for I felt sure Peg knew something of the Frenchman. 'Have you seen anyone like the man with moustaches that I described,' I pressed Peg.

'Lor' girl, can't yer listen when I tell yer? That's what I'm tryin' to say. Them foreigners stick together. Frenchie was on the Indian's boat. I seen them on the deck, arguin' loudly. Shouting and screaming at each other, they were. Then they went inside. I lost sight of 'em, I did. Anyway I 'ad to get on wiv me work. Can't stand around all day, I can't. I can tell you one fing, I never seen such a lot of strange folk.'

'When? When did all this happen?'

She shrugged, a massive rolling motion in her vast shoulders: ''Bout two hours ago.'

'Which one?' I asked urgently. 'Which barge does the Indian live on?'

Peg pointed one out to me, a few boats down. It had a strange name – the *Oudalali* –and was painted in eye-popping shades of turquoise and lime.

'Thanks so much, Peg,' I called, hastening to move down the banks to the *Oudalali*. But the boat-woman called me back.

'Yer too late!'

I halted.

'Ye won't 'ave any luck,' she said. 'They've scarpered. The whole lot of 'em 'ave cleared out.'

'What do you mean?'

'A carriage came for 'em. It took 'em, Frenchman, Indian, them two other gents, bags and baggage and all. I'll bet yer we've seen the last of 'em. The Indian and 'is rascally goblin.'

I stared at Peg confounded. 'What do you mean *goblin*?' I asked. 'Do you mean he had a dwarf?'

'Worse than that. 'E had a bleedin' monkey!'

Things were coming together in my head. Those claw-like tracks leading from Champlon's room to the river. Not made by some urchin at all, but by something far stranger. Something that could scale walls and dart through small openings with no problem.

A monkey!

❧ Chapter Four ❧

'A monkey,' I stuttered. 'Are you sure?'

'I am.'

'There aren't any monkeys in Oxford.'

'I knows what I saw.'

'But what was it doing here?'

'Thieving,' Peg snapped. 'He'd steal the knickers from under yer bottom, beg your pardon, young lady.'

I was glad the Minchin wasn't here. She would have fainted at the word 'bottom'.

'There wasn't anyfing that monkey wouldn't nick. Not nothing. When he looked at yer, with them beady eyes, grinning away, he looked wicked through and through.'

A thieving monkey. I had no time to lose. Thanking

Peg Leg for her information I hurried to the *Oudalali*. The boat was moored to the bank with a strong chain, the windows covered with check curtains and the cabin door firmly closed. It looked deserted. It was a simple matter to climb aboard. I was met with an odd sight. The deck was littered with rubbish; piles of twigs and leaves made into nests, bits of bright paper and scraps of material. I tried the door and to my surprise it opened.

At first glance the interior was typical of a canal barge. Panelled wood walls, a fold-down table and bunk. Gleaming pots and kettles. I've been inside many barges and I can tell you that they are usually cleaner than you would think, with cooking things, clothes, ornaments – all the meagre possessions of a bargee – scrupulously tidied away. But this place was something very different. It looked as if it had been owned by a mad magpie. Vessels and possessions were flung hither and thither. Piles of shredded cloth and paper littered everything.

It looked as though a hurricane had torn through the barge. Or there had been a vicious fight.

A heap of multi-coloured rags in the corner caught my eye. They were as higgledy-piggledy as the rest of the place, though seemingly of finer quality. I moved closer and knelt down to take a good look. Yes, I was right. Pieces of ripped velvet – rippling midnight blue – and fine lace were among this pile. Not what you would expect to find in a simple barge. I picked idly through the shredded stuff wonderingly . . . Then most unexpectedly my fingers felt something cold and hard buried deep. I clasped the thing and drew it out. It glistened, even in the gloom of the barge. I walked over to the window and looked at it in the watery light. Made of a dull metal, it was inlaid with bluish chips, which I recognised as lapis lazuli.

What could it be? A broken bit of jewellery? The handle of an antique teapot? I looked closer at the thing – and gasped. Most definitely, I recognised the engraving on the metal. This was a hieroglyph. An eye of Horus – also called a Wadjet eye . . . Could it really be? No, I told myself, it was simply too strange. But the more I stared at the curving piece of metal, the more I became sure. Yes, it was, it must be . . .

This was part of an ancient ankh, or Egyptian cross, the pharaoh's symbol of life.

This adventure was becoming stranger by the minute. What kind of man keeps broken ankhs in a heap of rubbish? For that matter, how could someone forget such a fine thing, a fragment though it was. But then, perhaps it had simply chipped off the ancient cross and thus been overlooked. You see, I already read the clues. The lack of clothes and luggage in this place confirmed Peg's story. The Indian had cleared out.

Carefully I wrapped the ankh piece, if that was what it was, in a rag that I found on the floor and popped it in my pocket. I would show it to the others. But before I hurried back to my friends, I needed to question Peg Leg a little further. I had the feeling that barge woman knew more than she was letting on.

'Where have you been?' Waldo demanded suspiciously. It was forty-five minutes later and the meeting in the Randolph was just winding to a close. Most of the press and audience had left but my friends were drooping by the door. Waldo and Rachel, in particular, are always complaining how bossy I am but it is interesting how aimless they become without me to take charge.

'Nowhere in particular,' I said airily.

'You've been up to something,' grumbled Waldo.

'The usual.'

'I know that smile. What's the big secret?'

'Have it your own way!' I paused a moment, just to tease. 'Actually, some rather interesting things have been *happening*.'

'I knew it,' Waldo groaned as the others burbled

about it 'not being fair'.

While they were moaning about the injustice of Kit Salter having all the adventures, I drew the slip of lace out of my pocket and unwrapping it, held out the fragment to my friends. In a shaft of light from the Randolph's chandeliers it gleamed mysteriously.

'What now? You've become a cracksman?' Waldo said, greedily plucking the fragment out of my palm, while I ignored his jibe. Obviously I do not shin up drainpipes to steal people's treasures.

He held the metal up to the light and we all stared, entranced. I marvelled that I could have thought, even for a moment, that it was worthless. This was a piece of a rare and beautiful antique.

Waldo suddenly let out a peal of laughter. 'We'll be rich,' he chortled.

'Less of the "we",' I said sharply. 'I found it.'

'Where exactly did you find this, Kit?' Rachel demanded.

'Why?' I asked, stalling for time.

'Don't you ever read the newspaper?'

We followed Rachel to the hotel's lobby where she picked up a copy of *The Times* from a table. Next to a headline reading: ANCIENT MAP TO 'EARTHLY PARADISE' DISCOVERED IN INDIA, was the following report:

Famous Lady Explorer Amelia Edwards robbed

Treasures were Gifted to the Crown Queen Victoria 'Unamused'

There was shock yesterday at the news of a robbery of Egyptian treasure belonging to the renowned lady explorer, Amelia Edwards. The robbery took place in a warehouse in the Egyptian capital, Cairo, where Miss Edwards was storing her collection, as she waited for it to be shipped back to England.

Guards were alerted by flickering lights in the warehouse and the noise of crates being moved. They intercepted the robbers, and shots were fired before the thieves made off.

When the treasures arrived in England, Miss Edwards found that some of her most precious treasures were missing. These included a scarab dating back to the reign of Thutmose II, a sarcophagus inlaid with gems and gold and a rare and beautiful ankh from the first dynasty.

'I am terribly upset,' Miss Edwards told our reporter. 'I was planning to give the ankh personally to Queen Victoria and the sarcophagus to the British Museum.'

'Yikes!' I gasped breaking off, for my eye had caught the drawing of the ankh below the news report. 'It's the same one.'

'I know.' Rachel nodded. 'I recognised it as soon as I saw the cross.'

The pieces of the puzzle were, if not exactly coming together, at least starting to form some sort of picture. But goodness, it was a confusing one. Champlon's disappearance. The man with the turban. Now Miss Edwards's ankh. I felt the strong pull of distant shores behind all this: Egypt . . . India. Which one was it? Swaying palm trees and burning deserts? Or Maharajahs and priceless jewels? In some muffled way these lands of heat and spice were calling to me. My pulse quickened with excitement.

'Kit, you can't have . . . er . . . just . . . *found* part of Amelia Edwards's stolen ankh.' Rachel looked at me pointedly.

'That's exactly what I did,' I said, grinning.

'How?'

'I've a pretty good idea of some, well, not person exactly. No, some *thing*, that is mixed up in it.'

'Spit it out then.' Waldo scowled.

'Hold on. We should be getting home. We don't want the Minchin to make it back before us.'

'You're just pretending,' Waldo muttered.

As we made our way through St Giles to our home in Park Town I filled my friends in on my adventure. Waldo was annoyed to have missed the fun, though he was forced to agree that the monkey was mixed up in the theft of the ankh. Rachel was all for going to the police straight away, but I had other concerns: I explained what I'd learnt from Peg Leg about the hansom cab that had taken the Indian, a seemingly willing Gaston Champlon and several mysterious trunks away.

We had urgent work to do, if we were to find out why Champlon had been kidnapped. You see, I didn't believe Peg's description of Champlon walking happily to the cab, I was certain that the Frenchman had not left my aunt of his own volition. Someone was coercing him. The mysterious Indian must be blackmailing him.

I was walking with my friends past the ancient sweep of St John's College, when I had an interesting notion about the identity of the Indian in the canal barge. Was my idea likely? Could I have stumbled on something important? Suddenly a low whistle from Isaac drew me up short. A lady was leaning against the stone walls, her shoulders heaving, her face mostly hidden by hair. She pushed a strand away and I realised the woman was Miss Minchin. She had been crying. Her face was all crumpled, her eyes reddened. Her hands were playing convulsively with something, a scrunched-up piece of paper, which I recognised with a pang of dismay as my forged love letter. She was completely oblivious to the stares of passers-by, lost in her own unhappiness.

'Not so clever now, are you?' a voice behind me murmured.

'I know, I know,' I said fiercely, to pre-empt a lecture from Rachel. 'I shouldn't have written it.'

My friend's face expressed exactly what she thought. The others were also looking accusingly at me as if it was all my fault, when Isaac and Waldo had goaded me on so. Anger boiled inside me. It was a joke, a joke. At the same time my stomach felt hollow and I had an unaccountable impulse to burst into tears. I'm sorry, I'm sorry, I'm sorry, I wanted to howl but I was silent and I could feel that my face was sullen.

Why was it always me in the wrong? Why couldn't Rachel be nasty or insensitive for a change?

Rachel's burning eyes made my insides feel watery.

'I'll go over to her,' I said, my voice wavering a little. 'I'll confess. Tell her I'm sorry.'

Rachel shook her head.

'No. That'll just make things worse,' she said. 'I'll see Miss Minchin back. Be off! Home! Now!' With that Rachel glided over to the wall. We saw her put her hand on Miss Minchin's arm and our governess look up, bewildered.

I began the walk home. The two boys dawdled, avoiding my eyes and whispering. I didn't care anyway, I told myself. But in truth I felt awful. Who would guess that Miss Minchin would take a silly prank so to heart? We went past the colleges on to the broad sweep of road which marks the beginning of our suburb. Still my friends hung away from me, as if I had a contagious disease. Part of me paid no heed; if they wanted to shun me now, so be it. Then suddenly I snapped, and a wave of rage washed over me.

This disaster was their fault, just as much as mine. I hadn't wanted to make Miss Minchin cry.

Finally outside our villa in Park Town I could bear it no longer. I turned around and walked savagely up to them. They were standing close together, wearing the same serious expression.

'What?' I demanded hotly.

Waldo shrugged.

'You egged me on!'

'I never –' Waldo began but Isaac laid a hand on his arm.

'All right,' Isaac said calmly. 'We're all responsible. We're all thoughtless. What we have to work out is how to make it right.'

'I'll apologise of course,' I muttered. 'Tell her it was a joke.'

Waldo shook his head. 'That won't help.'

'We've another plan,' Isaac added.

'What?'

'We, and especially you, Kit, are going to have to be extra nice to Miss Minchin.'

I nodded.

'It gets worse,' Isaac said, and he was not smiling. 'You'll have to make it up to her. There's only one way you can really do it.'

'What's that?'

'You'll have to find Miss Minchin a husband.'

'I hope you're joking. How can I find her a husband?'

'Evidently, it is what she needs,' Waldo said, firmly. 'The rest of us will help you. But you are going to find her a husband. We've already got one idea – your father.'

I stared at him, aghast. The very idea was impossible. Having to call the Minchin 'Dear Mama'. Seeing her sickly face every morning for the rest of my life over the ham and eggs. I am sorry but I was willing to live with any amount of guilt rather than that. Anyway I could not see poor Papa married to anyone who did not share his interest in ancient Aramaic and the preservation of parchments. Truth to tell, I could not see him married *at all*.

'No,' I said.

'Why not?' Waldo said. 'Your father is a widower. He's

lonely, Miss Minchin is lonely. They'd be perfect together.'

'Lonely? Whatever gave you the idea my father is lonely? He has *me.*'

Waldo exchanged glances with Isaac: 'That's what I meant,' Isaac murmured.

'And he has his books!' I said, hotly.

Now they were looking at me. Wearing their holier-than-thou-faces. As if I belonged to a different – more selfish – species of human being.

I felt sick.

'*You* marry Miss Minchin if you're so keen,' I snapped.

'I'm too young,' Isaac protested hurriedly, quickening his pace up the stairs.

'I tell you, she marries Father over my dead body.'

'We might have to murder you then,' Waldo replied. He wasn't smiling and for a moment I wasn't sure if he was joking.

❧ Chapter Five ❧

Opening the front door, I stumbled and fell, banging my knee upon the edge of a trunk. I groaned and looked around in bewilderment. Piles of luggage were strewn all over the hall, battered portmanteaux with rusty hinges and the labels of exotic destinations from Morocco to New York, leather handbags and carpet bags and bashed-about dressing cases and goodness knows what else. A foreign wind was blowing through our home. Our hallway looked less like an ordinary Oxford residence than some dusty way station in the African savannah.

'At once, Theo! I want it done yesterday!' my aunt's voice boomed and she swept into the hall, my father tagging behind her. Her frilly frock was gone, instead she was dressed in travelling clothes: serviceable tweed skirt and jacket, along with stout boots. Father was talking in so low a voice. I couldn't make out what he was saying, but from the nervous expression on his face, the gist was clear. He was pleading with Aunt Hilda. Begging her not to do something. But from the expression on my aunt's pug face she wasn't having any of it.

'Here's Kit and her pack of hangers-on,' Aunt Hilda said, spotting us. 'Well, my dear, I'm off. Going to take the train down to Portsmouth and away to India, on the boat tomorrow morning.'

'Pardon?' I stared at her. India again! It was becoming positively uncanny how strong the signs were pointing east.

'Are you a nitwit, girl? Can you not understand plain speaking?'

'But you haven't got the provisions for your expedition. You haven't even got a ticket!'

'Such trifles have never bothered Hilda Salter.'

'But, Aunt. How are you going to –'

'If you think I'm going to let Champlon steal all my best ideas and then rush to India before me, think again,' she interrupted. 'The rotter was stringing me along, Kit. Playing me like a blooming pianoforte. All that flattery, saying mauve really brought out my complexion,' she stopped abruptly, her hurt plainly showing on her face.

'It does,' I lied, gently.

'What?'

'Mauve does suit you.'

'Piffle. The man was using me. And I, Hilda Salter, Pride of the Zambezi, the only woman to ever conquer the North-Western Frontier, fell for it.'

I put my hand on Aunt Hilda's arm and gently drew her into the living room. Unhelpfully, father followed us. Though she was chuntering away in the familiar Hilda Salter style, underneath she was unusually unsure. I could feel it in the way she let me guide her. I propelled her to a comfortable armchair and almost pushed her down into it. She needed to hear what I had to say.

'I've something to tell you, Aunt Hilda, something about Monsieur Champlon.'

'Get to the point, girl.'

'I've got to ask you something first. What makes you think Champlon has gone to India?'

'He was seen. At the station with some Indian *thug* he has hired. He directed all the luggage to be sent to Portsmouth, for the *Himalaya*. It's a P & O steamer sailing for Bombay tomorrow.'

It was my turn to stare: 'It can't be true!'

'He gave the order himself. My groom happened to be at the station and saw him. Directed the porters to handle the trunks and supervise them on to the *Himalaya*. I know all about her. A fine steamer with the latest twin-cylinder engine. As sleek a boat as any in the Empire, blast it!'

'Language, Hilda,' my father tutted, while I reeled at her words.

All my certainties were collapsing around me. I'd been so sure Champlon was being blackmailed – or had been kidnapped by the strange Indian. But here was the Frenchman, by all accounts, ordering the luggage to be taken to India. It very much looked like he was in command of the whole operation and the man in the turban and the monkey, his minions. It didn't make sense. Why would Champlon desert my aunt? What did he have to gain by this strange behaviour?

I told my aunt my news, the strange story of the monkey and the stolen piece of the ankh. She gasped at the sight of the ankh fragment.

'I've seen that somewhere before,' she mused, gazing at the ancient metal.

'We think it was stolen from Amelia Edwards . . . you know, the famous explorer.'

'Poppycock.' My aunt's face set at the mention of her rival. 'That woman's no explorer. Tourist is a more accurate description.'

With that she turned her back on me and rang for the maid. With much muttering about how Champlon was clearly a thief as well as 'a bolter!', she ordered the girl to fetch the police. Sometimes I cannot follow my aunt's thinking. How could she blame Champlon for the theft of Miss Edward's treasure? The ankh fragment had been found on the barge, not in his rooms. But then again, it did look as though he'd bolted. Perhaps he had been using my aunt, discovering all her secrets, milking all her wealthy patrons and then leaving her slap-bang in the lurch. Perhaps he really was a member of a gang that stole antiquities. If so – and I really wasn't sure either way – what a villain the man was!

But I had made up my mind about something. 'I'm coming to India with you, Aunt Hilda,' I announced.

For the first time a smile crossed my aunt's face. 'Very well,' she said. 'S'pose you might be some help.'

I held out my hand to hers and we shook on it. In the background I heard spluttering. It was Father: his face red, his woolly hair in agitated disarray. He appeared to be dancing from foot to foot.

'Absolutely not, Kit,' he squealed. 'The dangers: cholera, typhoid, the heat, bandits.'

'I'm going, Father.'

'No. I must insist on this. There's is no way you are going to India. You will stay here and continue your studies with Miss Minchin.'

'Papa, do not be under any illusions. I'm going to India.'

'India is no place for a young lady.' My father halted and looked at me His eyes were pleading, soft with emotion. 'Dear Kit, please understand. You are the most precious thing in the world to me.'

Embarrassed, I tried to make a joke of it: 'More precious than your library?'

'What?'

'Your books,' I explained 'Do you really love me more than your books.'

'Yes, certainly.'

I laid a hand on his arm: 'Listen to me, Father. I am not being stubborn. *I love adventures.*'

'You know I never insist on anything,' he pleaded. 'This time I must. No father would let their child sail into danger.'

'Papa.'

'Do not attempt to tug my heartstrings, Kit,' he muttered as the bell rang and we heard the tramp of boots in the hall. The police had arrived to collect the stolen piece of ankh.

'Hilda will sail alone. You are most definitely staying behind.'

❧ Part Two ❧

✦ Chapter Six ✦

'JAM!' someone barked.

A lady in a saucer-shaped sun hat loomed over us as we reclined on the steamship *Himalaya*'s prom deck, deep in the latest books. Before either Isaac or I had time to react, she snatched away our novels. What on earth was the woman talking about and why, come to think of it, was she wearing a sola topi? True it was burning hot, for we were in the tropics now, but there wasn't a speck of sun anywhere in the gloomy sky.

'Pardon?' I gulped.

'You have jam on your chin,' a familiar voice admonished me. Squinting upwards, I saw my persecutor was Mrs Spragg, the mother of the dreadful Edwin.

'What does the state of my chin have to do with you?' I protested.

'Cleanliness is next to godliness.'

'I don't think Jesus spent his whole time washing his face.'

'Insolent girl,' she hissed. 'Remember you are no longer just Kathleen Salter.'

'What?'

'Don't say "What", say "I beg your pardon". As an Englishwoman Abroad you have a duty to represent the Whole of British Womanhood to the Empire,' she pronounced, thrusting a handkerchief into my hand. With that she stalked away, in the direction of the first-class cabins. Taking our books with her!

'It's a plot,' I muttered, for the books she had stolen were thrilling penny dreadfuls. 'She wants something exciting to read.'

Isaac groaned and turned over in his deck chair. It was a shame because it had taken a lot of persuasion to get him up here. He had spent all five weeks of our journey so far holed up in his cabin, moaning that the sea air was killing him. It was true a rash had spread over his face which made his skin look rather like a cooked chicken. But still, talk about making a fuss!

'Pull yourself together, Isaac,' I said. 'Why don't you do some inventing? Something to cure Miss Minchin would be a godsend.' For our governess was a fellow sufferer from seasickness.

'I'm done with inventing,' he moaned melodramatically. 'I will never invent anything, ever again!'

If you have ever contemplated a steamer voyage to

India, I beg you, do not. Your *idea* of the long journey to Bombay and the *reality* are, I am sure, very different. You may imagine a riot of shipboard entertainments: bowling and croquet in the afternoons, dances and theatricals in the evening, glittering saloons and bracing walks on deck with the captain. Most of all you may imagine sumptuous meals in the first-class dining rooms, with twinkling chandeliers and a menu that does *not* feature salt beef and more salt beef.

Pray do not get carried away!

In reality, life aboard the *Himalaya* was the last word in dullness. All the bores in England seemed to have flocked to our ship, the ladies being far worse than the men. I have never, ever, met such a stuffy, interfering lot. They would no sooner spot me than they would start spouting lectures. My insufficiently brushed hair, my dirty fingernails, my unladylike dresses, my forthright manner, my shabby shoes. There was almost nothing about Kit Salter that found favour with these memsahibs, the wives of tea planters and junior officials of our government in India. As far as they were concerned, I would let down the whole British Raj.

It almost made me long for the times when I only had Miss Minchin to nag me.

Before I go any further you may be wondering how I came to be aboard ship at all. Hadn't Father specifically forbidden it? Well, it may not surprise you that poor Papa, confronted by the combined forces of Aunt Hilda and myself, gave way and consented to our voyage. In fact, it turned out he was keen to travel to India himself, for he had heard of a remarkable archaeological discovery he wanted to track down. So my friends and I sailed east, for it was not hard to persuade Rachel and Isaac's absent-minded guardian and Waldo's spiritually inclined mother. Indeed Waldo's mother began to trot out all sorts of romantic mumbo-jumbo on hearing of our trip, including the hope that her son would find 'enlightenment' in India.

Frankly, I was dying to reach Bombay. Dark clouds were looming over the horizon and the waters were choppy. It looked like we were in for some bad weather. Leaning over the upper deck watching the waves, I spotted a bowls game below in the third-class deck. I made my way down, when the worst of the busybodies, Mrs Spragg, appeared. Clearly, she had pursued me to the lower deck.

'Quite out of the question,' she declared loudly. Behind her I spotted the whey-faced figure of her son Edwin and behind him their inevitable guards. It seemed there was no school or tutor in the whole of England good enough for darling Edwin, so Mrs Spragg had decided to take him back to India with her.

'Pardon?' I stammered, unable to believe my bad luck. To be caught twice by Memsahib Spragg in one morning!

'My dear Kathleen, you simply cannot mix with those on the lower deck. You are in danger of meeting steerage passengers and common sailors.'

'That's hardly a danger.'

'*What?*' she spluttered, forgetting her manners.

'I am merely going to play bowls.'

'With *them*?' Mrs Spragg asked, looking through her silver-rimmed lorgnette at the crowd enjoying the game. By this memsahib's lights they were a common lot, in threadbare clothes with rough manners. I thought they were far better company than the ladies and gentlemen on top deck.

'The young lady is a dab hand at the bowls,' a weather-beaten old salt who had overheard us declared. 'She's got a good eye and a steady hand.'

'This is scandalous,' declared Mrs Spragg, shaking her lorgnette at the sailor. 'If Miss Salter behaves like this in our cantonment in Baroda she will be cut dead! No one will receive her socially.'

'Not pukka,' Edwin said, with a sly glance at me.

'Pardon?' I asked, puzzled.

'Not the done thing.'

'My dear Kathleen, as you have no mother, it is up to

me to provide moral and social guidance.' Grasping me roughly by the arm Mrs Spragg drew me away from the bowls game. 'You must learn some decorum.'

I bit down the rebellious words I wanted to spit at Mrs Spragg, as I tried to wriggle out of her grasp. A moment later something hard hit me in the shin, causing me to topple over. It was Edwin, who had sent a bowls ball rolling straight for me.

'I do beg your pardon, Miss Salter,' Edwin smirked, offering his hand to me. 'I don't believe I know my own strength.'

I glared at the boy, knowing he had done it on purpose. Ignoring his outstretched hand, I rose. I could bear it no longer; I had to flee from the combined Spragg forces. It was especially irritating as I had a particular reason for going down to the lower deck. We had been aboard the *Himalaya* for weeks without a sight of Gaston Champlon, the strange turban-wearing Indian or the monkey.

That Indian. As I mused on him, a sort of foreboding took hold of me. I am an instinctive creature. My mind flies about making connections. Sometimes, even if I say so myself, they are spot-on. Sometimes my guesses are, well, wrong. But this time, I felt so *sure*.

This shadowy Indian. The missing evil Maharajah of Baroda. Somehow they were linked. Maybe the mysterious Indian was the Maharajah. Maybe he had kidnapped Champlon for some dreadful reason of his own. Or maybe the turbaned Indian was someone hired by Malharrao.

My aunt, who I had counted on being my ally and teasing out my thinking with me, was strangely listless. Like Miss Minchin, who had spent the whole voyage being seasick, she'd mislaid her spine. She hadn't even made a serious effort to find Champlon aboard ship – or plan what we would do once we reached India. Frankly, she was mooning about like a lovesick waif. Once she told me she believed the Frenchman had found passage on another ship. But I was not so confident. For a start there were no other ships sailing from Liverpool docks to India at the same time as the *Himalaya*. Furthermore, had not Aunt Hilda's groom heard Champlon order their luggage to be sent on to the *Himalaya*? It didn't make sense that he had suddenly decamped, sought a passage on another ship. They had no reason to believe that we were following them.

No. I believed that Champlon and the Indian were far removed from the gracious first-class world of dining-, drawing- and ballroom. I believed they were hiding among the dirt of the steerage passengers. That was why it was vital that I should make friends down there. So I could really search the ship.

But clearly today there were far too many busybodies on the warpath. I decided to return to my cabin. I shared a tiny space, equipped with three fold-down bunks, with Rachel and the Minchin. Sharing with Rachel was fun, but as you may imagine it was rather more difficult with my governess.

I opened the door, letting in a shaft of sunlight which cut through the cabin's stale air and gloom, only to be met with a groan.

'Is that you, Kathleen?' a feeble voice inquired.

'Yes.'

'Please shut the door immediately, my eyes can't bear the light.'

With that, the Minchin sank back on to her pile of pillows, eyelashes fluttering in her white, mute face. Beside her bunk – which was obviously the most comfortable in the crammed room – stood a tin bucket. With a sinking heart I saw my governess had been seasick again. The porthole window showed dark sky and boiling waves. We had been lucky to have got a port-side cabin, which are meant to be far more comfortable than those on the starboard side. I felt a surge of impatience with the Minchin. *Why* couldn't she pull herself together and get up? Immediately though, I felt guilty. Ever since the affair of the love letter I had been *trying* to be nice to her. Besides, she did look very sick, poor thing.

'Is there anything I can get you? A little beef tea? I can call for the steward.'

'No. Nothing,' she groaned. 'Last time I had beef tea it was cold and there were spots of grease floating on top. I was indisposed twice afterwards.'

'Indisposed?'

'I vomited, Kathleen.'

I shuddered. Still, if I stayed in the cabin I would be seasick too, so hastily I decided to brave the memsahibs outside. At least the air was clean on deck. As I emerged I ran into Waldo. Literally, I am afraid, for I banged smack into his chest.

'Whoa!' he roared, as if I was a mettlesome pony. 'Where are you going to in such a hurry, little girl?'

'What are you doing hanging about my cabin, little man?' I retorted. 'Can't you get along for five minutes without me?'

'You're late for luncheon.'

'I didn't hear the bugle.'

'You need to get your ears washed then.'

I followed Waldo to the dining saloon. The room was already filled up, most of the seats at the two long tables crowded with the chattering throng. One of the most eligible bachelors on the voyage, a Mr Charles Prinsep, who was rumoured to be the younger son of a baronet, was sitting at one of the tables. He was a nice young man, with wavy brown hair, a snub nose and a toothy smile. I thought him daft but Rachel said he was a good sport and tended to blush when he was around. Clustered around him were the 'Fishing Fleet'. No, not sportsmen, but well-bred young ladies shipped out to the colonies to find husbands among the British soldiers and government men who ran our Raj – our Empire in India.

The ones who failed to hook their gentlemen-fish went sadly home to England in the spring and were known as the 'Returned Empties'.

I slipped into a vacant chair only to have Mrs Spragg and the inevitable Edwin took the seats next to me. The woman could not let me alone. Thank goodness my aunt, father and friends were also at the table. The one person on ship Mrs Spragg was scared of was Aunt Hilda.

After grace was said, menu cards were passed around the table. I do not know why they bothered with the cards, for the choice was between braised and broiled salt beef. Since we left the Cape of Good Hope in Africa, supplies of fresh food had run low. It was days since we had seen such a luxury as a fresh tomato or a green bean. It was a huge relief that we were finally nearing Bombay, due to reach the Indian city in a day or two, I was told. Apart from all else, I was truly glad that I was going to

India. You see, it is the land of the sacred cow – where it is forbidden to eat beef. Personally I never want to swallow the stuff, in any shape or form, ever again.

Indeed I might even become one of those eccentrics they call 'vegetarians'. I would forswear all meat – except sausages, ham and steak and kidney pudding.

Gritting my teeth I went to work on the leathery beef, which was only slightly improved by mustard. Mrs Spragg meanwhile was rambling on and on about the 'White Man's Burden' – the duty of the English race to rule the world.

'The British are the noblest race in the world. That is why, Kathleen, your poor standards of dress and manner let down the whole Raj,' Mrs Spragg lectured, fixing me with her gimlet eye. 'You must understand, in India you are not merely a young girl, you are a representative of a race with divine rights. We have a sacred trust in India to –'

'Make money,' Aunt Hilda interrupted, loudly. 'That's the Englishwoman's only duty. Making money is all that matters, Kit. Blast your boots if you do it in a stained bonnet.'

'Surely you cannot mean it, my dear Miss Salter,' Mrs Spragg gasped. 'You cannot mean to praise mere grubby commercial enterprise over the uplift of the natives.'

'Give me a gold brick over an "uplifted native" any day

of the week. Including Sunday!'

Mrs Spragg cast a scandalised look at my aunt. But she was too frightened of her reputation, as well as her sharp tongue, to get into a fight with her. Shortly after, pudding arrived. To my dismay it was a lumpy suet concoction. I prodded it with my spoon and ate a few half-hearted mouthfuls. Much more of this food and I would be joining the Minchin in the sickroom. I threw down my spoon and pushed back my chair. Announcing that I felt a little ill, I left the table.

To my surprise Aunt Hilda joined me. As we walked on the promenade deck she seized my arm.

'Want to have a natter,' she said.

'Yes?'

'About –' she fell silent. This hesitation was not at all like my aunt.

'What is it, Aunt Hilda?' I asked gently.

'Well – look here, it's Champlon. Do you think he's run off with another woman?'

I was silent for a moment. As I've already told you, I had been thinking a great deal over the voyage. I couldn't really believe Champlon had stolen Amelia Edwards's ankh or been in league with the monkey and the turbaned stranger. I felt there was some link with the Spraggs' Maharajah. We had received a wire from Oxford, apparently the fragment I'd found was definitely from the ankh, and the police were full of praise for my actions. A grateful Miss Edwards had even promised me a reward.

'Aunt, you know what I think,' I said finally. 'He's been kidnapped.'

'There's no evidence Champlon has been kidnapped.' She paused for a moment, her eyes searching mine. 'You know what Frenchmen are like. They like to flit about from girl to girl.'

'You're hardly a girl,' I blurted. The words were out before I realised how tactless they were. 'I mean –'

'Yes, yes . . . Nonetheless, they like to flit.'

We were passing by my cabin. Dark clouds hung low and a strong sea breeze was blowing. I shivered, suddenly chilled and at that moment I heard a crash from within. Followed by a loud shriek. Hurriedly, I flung open my door.

Miss Minchin, dressed in a lavender tea gown, was sitting bolt upright in her bunk. There was terror on her face. She was pointing with a quivering finger, blubbering incoherently. I followed the direction of her finger and saw the porthole window was hanging open. Rushing over I looked out, but there was nothing there, just the frothing waves and the sting of sea spray.

I closed the window and returning to Miss Minchin took her hand. She clutched mine hard, still babbling. I made soothing noises and gradually she calmed down.

'Gibbering!' she wailed.

'You're not gibbering,' I murmured. 'Just a bad dream.'

'Not me, idiot. It was a *thing*. A creature looking at me,' she said. 'Right above me, Kit, I could feel its breath on my face. The most hideous thing I've ever seen.'

'You must have been dreaming. The window flew open and it startled you.'

'It wasn't human! Huge teeth and hideous rubbery lips and hair all over its face. A devil.'

Hair all over its face. Not a devil. Instantly my mind flew to another conclusion. The mysterious Indian's monkey. The barge woman had said it had a most evil face. What was it doing on board the ship? Where was it hiding? And what on earth had it wanted? We had no precious jewels! My eyes darted around the room, checking for missing things, while Aunt Hilda came in harrumphing disgustedly. Then I saw something strange. A large yellow envelope with a dirty smudge on the front lay on my rumpled counterpane. That wasn't there before! I rushed over and tore open the envelope. There was no sheet of paper or message inside. A few fragments of rubbish fell out. Fragrant seeds, a shiny feather, some coarse yellow hair and a withered petal. Nothing at all, just a strange collection of oddments.

Aunt Hilda however appeared to go berserk. She rushed towards me and clasped me so tight to her ample bosom I could hardly breathe.

'No, leave Kit alone,' she yelped to some imaginary enemy.

'Let go of me,' I puffed.

'Danger! The Shadow of Death!'

'Pardon?' I asked bewildered, casting a worried look at the Minchin. She was already scared half out of her wits. She didn't need my aunt to frighten her more.

'Don't you know anything, Kit? This is an Indian Object Letter. These are symbols. Warning you of danger.'

'How do you mean?'

'Object letters are an ancient and secretive language. These letters have passed among Indians for many years, often appearing when there is trouble ahead.' She leant over and peered at the jumble lying on my bed more closely. 'The lion hair stands for Kali, Hindu goddess of death. You must have seen pictures. She wears a necklace of human arms and a belt of skulls.'

A goddess of death festooned with skulls. I was quiet for a moment, for it was a frightening image.

'This is a peacock's feather,' Aunt Hilda continued, picking up the beautiful thing, blue in the centre, fanning out in a shimmer of yellow and green. 'A symbol of

India, an ancient, beautiful bird but proud and fierce.' She pointed at the withered flower. 'This is the flower of the dhak, a plant with blood-red flowers that grows wild all over northern India. It can mean several things but taken together with a symbol of Kali or death it means danger.'

I shushed my aunt hurriedly, for she was practically shouting, and tried to usher her outside. Standing in the doorway, she murmured ominously:

'This letter is a warning, Kit. Something very bad will happen to you if you enter India.'

'Nonsense,' I muttered, though a knot of anxiety was tightening in my throat.

'Your life is in danger.'

'All superstition.'

'It's my fault. I was selfish to bring you with me.'

'I'm not scared,' I lied, as Miss Minchin let out a horrible wail. Judging by her ghostly face, she had overheard the whole conversation. Hurriedly, I slammed the cabin door on my aunt, cutting out her moaning.

It was far too late for second or third thoughts. I was going to India and it would take more than the *threat* of death to stop me.

☙ Chapter Seven ❧

Back in our cabin, I turned my attention to Miss Minchin. It took all my tact and patience – all right these aren't my strong points – to calm her. Soothing words, camomile compresses, smelling salts . . . none of these remedies were enough to bring my governess to her senses. She only let me leave on the condition that Rachel would replace me by her bedside. She also consented, feebly, to a cup of beef tea.

Being nice to Miss Minchin was hard work.

It was with great relief that I joined my aunt on the promenade deck, where she was leaning against the rails gazing at our ship's great red and white funnel pumping out steam. I had my work cut out. First I had to calm her down, then fill her in on my suspicions. Most important, I needed her assistance in my plan. This object-letter business had made it urgent. The monkey must have been behind the so called death threat. You see I *knew* all the first-class passengers. There was no one like

Champlon, the Indian Maharajah/trickster or the monkey among them. We needed to get down and search the lower decks thoroughly. Only my aunt possessed that sort of authority with the ship's crew.

At first Aunt Hilda was dubious about my plan. She was still inclined to cling to her notion that Champlon had deserted her. But the object letter and the powerful message of danger it sent was a point in my favour. Finally, Aunt Hilda agreed to let me have my way.

So, ten minutes later, after I had done my duty in ordering the beef tea, I followed my aunt down the entrance from the lower deck to the steerage passengers' accommodation. In front of us walked a bewildered steward. This was probably the only time first-class passengers had demanded to inspect living conditions below deck. Though my aunt had told him we were searching for a missing brooch, the steward was clearly nonplussed.

As we followed him to the single men's quarters, I understood why he was so nervous. The place was foetid, thick with smoke, sweat, the smell of rancid meat and dirty underclothes. Men in vests lounged on the berths that were stacked like bookshelves under the low ceiling. Some were squatting on the floor, gambling, others were smoking pipes or simply lying down, staring at nothing in particular.

Compared with Aunt Hilda's luxurious first-class state room, I had thought my cabin was overcrowded, but this was a new definition of wretchedness. The *Himalaya* could take 1,500 steerage passengers, most of whom were crowded in here. Not that the men seemed glum. In fact, as my aunt and I entered, a great cacophony of hooting began. One hugely muscled fellow, lounging on his berth in underclothes, had the nerve to whistle at my aunt. The steward quietened him. My aunt, of course, can deal with any embarrassment, but I fancy she was a little flushed. Meanwhile, I concentrated on paying attention to every man, squeezed sometimes two or three to a berth. Champlon might be in disguise. There were plenty of Indians and all sorts of folk of every race. But no Gaston Champlon. I had so hoped to find the Frenchman hiding in the men's berths! We moved to the family berths and then on to the single-women quarters. The women were still eating lunch, and I must say their food looked even more unappetising than ours.

Finally, when we had even ransacked the latrines, I was forced to admit defeat. The stench was overpowering. There were too many Indians below deck to find our suspect. It was like looking for an Englishman in London. Sick at heart, we climbed up to the promenade deck.

'Oh my sainted aunt!' Aunt Hilda exclaimed. 'What's going on?'

Sailors were running about hollering, ladies were fainting, gentleman were rushing to the sides of the boat. The promenade deck was lurching in the wind and billowing white sails blocked my view. A red and yellow diagonally divided signal flag was fluttering. In the distance a cannon exploded. The steward cursed and broke into a run. Aunt Hilda saw the flag and spat out an oath.

'MAN OVERBOARD!' a sailor shouted.

'It's a lady, you lummox,' another seaman yelled.

I rushed over to the rails but someone elbowed me out of the way. It was a gentleman who had thrown off his jacket. Gripping a rope, tied at one end to a life preserver and at the other to the mast, he jumped overboard. He disappeared into the churning waves, as I realised that it was the Fishing Fleet's favourite, Charlie Prinsep.

That meant the woman must be one of those who gushed around Prinsep in the salon.

Hanging over the rails I watched Mr Prinsep descend into the waves on the rope. I could see no sign of a body, in the churning of froth and waves. Waldo and Isaac had joined me in the watch.

'He sure is brave,' murmured Waldo, who had appeared.

Mr Prinsep was thrashing around in the sea, swimming in ever wider circles, while one hand clung to the life preserver. We spurred him on with our shouts of encouragement, but increasingly I felt that his task was hopeless. All we could see was a group of seagulls skimming the spray, scything in and out of the water. Surely the lady, whoever she was, would have drowned by now.

I felt a hand gripping my arm. It was Rachel, her eyes wide with terror.

'Where's Miss Minchin?' She blurted.

'I don't know.'

'She's not in the cabin. Kit, this isn't right. She hasn't left her bunk for days.'

'Maybe –' I began but Rachel cut me off.

'Oh, Kit, she's been sad ever since –' Rachel stopped dead.

Her words bludgeoned me in the head. For a moment I just gaped at her.

Thing is, I knew Rachel was right. I *knew* Miss Minchin's spirits had never recovered from the forged love note. I shook off my friend's hand. For one lunatic moment, I thought of jumping into the waves. But I was halted by a volley of shouts. Down below Prinsep was signalling for the rope to be hoisted. How could I ever forgive myself? Prinsep was being winched up, dripping sea slime. He had done his best. It just wasn't good enough. Tired and exhausted, he had given up the rescue attempt.

Which meant I might be responsible for something truly awful. It was meant as a joke, I told myself. But I felt so heavy I could scarcely stand up. I watched a soggy Prinsep rise on the rope. Attached to him was a bundle, a shapeless, dripping pile of clothes. My heart jerked suddenly. A skein of hair hung down from the sodden mess, or was it seaweed? Strong hands pulled up the rope and Mr Prinsep and the bundle were laid on the deck. There was too much of a press in front of me. I caught a glimpse of lavender gown and dripping hair. Then the human throng edged me out. Angrily I pushed my way through, using elbows and fists, anything.

Mr Prinsep was bending over a lady, whose hair was fanned out on the deck. His mouth covered her lips. He jerked upwards and a spray of water spurted from his mouth.

The lady – Miss Minchin – was corpse still. Her features had a bleary look, as if they were covered with gauze.

Mr Prinsep bent over her again, desperately giving her the kiss of life. But to the circle of onlookers it was quite clear that his attempts were futile. Her skin was waxy, mottled with bluish veins. Like the underbelly of a dead fish. Again the gallant man surfaced, to spit out water, and again bent over her, striving to will her to life. I knelt down at her side, urging her on. My fingers brushed her hand, which was lying limp on the deck. It was clammy, sea-water cold.

All was lost. The seconds were ticking on and she hadn't stirred, hadn't given any sign of life.

Then, quite miraculously, Celestina Minchin opened her eyes.

'Thank –' I began, then fell silent, for Miss Minchin was not looking at me.

'You saved my life,' she murmured, gazing deep into Mr Prinsep's eyes.

Mr Prinsep blushed red as a beetroot. 'Always wanted to do it,' he sputtered.

'Do what?' I butted in, interested.

'Rescue a damsel in distress.'

A blonde, whom I had seen hanging on Mr Prinsep's arm at every dance, snorted, her nostrils flaring like a thoroughbred stallion. Then a man with a black bag pushed his way to the front, ordering everyone away. The doctor had finally arrived.

'Clear the decks,' he ordered.

The drama was over. Reluctantly the crowd drifted away, while Miss Minchin was loaded on to a stretcher. Only my aunt, my friends and Mr Prinsep, were left. Before she was taken away Miss Minchin opened her eyes. This time she *was* looking at me.

'I'm so sorry,' I murmured. 'I'm sorry about not

sending Rachel to you, sorry about everything.' I paused a moment, unsure and went on, 'You shouldn't have done it.'

'Done what, Kathleen?'

'Er . . . jump.'

'I didn't *jump*,' she snapped. 'I was frightened in that cabin. Frightened that evil thing would come back. So I came out to the prom deck. I leant over the rails for a breath of air, the ship lurched and before I knew my head was under water.

'All I wanted was a breath of fresh air and suddenly I was drowning!'

❧ Chapter Eight ❧

'We really couldn't accept, Mr Prinsep,' Miss Minchin twittered. 'It's quite impossible.'

The damsel who had lain in a soggy bundle on the deck was gone. She had transformed into this fluttering figure, gazing wide-eyed at Mr Prinsep, as she organised the removal of our luggage. Though she was refusing something, her eyes signalled she badly wanted to accept.

'We couldn't impose on you, Mr Prinsep.'

'Oh I say,' protested her saviour, 'call me Charlie.'

'We just couldn't,' she persisted.

'Least I can do. Hospitality to strangers. All good folk mucking together in the Empire and all that.'

'What's this?' my aunt enquired, bustling up behind us all as we stood on deck, awaiting the coolies who would unload our luggage on to the docks. For you see, we had arrived at Bombay! The gateway to India and a whole new continent of adventure.

'Mr Prinsep . . . Charles . . . is so generous,' Miss Minchin replied. 'He has offered to put us up. He is engaged as tutor to the young Maharajah of Baroda and he has a whole lodge in the palace grounds at his disposal.' I hadn't seen so much pretty colour in her face for the whole voyage. 'Of course I've told him it is quite impossible for us to accept.'

'Providential. We're heading to Baroda anyway. Save on hotel bills,' Aunt Hilda announced. 'Has the Maharajah sent his carriage for you?'

'Er yes, I believe I've a two-horse . . . tikka gharry,' Prinsep replied, pronouncing the words unsurely. 'His Highness has also been so good as to send me the Royal Carriage on the Great Indian Peninsular Railway. The very latest word in modern colonial travel.'

'Splendid.' Turning round, Aunt Hilda shouted for a coolie to convey our boxes to Mr Prinsep's carriage and so the thing was done. Poor Mr Prinsep. He had wanted his damsel in distress. Well, he had got her. He'd also got Aunt Hilda, Father, myself, Rachel, Isaac and Waldo. Rather more than he'd bargained for. From our point of view the offer was providential, for the archaeological treasure my father was interested in had been unearthed in the grounds of the Maharajah's palace.

'The heat, Kit. I don't know how I am to stand it.' Father appeared, looking even woollier than usual. I took his hand reassuringly, than quickly released it – too damp and sweaty.

'You could take that off,' I said, indicating his tweed jacket.

'Really?' he asked surprised.

Soon the stewards were ushering us off the ship. What an explosion of colour, noise and smells greet us. Swarming coolies and crying babies. Friends and relations of the passengers waiting on the docks, penned behind bars like cattle. There was no hiding from the sun, it bathed everything in white, fierce heat. My clothes were clinging to me with perspiration and a fly had settled on my face. Swooping in and out of the crowd, with a flutter of ebony wingbeats, were a flock of carrion crows. Their harsh caws mingled with the babble, pressing confusion on us from every side.

Odd and unnerving though this was, I was exhilarated. Of course, I had been to Egypt, but this was an utterly different land! India – this vast, teeming, spicy continent! A fever of excitement coursed through my veins. My friends felt it too, even Rachel. Our senses quickened, our minds were alert. Only father stared round with bewildered eyes, clearly more at home in the library. I would have to take care of him in this strange continent. My first task, though, was to find Champlon and his Indian.

All around us on the docks were clumps of travellers, saying emotional goodbyes to the ship-board friends. My way was blocked by Mrs Spragg who was saying a prolonged farewell to at least a dozen bosom friends. Her cambric handkerchief fluttered at her eyes, tears flowed down her plump cheeks, but finally she moved aside and I saw something so strange I stopped dead in my tracks.

White-jacketed stewards had cleared a wide path through the crowd of passengers. A special ramp had been laid from the ship to the dock. Now as we watched, more sailors came and formed a human shield, blocking any hope of getting beyond their lines. At the end of the ramp waited a tikka-gharry with darkened windows. Before my amazed eyes two wheezing figures in wheelchairs, bundled in layers of blankets despite the heat, were pushed down the ramp. Following them was a hobbling individual, whose face was so bandaged up with linen that he looked like a walking mummy. Last of all came an Indian. A splendid figure dressed in a gold-and-white footman's costume.

I had just a moment to study the Indian. He had a sallow face with a proud beak of a nose and pop eyes set in shadowed sockets. His mouth, curved now in a sneer as he glanced neither left nor right, was full and sensual. Just a glimpse was enough to convince me that here was a man of deep selfishness, one who put his own pleasures above all else. This was not the face of a servant.

On his shoulder perched a small, gibbering thing. Its face was trimmed by a ruff of white fur. Its eyes, black points in flaring yellow, peered left and right with wicked intent.

The monkey!

It looked straight at me and I saw that in the centre of those beady pupils there was a pinpoint of white light. I could have sworn that the monkey was laughing at me. No, worse, it was looking down on me.

'Who are they?' I burbled to my aunt, clutching at her sleeve. 'Where did those people come from?'

'I don't know. Perhaps they were in the sick bay.'

The sick bay! I had never thought of that. I'd foolishly reckoned I'd known all the first-class passengers aboard ship. I'd never imagined the people I was looking for could be hiding among the diseased. That man with the swaddled head was passing me by now, so close that if I could have got past the naval security cordon, I could have ripped off his bandages. A waft of scent hit me in the nose. A sickly mixture of jasmine and musk that was all too familiar. Champlon claimed it was cologne-water for use after shaving, but anyone else would call it by another name.

Perfume.

The turbaned Indian was walking right by me. He

turned his head and gave me a sideways look. I believe he too was laughing at me. Then he was gone and the passengers in wheelchairs were being helped into the tikka-gharry.

Aunt Hilda had also smelt Champlon's perfume, for suddenly her expression changed. A stillness came over her face and she raised her nose to the air and sniffed. She looked, for all the world, like a hound scenting a fox.

'Champlon,' I gasped.

'The cad!'

We acted at once; surging through the cordon of sailors guarding the 'sick passengers', as my friends and father gaped in astonishment. We caught the sailors off guard. I got through and ran towards the tikka-gharry but a sailor had caught hold of my aunt. The doors, black-painted like the rest of the carriage, were closing. My prey was safely inside, but I wasn't finished. I grasped the door handle and wrenched it open. I had a fleeting glimpse of astonished faces, then the Indian raised his cane and slashed me viciously. Just in time I raised my hands, which took the brunt of the blow.

'Ouch!' I yelled, clutching my throbbing hand.

'To Bori Bunder,' the Indian shouted at the driver. The brute slammed the door of the carriage in my face. With a flurry of whips and wheels it was off.

'Stop!' I yelled, but a sailor-guard had caught up with

me and was grasping me roughly by the arm.

'What you playing at?' he shouted. 'Are you a lunatic?'

'I thought I saw a friend,' I mumbled.

'No friends of the likes of you. Them's very important passengers. You're lucky I'm not arresting you for creating a nuisance. Off with you now. Go on, get lost!'

I sped away, back to my friends. Whoever they were, the mysterious strangers clearly had a lot of power, for the traffic had been cleared for their carriage. Bullock carts, rickshaws, tikka-gharries, tongas – all sorts of strange rickety vehicles – moved to one side. It was like the seas parting. Their black-and-gold tikka-gharry sped off. After it was lost from view, the traffic surged round them.

The villains had escaped.

My hand was stinging, and a weal was purpling my flesh where that man had struck me with his cane – but this was no time for self-pity.

'What's Bori Bunder?' I asked my aunt.

'The train station.'

'Quick! We have to follow them.'

❧ Chapter Nine ❧

When we got to the station there was no sign of Champlon or his strange companions. Everywhere we looked was a heaving mass of people, of porters balancing huge trunks on their heads, of families trailing straggling children. The sticky heat, the crush, made my head feel as if it was alive with buzzing flies. Above the constant din of people and steam engines, was the bawling of vendors carrying trays of scalding drinks – 'Kaapee, kaapee', 'Chai, chai' – for that is how they sell coffee and tea in this strange land.

'We will never find Champlon,' I sighed, looking around despairingly.

I must confess I had rarely felt so utterly bewildered by any sight as that inside Bori Bunder. What a steaming, rickety place it was. Only the trains struck a modern note.

'Of course not,' snapped my aunt. 'Might as well look for a maggot in a rotten tree.'

'Maybe we can find him in Baroda, maybe the Maharajah will help us.'

'Cease your dreaming,' my aunt said, turning away.

Prinsep was helping Miss Minchin into the Maharajah's carriage, handling her as if she had still not recovered from her bath in the sea. Unlike all the other train compartments, which were dirty and crammed with people, the royal carriage was the height of luxury, draped in gold-embroidered curtains, the soft leather seats plump with cushions. It even had a small golden throne, which stood in the middle of the panelled room. Porters were attending to our luggage, which they loaded just in time, for the whistle blew and with much puffing of oily black smoke the train made its way out of the station.

As the train chugged through a flat landscape of rice fields, palm trees and mud huts, a small boy dressed in the red and gold livery of the Maharajah pulled a flat fan made of palm leaves over our heads. This 'punkah' did little to ease the stifling heat inside the carriage, merely moving the hot air around a little. I gazed out of the window. Squatting dangerously close to the sides of the rail tracks were hordes of villagers. They were stick thin, the women dressed in coloured sheets called saris, many of the men wearing a garment I found hard to describe. It looked like a knee-length *skirt*. Wherever the train went, crowds watched.

I watched them in turn, sipping the sugary, spicy chai. I felt lost, for India was blisteringly hot, crowded and so foreign. Even the chai, sweet though it was, tasted peculiarly different from my normal tea. For a moment I felt homesick for the rain and grey familiarity of Oxford.

Mr Prinsep, who had been talking in a low voice to Miss Minchin, suddenly cleared his throat, attracting our attention.

'I say,' he said and abruptly stopped, his mouth hanging open. Prinsep was apt to behave like this, suddenly forget what he wanted to say in the middle of a sentence. Miss Minchin began speaking to him in an undertone, perhaps urging him on.

'Maybe he's going to declare his love for the Minchin,' Isaac murmured in my ear.

'Wouldn't that be wonderful,' I muttered. 'No more sums.'

'He saved her life. Maybe now he can save her from turning into an old spinster,' Waldo said meanly.

I glared at him.

'At least it would let your father off the hook,' Isaac added.

I switched my glare to Isaac.

'I say,' began Prinsep again. This time he managed to get his words out – and sadly they did not concern our governess. 'I want to talk to you a bit about Baroda. You see, as I expect you all know, the last Maharajah, Malharrao, was a bad egg. A nasty chappie. Gambled, drank, spent the state's gold like water; for example he had a carpet of pearls made for his bedchamber! Worst of all he wasn't above chopping a head or two off just for the fun of it. Well, things really came to a head when he tried to poison the British Resident. A tad of arsenic in the poor fellow's lemon sherbet.'

'The Resident was Mrs Spragg's husband,' I interrupted. 'She told us all about it.'

'Well, then, I see you know the background. Thing is, the Queen Mother, the Rani, decided they had to have a new Maharajah. So she had her spies find three humble village lads and bring them to the palace. The boys were scared stiff. I've been told they'd never seen a chair before, some of 'em, never mind a whole palace. Each boy was asked the same question – why had they been brought here? The first didn't know, the second replied, "To see the sights."

'Only the third boy, Sayaji, replied, "To rule." He's rather a bold little chap. Of course he became the new king!'

'That's all very well,' Aunt Hilda cut in, 'but my brother, Professor Theo Salter, and I have a special reason for visiting Baroda. That is why your offer to put us up was really very fortunate.'

'Yes?' Mr Prinsep asked, bewildered.

'We are interested in the recent discovery in the palace's treasure vaults. They are said to include a map to the legendary mountain paradise, Shambala.'

At the name Shambala, my father woke up. 'You must help us find these papers, Prinsep. They belonged to the famous Jesuit traveller Father Anthony Monserrate. He was in India three hundred years ago and wrote a diary. It is said that he may have even found a very old stone table or parchment – we don't know which – that shows the way to Shambala.'

'I don't know anything about Sham-whatsitsname or any paradises,' replied Prinsep, who was starting to look a bit harassed. 'Of course I will help you all I can, but you see things are a bit delicate at the moment in Baroda. The crops have failed, there's been a bit of a famine and, well, the old Maharajah – he just made things worse. Thing is, revolution hangs in the air. There're all sorts of bandits on the loose who want to kill the new king.

'There have already been six attempts on the young Maharajah's life. He is surrounded by armed guards day and night. The palace is seething with talk of plots, the staff constantly on the lookout for would-be killers. You must be very careful for, you see, he's only a lad, just twelve years old.' He came to an abrupt stop and we smiled encouragingly at him.

'Hope I've not put my foot in it or anything like that,' Prinsep suddenly gave one of his foolish grins – this one directed at Aunt Hilda. 'See, we're jolly lucky to be allowed in to see the Maharajah. So the thing is, folks, pretty important to show the proper respect to the little lad.'

'Am I showing the proper respect?' I mouthed silently to Rachel. Bowing so low my nose scraped the floor, I inched snail-like towards the boy king.

'Behave,' Rachel whispered, though she could not help grinning.

I caught my first glimpse of the Maharajah, Sayaji – a boy perching on a throne made for a man. His face was round as a full moon, teeth flashing white in skin with the sheen of polished walnut. His puffy cheeks were fringed by feathery eyelashes. He surveyed the world from under those lashes. In fact, at first glance he looked as if he was dozing on his throne.

What a throne! Like a curved golden shell, set with glittering gems. The throne dominated the enormous first-floor chamber, which was crowded with courtiers, open to the sun and rain on all sides. Birds fluttered in and out, graceful swooping things with scarlet tails and ruffs. Above the chatter of the courtiers was the melodious twitter of these bulbul songbirds, India's nightingales. But the boy was apart from all the hullabaloo, ringed as he was by five bodyguards. I was told these men shadowed him day and night, on the watch for assassins. How small he looked among those burly men, bristling with knives and swords! Like a child at the dress-up box. A boy playing at king.

Rachel murmured, 'He looks so sad and lonely.'

'I wouldn't be sad. Not if everyone had to grovel to *me*.' Waldo grinned.

As we approached, the boy opened his eyes and I saw what Rachel meant. He did look sad, somehow. There was a lost look in those bulging brown eyes. The Maharajah was dressed in the simplest white linen tunic and pyjamas, though his chubby hands were be-ringed with glittering gems. Nothing save the huge diamond – the legendary Star of the East – glittering on a chain around his neck marked him out as the king. What an odd ruler.

I felt sorry for the young Maharajah. How many of the courtiers circling around him must be plotting to seize power for themselves? How many supposed friends were just waiting for their chance to plant a knife between his shoulder blades? The looks, the whispers, the courtiers bristling with swords. Easy to imagine the dagger glinting in some shadowy corner. What a strange mixture of glamour and decay the Ran Bagh palace was.

'What is these, Charles?' the Maharajah asked, turning to his tutor. I had been told that he was learning English, but he spoke remarkably well.

'The travellers I told you about, Your Highness' Prinsep replied. 'The archaeologists.'

'They make archaeologists young in England,' said a diminutive man standing by the throne. He peered at us doubtfully. Later I learned that this was the Dewan, the king's adviser and the real power behind the throne. He was bald as an egg and had a funny, crinkled face. But his green eyes were shrewd.

'No, these are their children.' Prinsep pointed to my father and aunt. 'Here are the archaeologists.'

'A woman?' the Dewan gazed thunderstruck at my aunt, who, clad in puffy bloomer-style trousers, stood in front of my father, blocking him from sight. 'She goes about in *that*?'

I suddenly realised what had struck me as strange about the palace. There were no women, anywhere, though coming up the stairs I'd heard the faint tinkle of laughter. Through a moon-shaped fretwork in the wall I glimpsed slanting, almond-shaped eyes watching me. A swirl of pink silk. Then more bell-like laughter and the eyes disappeared. Aunt Hilda had explained the vision to me: in this palace, the ladies kept 'purdah' and had to keep to their quarter of the palace which was called the Zenana. For all their silks, gold and baubles, they were but beautiful caged birds. Like the Maharajah, they were trapped.

Of course no Zenana could contain Aunt Hilda, who announced:

'I am the most famous explorer in England, Your Majesty. You've heard of Hilda Salter? . . . Modern enlightened thought holds women to be as good as men. We don't keep ladies locked away in Britain. All sorts of women are becoming doctors and so on. Many of them rather look up to me.'

I'm not sure how much of this speech the boy Maharajah understood, though he nodded politely. I saw his dewan whispering to him and then my aunt was introducing my father. Shortly after that, my aunt, never one to waste time, got down to business.

'Your Highness, your fame and goodness is known throughout the Empire. We have come here because we've heard of the exciting discovery in your grounds. We are dying to see Father Monserrate's famous diaries. What a thrilling find! We have heard they include a map to Shambala – perhaps the way to paradise on earth.'

The Maharajah held up a chubby, glittering hand. Instantly all chatting and laughter in the court was stilled. The gesture was so unexpected it even silenced my aunt.

'NO,' he said.

'Pardon?' my aunt spluttered.

'Why should I allow you to see these things?'

'Er . . . I am a famous explorer; my brother Theo here is a renowned archaeologist.'

'You don't want look. You want take,' the boy king declared.

My father had stepped forward. I saw he was trembling as he attempted to speak. 'Your Majesty . . .' he managed to mutter before the boy interrupted:

'Britishers are always stealing India's treasures.'

My aunt drew herself up to her full five feet: 'Your Highness! We are not thieves.'

'Madam, you are most welcome to my palace. But not to my treasures.'

'I assure you, my interest in these old papers is purely scholarly,' my aunt protested.

'I believe you, madam. But even your great Queen Empress is . . .' he waved his hands around and then paused a moment for a whispered discussion with the Dewan. When he began again the Maharajah was grinning. 'Even Queen Victoria is light-fingered. She has stolen India's greatest gem, the Koh-i-noor diamond, from my brother Maharajah.'

My aunt was momentarily speechless. Perhaps to make up for his charge's rudeness, the Dewan stepped forward, smiling. With a few gracious phrases he invited us all on a great shikar, or tiger hunt. We would start off for the jungle, tomorrow morning, at the very crack of dawn.

With that we were shown out of the court.

Gazing back at the palace we had left, I saw it was really the most splendid building, sprouting fairytale turrets, domes and minarets. Look a little closer and you could see the marks of woodworm, devouring the mighty wooden edifice from the inside. It might be a metaphor for the whole court, I mused. Glittering on the outside, but eaten up by greed and suspicion.

What a relief to be away from the court. Here in the glorious grounds, we could enjoy the plash of fountains and the screech of peacocks. Feast our eyes on vast banyan trees that sent misshapen limbs into the grounds, twittering birds and chattering monkeys. Instead of the birch trees and cedars that you would find in an English park there were mango trees – plump with juicy golden fruit – peepul and burning orange Flame of the Forest. The sweet scent of jasmine was everywhere. Truly we felt we had been transported into the pages of some exotic tale.

As we stood in the shade of the banyan tree growing

over our lodge, Mr Prinsep said, consolingly: 'Do not fret about the journals. Most people would give their right hand to go on one of the Maharajah's tiger hunts.'

'I have use for both my hands, thank you,' Aunt Hilda snapped. She paused a moment, letting Mr Prinsep feel the full force of her anger. 'I'll tell you one thing for free, Mr Prinsep, I consider your tinpot Maharajah most precocious. Not to say disrespectful!

'I will have that journal. Even if I have to break into the treasure vaults to get it.' With that Aunt Hilda turned her back on us and strode into the lodge. We all followed a little nervously, for my aunt in a mood is as dangerous as a rogue lion. As we entered the corridor I stopped and gasped.

There was an oil painting on the wall in front of me of an Indian reclining on a tiger skin, a rifle lying on his lap, a thick rope of pearls around his neck. He had a moustache almost as full as Champlon, this man. Something about the face under all that hair pulled me up short. That plump, pleasure-loving mouth, thin cheeks, sallow skin, was all familiar. Above all, the expression in the bulging eyes, reminded me of someone. The artist had captured exactly the look in the man's eyes.

I had seen him somewhere very recently. Cleanshaven, but most definitely the same man.

'Who's that?' I turned on Prinsep urgently.

'I thought they'd got rid of all the paintings of him,' he replied.

'Yes, but who is it?'

'That rotter Malharrao, of course. The old Maharajah.'

❧ Chapter Ten ☙

As we travelled towards the jungle in search of tigers the next morning, my mind was still buzzing with my discovery. Of course I hadn't been able to keep it to myself. I instantly told the others I'd recognised Malharrao as the supposed 'footman' disembarking from the steamer at Bombay. My aunt believed me, as did my friends. But I could tell Prinsep was sceptical. I felt frustrated with him, for the implications were huge.

It looked very much as if Malharrao – the wicked, former Maharajah of Baroda – had kidnapped Champlon and brought him to India. Why, I had no idea. I also had no real clue as to the identity of the two invalids in wheelchairs with the travelling party. I had my suspicions, though. Sick suspicions that were curdling in my stomach.

Could those two sick invalids be a pair of brothers we had met before? Rich, evil and ruthless, they were the perfect candidates to have sprung Malharrao from gaol.

But what did they want with him? Why, if it was indeed the Baker Brothers, were they in India? Where did the thieving monkey fit into all this? It was all most perplexing. I had questions, questions, questions – but so few answers.

In England I would have been able to make a better go of understanding it all, but India was so very *foreign*. The sights and smells of the palace bewildered me, the heaving mob of people outside the gates even more. The very air was different; hot and musky, filled with stinging particles of dust. With the royal party I was cocooned in luxury, swaddled in silk and ivory and fed fifteen-course meals. Outside the palace gates there was danger, rebellion, poverty. Yet it wasn't as if we were so safe within the palace. Yesterday I had cannoned into a man lurking outside my door. His gold teeth glinted as he accepted my apologies, but the expression in his eyes made me shiver. Who was he? A bodyguard? A spy? I had no idea. There were so many undercurrents I was grasping to understand. High intrigue involving the fate of kingdoms and princes, and something more tantalising in the background, something my fingers would clutch and then it would all slip away.

What could the plotters want with Champlon? What did he have to offer them? Then there were those threatening letters to me – oh, why couldn't life be simpler?

'Kit! You're talking to yourself.' Rachel prodded me in the side, while, sitting in the palanquin opposite me, Waldo grinned slyly.

'Oops, sorry.'

'Planning to solve the world's problems?' Waldo asked. 'All by your little self?'

Scowling slightly, I ignored him and glanced through the silk curtain that draped our golden palanquin. It was strange to be riding an elephant, but the beast had made good progress across Baroda. Through paddy fields and coconut groves, through villages of squat mud huts, till we plunged into jungle. Here the sights were so wonderful my worries fell away. We were engulfed by a canopy of trees, swarming with creepers and thick with the cries of exotic birds: racket-tailed drongo, paradise flycatcher, black-headed cuckoo shrike. The only sound I recognised was the reassuring tap-tap of woodpeckers.

As our beasts swayed under us, I spied a herd of antelope with the delicate legs of ballerinas. They watched us from the edge of the clearing, their curling horns quivering, appearing too graceful to survive this jungle. Then, in a startled rush, they fled. Monkeys crashed through the branches overhead and once I thought I saw a flash of yellow and black spotted hide, a cheetah perhaps or leopard.

Finally we arrived at a tangled gully from which a

bank sloped down to a water hole. At the moment it was a dried-out pit, only a little moist mud at the very bottom to show how it must swell during the monsoon rains. On the other side of the gully a screen of creepers draped the trees and bushes like enormous fronds of clinging seaweed. We were surrounded by the screech of parakeets, the whisper and crackle of prowling creatures: tigers, panthers, boar, black buck.

My father had been travelling with the Maharajah and my aunt on the other elephant. Now his head emerged, blinking, from his palanquin. 'There's nowhere to picnic,' he called, panic stricken at the idea of crouching in snake-infested grass.

'Nonsense.' The Maharajah waved his hand airily: 'We will sit on God's earth.'

It was all right for the Maharajah. His servants produced a charming gold chair for him to sit on. The rest of our party, which included Mrs Spragg and her bodyguard, had to make do with rugs. The swaying motion of the elephant ride had obviously been a bit much for some of my friends: Isaac and the Minchin were both delicate shades of green.

The Maharajah dismounted and placed one arm round his favourite elephant, Sonali. A beast the size of an omnibus, with great baggy eyes, surrounded by rolls of wrinkled flesh, she looked at you so sadly you could have sworn she *understood*. The Maharajah stroked her flank lovingly, as he fed her slices of mango.

'Sonali, my little one,' he murmured to her, as he scratched her wrinkled hide. We watched a little nervously, for one swish of the elephant's trunk would send us flying on to the forest floor. Her feet could crunch your skull like a teacup. The Maharajah turned and saw us watching him anxiously.

'Don't fear.' He smiled. 'Sonali does not hurt a mosquito . . . Go on, stroke her.'

This was a royal command. Waldo came forward, but I was quicker.

Which is how I came to stroke a real live elephant. Her skin felt scabby and rough, it was a little like patting an old leather bag. A beast that weighed over 7,000 pounds, but was gentle as a lamb. She curled her trunk with pleasure, as my friends and I patted her sides. She seemed to be smiling at us.

While the mahout tended to the beasts, the small army of servants that accompanies the Maharajah everywhere, even to the middle of the jungle, got to work. They unpacked a vast array of hampers: inside were silver tureens breathing steam, tiffin tins, jars of pickles and chutneys; bottles of fresh candy-coloured sherbet. My mouth watered at the sight of the sumptuous spread. Even a picnic with a Maharajah was an impossibly grand affair.

'Mulligatawny!' the Maharajah announced to our party. 'I know how you Britishers love your mulligatawny!' He pointed at one large tureen in which churned a pool of brownish liquid, floating with odd, slimy things. Stomach churning.

'Most thoughtful, Your Highness,' simpered Mrs Spragg. 'Mulligatawny is just the thing in this awful heat.'

It might have been just the thing for her but I loathe mulligatawny soup.

Of all the curious dishes I have tasted in this country, it is the worst, a weak mix of the dregs of English and Indian fare. Sadly Indians are convinced that us 'Britishers' love mulligatawny, though it is so watery and plain horrid my gorge rises when I taste it. I cheered up a bit when I saw the servants unpacking the trimmings that go with mulligatawny. Quartered hardboiled eggs, shredded vegetables, cold slices of curried meat, savoury poppadom biscuits and so on . . .

'Mmmm,' I burst out, catching a hint of a delicious, sweet spicy scent.

It was the steam wafting from the Maharajah's huge plate of spiced rice. Arranged in small silver bowls around his plate were the condiments: sauces, chicken pieces, pickles, pastries, chutneys. My mouth watered looking at the Maharajah's plate and I couldn't help another small gasp of hunger escaping. Rachel glared at me warningly; she was convinced that all India was trying to poison us. It is true the poor girl has suffered from the upset stomach called 'Delhi belly' since arriving. But my stomach is made of cast iron! The Maharajah noticed my greedy look and made a surprised movement, as if to offer me some.

But Mrs Spragg stepped in: 'No, dear Kathleen,' she snapped. 'That will be far too spicy for you. Better stick to plain English food.'

I was about to protest when my aunt saved me.

'My niece Kit and I love your Indian cooking,' she announced to the Maharajah. 'We would be honoured to try some of your fare. What is this?'

'Chicken biryani,' he said, beaming.

Though Mrs Spragg looked cross, I got the feeling the Maharajah was pleased. Smiling, he waved a hand at the servants and soon heaped plates were set in front of me and my aunt. Sitting on silken rugs we tucked in. The rice was fragrant with the sweet tang of coconut and raisins. The curry sauce rich and dense and the pickles so hot they burnt the roof of my mouth. All in all it was one of the most gorgeous meals of my life and I can assure you I did full justice to it. That is to say I polished off my plate of food and had seconds and thirds, managing to ignore Rachel's doleful looks. Indeed Waldo, Isaac and my slightly nervous father joined us in the meal, though Mrs Spragg and Rachel were extremely suspicious.

Perhaps some day I will open an Indian curry eating-house in Oxford, for I am as adventurous with strange foods as foreign lands. It will introduce those timid souls brought up on a diet of boiled vegetables and suet pudding to the tempting treats of the Orient.

After the main course came puddings and here I must confess to disappointment. We had round pale sweets that tasted a little of condensed milk and were called 'barfis'. They weren't bad, better than the dry and crumbly orange things called 'ludos'. Horrible. I must confess my mind went back to cook's treats: creamy sherry trifle, or her cake – oozing melting chocolate, rich and moist.

Indian main courses may be tastier than ours; but I am glad to say that their puddings are not a patch on British ones!

Too soon the meal was over and we remounted our palanquins. Our convoy of elephants moved on, heading into the thickest part of the jungle. We were under a dense cloak of palms and creepers that grew over our heads, almost cutting off the light. The elephants moved with difficulty, trampling their way through the undergrowth, swinging their long tusks from side to side. Suddenly there was a screeching right next to my nose and a paradise flycatcher, exploded horizontally out of the bushes and zoomed away, trailing a blur of snowy tail feathers.

We were nearing the tiger hunt. The beaters had been out in force over the last few days, looking for tiger prints. They had spotted some in this part of the jungle and had tethered a live goat to a stake to attract the beast. They claimed it was deadly, a man-eater who had carried off a young girl from a nearby village.

We came to a clearing and the beaters gestured to us to be silent. The goat was chained to a stake by a tussock of grass on the edge of the clearing. Poor animal. All that remained of it was its head and a carcass, oozing blood. Only a savage creature could have done such damage to the goat. My breathing became more ragged, the thrill of the chase infecting me. Rachel, however, was disgusted. She turned her soft eyes on me and hissed:

'It didn't have a chance.'

'Hardly my fault.'

'This isn't about you, Kit. Imagine its agony.'

The chief hunter slid down our flank, followed by the Maharajah. Even here, in the midst of the jungle, he was a semi-captive, ringed by bodyguards alert for assassins.

Waldo, my aunt and I stalked after them towards the tussock. Isaac, Rachel and the others preferred to watch the hunt from the safety of their palanquins. We crept on cotton-wool feet, for tigers do not give you second chances.

The hunter reached the tussock and signalled to us to come no nearer. We stopped. I looked around. Out of the corner of my left eye, I caught a flash of orange in the midst of a thicket. Suddenly, something was surging towards me. Boiling eyes, ears flattened, claws outstretched. I lurched blindly as the tiger leapt at my face. A half-scream gurgled from my throat. I could hardly breathe. Choking, I cursed my aunt who had forbidden me to carry a gun. The Maharajah shrieked. Instantly his bodyguards clustered around him in a protective huddle, ignoring the tiger attacking *me*. A claw was at my face. It loomed before my eye as I cowered against the bush. A shot rang out. The claw fell, grazing my face. Another bullet went whistling past, so close it scorched my ear.

There was blood on my face. Then a thud on my feet. The tiger had fallen on to me, its body crumpling in a heap of black stripes.

'Thank you,' I sobbed, struggling away from the heavy beast, my left ear zinging from the bullet that had so nearly ripped it off.

The tiger was magnificent. It lay at my feet in death

agony, its powerful muscles pulsing under its orange hide. It would have crushed my skull with one blow.

'Waldo, you saved my life!'

'It wasn't me,' my friend yelled, wildly. 'Where'd the shot come from?'

'Aunt Hilda?'

'Quiet, child,' she screeched.

Tension crackled in the air. The Maharajah's five bodyguards encircled him, their eyes swivelling from side to side, searching for the gunman. Mrs Spragg's guard was at the side of the elephant where she was cowering in the palanquin. Somewhere, a twig crackled, setting my teeth on edge.

'Who fired?' I blurted. But almost as the words were out of my mouth another bullet spat out, whizzing past me. Heading straight for the Maharajah.

The Maharajah froze. Time hung suspended. The bullet was followed by another and then another. The bodyguards fired in wild panic. But these were like no normal bullets, they swooped and curved round the bodyguards. They made their way straight to the Maharajah, like pins flying to a magnet.

One bullet whizzed through the middle of the Maharajah's turban, leaving a blackened hole. Another bullet was within a whisper of his soft, plump throat.

The Maharajah howled, the screech of a scared

animal. His whole body trembled, in face of this bewildering splatter of death. But he didn't duck and he would have been killed if a bodyguard hadn't pushed him to the ground with the butt of his rifle.

My eyes desperately scanned the sprawl of bush, tree and creeper, the whole teeming jungle. The man with the gun could have been anywhere. In that neem tree over there, crouching behind that wild jasmine, anywhere in the dark of the encircling jungle. There might be a number of bandits attacking us, they might have led us here, only to surround us and pick us off at their pleasure. An ambush. Panic rose sour in my throat, as my eyes flicked this way and that. But nowhere could I see the glint of a hidden gun.

❧ Chapter Eleven ❧

A roar came from behind me. I spun round. Waldo was screaming, holding his gun in front of him like a sword. He's been shot, I thought. I wanted to run to him, but my feet would not obey my brain. As I watched, frozen, Waldo raised his rifle and aimed at a large tree. It was a wild almond, sprayed with red flowers, like splatters of dried blood.

His rifle stuttered. A moment later a pistol fell out of the tree, followed by a dark figure which landed with a thud in a thorn bush. The Maharajah yelled, Aunt Hilda bellowed and the bodyguards continued to fire into the jungle. Scared out of their wits, the elephants made a deafening honking, which almost drowned out the rest of the commotion.

Finally my feet moved. I rushed to the wild almond, just a second behind Waldo, to see two brawny guards hauling a man to his feet.

A stick-thin figure, with a huge moustache, clad in a

grubby shirt and loincloth. He looked befuddled, eyes peering dully from above wrinkled brown skin. The guard slapped him viciously across the face. But he barely reacted.

I was hit by a horrible stench – the wild almond as pungent as an open sewer. I staggered back, reeling. Mingled with this stink was a more delicate scent: rich, flowery, sickly sweet. A mixture of jasmine and musk. A familiar smell.

Champlon!

I blinked and gazed at the man, hanging like a skinny rag doll from the bodyguard's hand. It couldn't be! But it must. Those curving bullets. No one in the world could shoot quite like our French friend.

I went up to the bodyguard and shook his prisoner by the arm. 'Monsieur Champlon, it's me.'

Was I right? There was no flicker of recognition in the man's eyes. He was seemingly unaware – or indifferent to – the commotion all around him. But the moustache, the jutting nose – the Frenchman was unmistakable. Champlon's hand was dripping blood: the bullet had nicked one of his fingers. Why didn't he feel the pain?

Waldo gazed at the Frenchman and gave a grunt of surprise. 'It's him,' he squealed. 'That rotter Champlon.'

At that my aunt came scurrying forwards and when she recognised Champlon such was her surprise that for a moment I thought she was going to faint. But she pulled herself together and glared at him, trembling slightly. Suddenly, she slapped him.

'That's what you get for running out on me,' she hissed. 'You rat!'

Champlon blinked in surprise, staring at Aunt Hilda without recognition. Aunt Hilda's lower lip had begun to tremble at his lack of reaction. She stared at him unblinking, but his gaze back at her was dull.

'Gaston! It's me!'

He was blank.

'Gaston. It's Hilda!' her voice broke. 'Speak to me. Please.'

By now the bodyguards were roping Champlon's hands together, tying them so tight that the rope bit into his flesh.

The Maharajah held out his hand to Waldo, his moon face beaming:

'You saved my life.'

'No.' Waldo blushed. He was glowing with pride. 'I mean . . . um . . . yes, but it was only –'

'A stroke of luck,' I interrupted, a bit meanly. But I could see how this would go to Waldo's head. He must have blasted the gun out of Champlon's hand! 'Your Highness, that man is a sharpshooter. My friend has only just begun –'

'Hey,' Waldo bridled. 'I *aimed*.'

'You are hero,' the Maharajah said, ignoring our tiff. He had a fluting sing-song voice, which rose over our squabble, like one of his own bulbuls. 'It is because you are American, the New World they call it, no?'

Waldo nodded proudly. 'It is a mighty fine country,' he said.

The Maharajah turned now to his dewan. But Aunt Hilda had intercepted the minister and was talking frantically to the king.

'I know this man, Your Highness,' Aunt Hilda blurted to the Maharajah. She towered over him, but despite his tiny, plump frame the boy king had dignity. 'Something is wrong.'

'How can this be?'

'He is a Frenchman. A famous explorer.'

'He wanted to kill me.'

'There must be some mistake.'

'He will be execute at dawn tomorrow. Sonali will take care of him.'

'How do you mean?

'She will crush him.' He brought one plump hand down, slap bang on the other. 'His head will be crushed under her feet.'

I had a sudden, sickening vision of Champlon's head disappearing under the elephant's massive, trampling feet.

'No!' my aunt and father wailed in unison.

'Silence.' The bald Dewan held up his hand imperiously. 'It is the law of the land.'

For a moment a hush fell on the scene, above which could only be heard the snorting of the elephants and the soft shushing and crackling around us. We could not let Champlon die in India, whatever he had done, so many miles away from his home.

'Your Majesty.' My aunt's gruff voice rose in desperate appeal. 'Of course you must execute anyone who dares to threaten you. But something is wrong. *I know it*. Something is not right with this man . . .

'Look at him. Your Highness, he looks like a sleepwalker.'

'A what?'

'He is not himself. I know it.'

She had piqued the Maharajah's attention. He went up to Champlon and gazed at him closely and the Frenchman gazed back dully, as if nothing unusual was happening. As if he was at The Travellers, that famous gentleman's club in Pall Mall.

The Maharajah said, 'This is strange.' He said something in his own language – which I have learnt is called Gujarati – to the guards who were holding Champlon. They seemed to protest but a sharp word from the Dewan was enough to silence them and they undid the

121

ropes that bound the Frenchman, but remained close by his side. The Maharajah held out his hand and grasped Champlon's in a kind of handshake. 'I have seen this in my village once, long time ago. Before I was Maharajah.'

Champlon scarcely seemed to notice the king taking his hand. His bony fingers limply in the Maharajah's plump palm and now the boy king did something very strange. He began to stroke the Frenchman's hand, pudgy fingers flickering.

'This is fakir's work. I have seen it in the village,' the Maharajah declared. He began to gabble excitedly to his dewan and the adviser translated:

'The Maharajah says that this man has been hypnotised. He has been put into a trance. The Maharajah believes he is doing another man's bidding.

'The man is like a puppet on a string. Dancing to his master's tune. The Maharajah saw this as a boy, a man driven out of his wits by a fakir.'

Aunt Hilda exclaimed angrily but the Dewan held up his hand to silence her.

'Do not despair. The Maharajah, he has learnt it from his parents. How to bring someone out of a trance.'

The word 'trance' gave me a jolt. Indeed there was something trance-like, about the Frenchman's strange behaviour. His lolling, vacant eyes, his drooping mouth. Not at all the energetic and impatient explorer, the

Gaston Champlon we knew so well.

'It is a very powerful fakir who has done this,' the Dewan continued.

In the tangle of creepers above us I had a fleeting glimpse of a pair of yellow eyes. A wrinkled face. Almost human, but so old and ugly it couldn't be. A powerful smell of evil surged down to me and the tiger scratch on my face throbbed, with a sudden fierce pang. *The monkey*, I gasped. I looked up into the screaming maroon and green of the wild almond but the thing was gone. Only the caw of the racket-tailed drongo, the whir of lizard and shrike. How could I spot one evil creature here in the midst of this flurry of animal life? I wasn't sure if, after all, it was only an illusion.

All the while, the Maharajah held Champlon's hand. The Frenchman drooped, his body limp, his eyes blank. Then he dropped the hand and the Frenchman gave a great cough. His head moved from side to side, his eyes darting wildly. In a heartbeat Champlon changed. Animated and anxious, he pulled away from the startled guards and trotted over to Aunt Hilda and blurted, 'Madame, we must hurry. The Randolph Hotel. It is a bad business to be zo late.'

'Gaston,' Aunt Hilda gasped and the word struck him like a whiplash. He stopped short, gazing around in astonishment.

'Where am I?'

'Hyde Park?' my aunt replied tartly. 'In the jungle, of course.'

'*Ze monkey*,' Champlon murmured. 'Where is ze monkey gone?'

❧ Chapter Twelve ❧

I waited till the next morning to visit Champlon, wishing to give him a little time to recover from his ordeal. Kidnap, hypnotism, an assassination attempt on a king – quite a lot to cope with even for a seasoned explorer. His bedroom was guarded by two fierce-looking soldiers. When I entered, despite the gravity of his situation, I had to suppress a smile. I had never seen anyone look *quite* so ill. His wrinkled face was just visible under the towel wound about his head and tied, like a lady's bonnet, under his jaw. How could he bear to be muffled in blankets in this heat? The room was stifling with only a breeze now and then from the steady movement of the palm-leaf punkah wafting across the ceiling.

'My 'ed is ache,' he moaned.

'Not your 'ed, monsieur,' I snapped, for I was angry and frustrated with our French friend. 'Your head.'

'Is what I says, my 'ed,' Champlon replied.

A small boy – the punkah wallah – was pulling the

punkah. In a moment another boy – the pani-wallah – would replenish the jug of ice-cold water by the Frenchman's bed. There was a boy for every job in this palace, servants everywhere. Giving up on the impossible task of correcting Champlon's English, I dropped my voice. What I had to say was sensitive, and I did not want to be overheard.

''Ed or head,' I said sternly, 'you're lucky that moustachioed lump of flesh is still attached to your body.'

Unconsciously, Champlon's hands fluttered to his neck.

'Most rulers would have it off,' I made a chopping motion with my hand. 'Listen, monsieur, you're in a very tight spot. Aunt Hilda is pleading for your life, right now. Most of the Maharajah's advisers are begging him to squash your head under the feet of his favourite elephant.'

'Mon Dieu!' Champlon moaned. 'I have ze memories not at all.' He gave me an odd look. 'What is zat on your face?'

My hand flew to my scar, the vicious scratch the tiger had left on my cheek. It throbbed day and night; I was horribly self-conscious about it.

'Nothing,' I barked. 'Look, Monsieur Champlon, what were you thinking of? We have all been so worried. Trying to shoot the king!'

'The 'ed explodes.'

I shot him a suspicious look. I'd never heard him speak such broken English. He sounded like a pantomime Frenchman.

'Anyway, one thing is clear,' I said.

'What is zat?' Champlon stuttered.

'I thought you were meant to be a brilliant shot but even *Waldo* took you out.'

He glared at me. 'This was not ze true Champlon.'

'I'll say!' I knelt down by the bed and stared the Frenchman in the eye. 'Monsieur Champlon,' I said, softening my tone, 'you must try to remember. It's very important. Let's start with the monkey. And the boat.'

He turned a troubled face towards me, his moustaches trembling. 'What boat?'

'I know you were on the boat with us, monsieur. The steamship *Himalaya*. In the sick bay.'

'It is all so strange in my 'ed. Like I am walking through ze dream. Everything is cloudy and I floats. I see a man who I know. It is myself but I am not myself. I am looking at zis man and I am thinking who is he?'

'Monsieur.' I took his hand. 'Pull yourself together.'

'Questions, questions, questions . . . First your auntie and now you. But I do not know what zat man did. He, or I should say me, was sick, on the boat. He was sick all days and the other men, ze brozzers, were sick too.'

'Brothers?'

'Wheezing men. Ghosts.'

Instantly my mind flew to those villains, the Baker Brothers. I had suspected their hand behind the vanishing Maharajah. The uncanny way that Malharrao escaped from Walton Gaol was so like the Brothers. They floated behind the scenes, pulling strings, paying the bills, furthering their own evil schemes. They preferred to operate through henchmen. From Champlon's words – 'brothers', 'ghosts' – it sounded very much like our old enemies. Something big must be afoot, if they were in India. However, Champlon knew these men. Wouldn't he have told me if it was indeed the Baker Brothers? I stole a glance at my sick friend, while he continued to speak. Everything about him was hazy; like a pencil sketch that was half erased. In this state, I was surprised he even recognised me.

'One of zees men, he 'ad 'orrible skin, like ze burnt rubber. He was sick. We were all sick. The monkey, the Indian, me. I don't remember a thing – have pity, Kit.'

Champlon was so wan I was loath to press him further. He was sick, for sure. I was cruel to come here and press him for answers. But then, I had to find a way to save him from execution. Awkwardly standing there, my fingers pressed against the scrap of lace which I'd found with Amelia Edward's lapis lazuli cross. I'd carried it all the way from Oxford with me, out of some odd super-stition.

'I found the ankh!' I murmured, absent-mindedly.

My words had the oddest effect on Champlon. His fuddled manner vanished. He glanced at me, then quickly looked away. Just a fleeting impression, but so crafty. The very hair on my scalp began to prickle. All my instincts warned me to be very, very careful.

Something was not right.

I could not mistake the cunning in that glance. So, was he merely *acting* sick? I knew I had to pounce.

'It was very precious,' I said, quietly.

'Lapis lazuli is only a semi-precious stone . . . Not so –' he began and halted.

'But so old, that's what made it so valuable.'

'Please. Spare me, I beg you. Do not tell your aunt,' he blurted, in perfect English.

Champlon was sitting bolt upright, the towel had fallen off his head and what little colour there was in his face had drained away. He was very frightened.

'So old . . . and . . .' I said, feeling my way. Then suddenly, savagely I *knew*. 'But it is not just the money, it is a matter of trust.'

He fell back, his face ghastly against the white pillows.

'You betrayed Aunt Hilda, didn't you? Why?' I had no mercy. 'Was it greed? Treachery?' I moved closer to him and he flinched away. 'This is all an act, isn't it? The whole hypnotised bit. *You were never hypnotised. You were no more in a trance than I was.*'

He took a deep breath, steeling himself. When he spoke his voice was cracked. 'You're a child. You don't understand.'

'I am going to tell: Aunt Hilda, the Maharajah, the police. Public scandal.'

'Please.'

'I will tell all,' I said firmly.

'You wouldn't do that to me. Your own dear Champlon. Why I 'ave always looked out for –'

'Monsieur,' I cut his bleating off. 'There is only one way. Tell me everything. *Everything*, mind. I will see what I can do for you.'

'You're a cruel girl, Kit.'

'Everything,' I said coldly.

He sighed. 'We were shopping, your aunt and I, in the old market in Cairo. At the same moment we both saw an ankh lying on a stall along with a pile of fakes.'

'Fakes?'

'Antiquities created for the stupid travellers. Not so valuable at all.'

My mind flew back to our visit to Egypt. My gang of friends, along with Champlon and my aunt, had become embroiled in an adventure revolving around a stolen scarab. I recalled the day my aunt and Champlon had gone to the market together.

'Your auntie claims to be Egyptologist but she knows nothing. Not like Gaston. She wanted to buy ze ankh, but I told her it was worthless. I teased her. "Can't you tell a fake?" I asked. When I got it back to my hotel room and checked in my book I found ze ankh was a brilliant thing. A genuine Old Kingdom ankh. Worth 'undreds of pounds. Later, I sent out my servant to buy it. He got it very cheap.' The crafty smile was back.

'Your auntie would be hopping mad! She would never forgive me! But, of course, I had no intentions to tell her how I trick her.'

'You double-crosser!'

He shrugged. 'Anyway, perhaps your auntie look in ze same book. Poor lady, she brooded on ze ankh. She told me next morning at the breakfast, she was going back to buy it – pah . . . it was gone. Luckily she never found out I trick her – for the market man tell her Egyptian boy buy it.'

'So it ended. I took my ankh everywhere. Then, disaster. I saw something in the newspaper about that terrible woman, Amelia Edwards. You know her?'

I nodded. Miss Edwards, as you will remember, is a great rival of my aunt, a famous lady traveller and Egyptologist. In fact, I believe she is better known than

Aunt Hilda, though of course my aunt will dispute this.

'Miss Edwards she 'ad a big collection of Egyptian antiquities in Cairo – waiting to be shipped to London. She 'ad given much to ze British Crown.

'But zen in Cairo, robbers 'ad struck and half the collection 'ad been stolen from the warehouse before the guards chased –'

'I know,' I interrupted. 'I read about this in *The Times*.'

'Oh – I see. Well, when the remains finally arrived in England, Miss Edwards found that an ancient mummy and my ankh were among the stolen items. My ankh, Kit. I saw a drawing of it in *The Times* that terrible morning. Definitely my ankh!' He paused a moment, then went on, 'Well, I had not stolen it. I 'ad bought it fairly –'

'If you say so –' I mumbled, thinking of how he'd cheated my aunt. But Champlon continued: 'I paced around my college rooms, my mind shattered. What was I to do? There was only one way out. A few weeks ago I 'ad been bargaining with a well-known collector for some of my antiquities. He seemed to know about my ankh. But I refused to sell. Now I would have to sell ze ankh – on ze quiet. But I was not happy, no not at all.'

You could have reported it to the police rather than trying to make money out of stolen goods, I thought. But I held my tongue and listened to his tale.

'I was dressing that morning in my college rooms,

when suddenly a strange creature appeared. Gibbering, yabbering. A monkey. It pounced on my ankh which was lying on my chest. Grabbed it with dirty paws. I chase this monkey, down ze creeper, across ze college lawn, down to ze canal – and on to a barge. The owner is zere, an Indian. And two pale men. I know zem. 'Oo do you think it is, Kit?'

'The Baker Brothers,' I murmured.

He stopped a moment, reliving the moment. 'A trap.' His voice trembled. 'These brothers, zey kill me with zeir eyes.'

I nodded, recalling how Champlon's wizardry with his pistol had humbled the brothers and left them fleeing from the scene of the ruined temple in Siwa.

'So I fight zis monkey. It is a beast, most ferocious, spitting, hissing. I seize my ankh back. It breaks. I stop, my heart is break too. One brother, 'e grab the monkey, make it stop. He take ze ankh. Then 'e tell me they have evidence I steal zis ankh from Miss Edwards. "No, No," I protest. "I buy this fairly from market." But the one with ruined face he just smile. "No one will believe you," 'e say in his wheezing voice. "After all, my brother and I are highly respectable, we are friends of the Prince of Wales. We will testify you are a contemptible thief. A lying, low-down, rotten, French thief stealing from treasures meant for ze Queen. Why, I have no doubt you will be tried for treason."

'"With any luck," say the other brother, "zey will hang you."'

Champlon's voice cracked as he relived the moment. 'Believe me, Kit, I had no choice. They had me already on the guillotine. You see . . . well zere had been another instance . . .'

'Another instance of what?' I asked sharply, though I could well imagine. Clearly Champlon had double-crossed someone else before. Maybe he had even stolen something! Collectors have the loosest morals of anyone I know.

'Nothing was proved,' he replied swiftly. 'I was a young man then . . . still . . . ze . . . mud, it sticks close.'

'What did you steal? How long ago was this?'

Champlon flushed, evading the questions: 'Accusations, articles in newspapers. Even if I didn't hang – they would ruin me. So, the rest you know, Kit. It was blackmail. Foulest blackmail. But I 'ad no choice. I would be finish. Your auntie would never forgive me . . . I've never met a woman like zis, zis Hilda Salter. She steal away my heart, Kit.'

'So you say,' I said sourly. My mind whirled. 'You were never hypnotised. It was all a pretence . . . Gosh, Monsieur Champlon, you are the very best actor I have ever met.'

'I . . . am dazed, ze whole time,' he said hurriedly. 'Like the monkey was in my 'ed.'

'Head,' I snapped automatically. 'I'd believe you . . . if you hadn't told us such a packet of lies. So let me get this clear. They, the old Maharajah Malharrao and the Baker Brothers, they *made* you assassinate the new King . . . little Sayaji.'

'I missed. I missed on purpose. Also, I saved you from the tiger, Kit. Don't forget that!' His voice had sunk to a pleading moan.

'These criminals wanted little Sayaji out of the way for some reason,' I went on. 'They had an elaborate plot to rid themselves of him – and so they blackmailed you. But why you? Why not just hire an assassin out here?'

'I asked myself that. Obvious, I am ze best shot in ze world.'

'We've heard quite enough about that,' I cut in.

'You 'ave to understand these men, ze Baker Brothers. Zey know how to hate, Kit. Later, I was with them on that ship, in the sick bay and I know it. They 'ardly spoke two words to me. I felt such ice in them it nearly froze my bones. I was a trapped bird. All zey wanted was to torture. It delight them to 'ave me wriggling in their power. Zey have never stopped hating me for making them small in Egypt, Kit, and zey never shall.'

He fell silent after this outburst. I thought back to

Egypt: scorching sand, burning heat, miles of nothing-ness and two frozen men. Truly, they were artists in revenge, those brothers.

'But why do the Baker Brothers want to kill Sayaji?' I asked.

He hung his head. 'I don't know. Zey 'ave schemes within schemes. Zey use that fool, Malharrao.'

I believed we were seeing only a portion of their grand plan. Whatever they were plotting, the assassina-tion of the Maharajah of Baroda might be only be a small part, a means to their greater – and more evil – end.

'Your position is very grave. The Maharajah's advisers are clamouring for your blood,' I said. 'I will have to think about my –'

I got no further for at that moment there was a knock on the door and Waldo burst in, flushed and excited.

'Where have you been, Kit?' he burbled. 'I've been looking for you everywhere.'

'Here, of course,' I answered.

'Oh give up the smart talk. This is too exciting!' Perspiration was dripping off Waldo's face and his shirt was damp. 'The Maharajah has asked to see us. We're going to the treasure vaults.'

'Why?'

'I don't know . . . *Come on!*'

With a last glance at Champlon who had sunk back on his pillows, his face crumpling, I raced after Waldo.

'Please,' Champlon mouthed at me. 'Please keep my secret.'

The Maharajah paused at the top of the stairs leading down to the lower levels of the palace and the treasure vaults. 'You have heard the terrific news?' he asked.

'No, Your Highness.'

'Mercy doesn't grow on trees.'

'No.'

His round face broke into a delightful smile. 'But in Baroda it does grow on trees! We have decided to pardon your friend Champlon. I tell my advisers the better part of wisdom is mercy. Let mercy temper the fruits of justice.'

'Oh, thank you, Your Highness,' I said, rejoicing with all my heart.

He waved his hand airily. 'It is done already. Besides I am too pleased with my friends, Waldo. This is all you want, Waldo? Just look old journal?'

Waldo nodded.

'Young man,' the Dewan intervened. 'The Maharajah feels you are too humble. This is too little to thank you for saving his life. He will give you rubies, diamonds, gold, tigers . . . name your price.'

'You have already done enough, Your Majesty,' my aunt interrupted. She didn't approve of anyone but herself being showered with riches. 'Pardoning Monsieur Champlon was merciful indeed.'

'It is right that I personally must thank you, Valdo the American,' the Maharajah insisted.

Waldo hesitated a moment. He was very, very tempted, I could tell, by the diamonds and tigers. I kicked him from behind on the shins. 'Ouch,' he muttered and then after a moment's sullen silence he replied:

'It's very kind of Your Majesty to offer me gifts but I must refuse them.' He gave me a quick sideways glare. 'It is very important to *my friends* to see this journal.'

The Maharajah nodded and we all followed him single file down through winding corridors till we came to an iron door engraved with swirling patterns. Three sentinels, richly garbed in scarlet and gold uniforms, curved scimitars in their belts, were lounging outside the door. When they saw us they sprang to attention and we were let into the treasure vaults.

It was a vast, soaring chamber. Cobwebs wreathed fluted pillars, trailed from wooden beams carved with wondrous birds and beasts. I gazed around in wonder, though I could see but dimly. The Dewan uttered a word in Gujarati and more sentinels sprang into action, throwing open the shutters with much clanging. As the room was suddenly flung into bright relief, we all gasped with awe.

Treasure. More treasure than we had ever thought to see! An Aladdin's cave, crammed with chests of gold, silver, wood and ivory. Glistening pearls spilled from one. A golden cup, coiled with ruby snakes, sat carelessly on top of another. The Maharajah opened a bronze box brimming with gems. What a world of wealth they conjured: sapphires and emeralds hinting at the watery depths of the ocean, rubies rich as the reddest wine. Casually he reached inside and pulled out a glittering rope of gems, sapphires coiling around one huge diamond.

'The Star of the South,' the Maharajah said, pointing to the sparkling thing.

The diamond was multi-faceted, gleaming with a strange secret light. To my dazzled eyes, it looked as if the Maharajah had caught a little piece of the moon – and held it trapped and blinking in his hand. This sounds foolish I know, but I had never seen something *so shiny*. We stared at the diamond, mesmerised. Rachel, Waldo, Isaac, Mr Prinsep, Miss Minchin, my aunt and father. A circle of worshippers.

'Best necklace in the world,' the Maharajah said, casually replacing it in the box.

I glanced at Waldo. His face was ashen. Now that he had seen the Maharajah's treasures he was clearly regretting his decision not to be showered with gifts.

'Um,' he began, clearing his throat.

'Don't even think of begging for gold,' I hissed at him. 'Aunt Hilda would never forgive you.'

'What you think of this? My royal robes.' The Maharajah had wandered over to the corner of the room where a court dress was laid out on a silver chair. There was a coat of deep blue silk with a high stiff collar and covered with delicate embroidery of pearls and gold thread. A matching set of pantaloons. A waistcoat even more richly embroidered with emeralds and rubies, and perched above, a turban speckled with more diamond fire. The costume was far too big for the Maharajah, he would be swamped by it. These rich robes must have been ordered by his wicked predecessor.

'Why don't you wear these things, Your Highness?' I asked. The Maharajah was wearing cream linen pantaloons and a matching shirt. Though gleaming with starch the garments were very simple.

For a reply he burst into giggles. 'Most uncomfortable, Miss Salter, I could hardly move my neck.' Then his face sobered. 'I will be different kind of Maharajah . . . a modern king. I will build schools and hospitals for my people.'

Mr Prinsep was glowing with pride. 'You'll show 'em,

Your Highness.'

'Most surely.'

'You'll be a lot better than that fellow.' Mr Prinsep gestured to an oil painting shoved in a shadowy corner of the vaults. I went up to it and took a good look. It was of a bearded, slightly pop-eyed man. Unmistakably our old friend, Malharrao, the wicked former Maharajah. He seemed to have a positive mania for posing atop dead animals, for here he was lying on a lion skin, the Star of the South gleaming round his neck.

'Have you any news of him?' I asked, cautiously. My aunt and friends knew of course that he was behind the plot to kidnap Champlon and assassinate his successor. But what had they told the palace? I didn't want to get the Frenchman into more trouble.

'We think he is here, in Baroda,' the Dewan said, a grim look on his face.

'Why?'

'You can take that innocent look off your face, Miss Salter,' he replied. 'We are not fools. Mr Prinsep told us you recognised Malharrao, leaving the boat. Somehow Malharrao is involved with your Frenchman and this whole to-do about hypnotism.

'It is very simple really. No one wants Sayaji dead, like that rotten man.'

We were all silent – glancing at one another guiltily.

141

The tension was palpable, in that vast gloomy hall. I felt as if I was in a room full of smoke and mirrors. What did the palace know? What did they know we knew? *Who knew?* It was an impossible situation, heavy with guilt and secrets. Then the Maharajah clapped his hands.

'You all worry too much!' he trilled. 'I have idea. Waldo, you must try on royal robes.'

'No, sir . . . I mean Your Majesty.'

'Yes, yes!'

'I couldn't.'

'You must. It will be a great joke.'

With a foolish grin on his face, Waldo agreed to the Maharajah's demands. He shrugged on the heavy robes with a proud air. I hate to admit it, but he did look rather handsome. The dark silk set off his blue eyes and blond hair. He lifted his head in the pose of a king.

'My, you look handsome,' Miss Minchin gushed. Her admirer, Mr Prinsep, cast a jealous look at Waldo.

Then the beaming Maharajah placed the turban on Waldo's head and the royal likeness was complete.

'His Supreme Highness Waldo the American,' said the Maharajah. 'Bow down.' Everyone, down to the last sentinel played along with his game. I grovelled along with the rest, though I felt slightly sick when I caught Waldo's smirk.

He was loving this.

'I know!' the Maharajah exclaimed. 'I vill give this turban to you, Waldo. Wenever you put it on you vill be King and everyone will have to listen to you.'

That was the worst idea I had ever heard! The Dewan took the Maharajah aside and whispered to him agitatedly, but I could see the boy was adamant. The turban must be worth a fortune, speckled as it was with diamonds.

'It is too much,' my aunt said, echoing my thoughts. Though as it was her, she was probably wishing she had been presented with gems. 'The diamonds are –'

'Only small . . . nothing.' The Maharajah waved an airy hand. 'Waldo, when you put on this turban, you remember that Maharajah of Baroda is always your great friend,' he said and that was the end of the matter.

I could see my father, who has a one-track mind, was thinking of Father Monserrate's journal. Coughing now, he brought it up. 'The manuscripts, Your Highness.'

'Ah yes.' The Maharajah wandered past some glossy oil paintings – one of a golden angel bathed in a halo of light looked Italian – till he came to a dusty wooden box. This was a broken-down old thing, fragments of earth still adhering to it. It was out of place amid the riches of the royal vaults. He picked it up and handed it to my father, who was trembling with excitement.

I must confess I was trembling too.

Inside there was a leather-bound journal filled with yellowing paper. Nothing precious. Though, to my father, this was the most amazing thing in the room. He was a dusty old scholar again, the lure of diamonds forgotten.

The paper gave off a dry crackle as he extracted them from the box. We crowded round him as he opened the book up and started to leaf through the pages, glancing at the spidery black writing.

I had glimpsed something that my father had missed in the depths of the chest. A rusty-red roll of paper. I reached in and felt the dry texture of parchment. As soon as my skin touched the thing a jolt, a marvellous shock, travelled up through my fingers, sparking along my nerves till it reached my heart. I felt alive, alert. I knew this was vital. In that tiny twist of a second I felt that *it* would change my life. Carefully I took out the paper, which was folded up into quarters. On the face of it, it was pretty unremarkable, something old, long-forgotten. When I unrolled the thing, it began to glow, moon-like. It was a map. The parchment faded with the ages, but the ink still vibrant oranges, turquoise and scarlet.

I had only to brush this object with the lightest of touches, for it to claim me. This map and I were connected. It had *chosen* me. I was destined to be here, to hold this precious, secret thing in my hands. No one was taking the slightest notice of me, they were all crushed around my father. My heart was thumping with excitement, as I began to read:

SHAMBALA

A guide to the Moste Secrete and Beauteous Idyll

Now my aunt had noticed my find and looked curiously over my shoulder. 'Theo,' she gasped. 'It's here. Shambala. Paradise on earth.'

She had attracted the others who now all crowded around me. Shaking them off, I walked over to the window so I would have more light. I smoothed the map out and carefully held it up, stretched between my two hands. There was silence in the room, as we breathed in the aroma of this old legend. I could just imagine the missionary venturing across the seas many centuries ago to the court of the great Mughal king, Emperor Akbar. There he had heard tales of marvellous doings. Whispers of mysterious rites and secrets.

This map was special. But it did not belong to my father, or aunt or the Maharajah. I knew that only I, Kit Salter, could feel the call of time and magic swirling beneath the surface of the rough parchment, the presence of the fakir who had inscribed these secrets. It was beautifully designed, covered with ultramarine lakes and mountains with icy white-inked tips. I looked at them and was drawn into the map. I felt a longing, deep inside me, a sort of wrenching in my gut and snarling in my heart. –

It was as if the map was pulling me. Somewhere, a voice whispered, there is something *better*. I would be . . . happier . . . oh, I didn't know. Along with the pull of a dream, I also felt sharply dissatisfied. I had to shake off my clinging friends and family and make a break for myself. I had to find out who I was, and what real freedom meant.

Was there really a promised land?

Abominable Cave – beware all ye who . . .

I was reading when my hands were joggled. I felt a sudden, sharp pain in my neck. I shrieked as a pair of claws grasped the map. There was something on my shoulder, yabbering in my ear, nails digging my flesh. I turned my head and I was inches away from a furry white face. It had leering ochre eyes, its raven-black pupils dilated. There was a tiny point of light in the centre of each eye.

The monkey grinned away at me. A gibbering envoy from hell.

'No,' I screeched, pulling the map away from the creature. It grabbed back, ripping the parchment in half.

A lightning bolt of pain streaked across me, causing my legs to buckle for an instant.

Yelling guards rushed towards us, as the monkey gave a harsh cackle. But the soldiers were too far away. It was up to me. My hands gripped the monkey's leg, but it wriggled out of my grasp, clawing viciously at my arms. Its tail lashed me across the face, making my scar throb. With three bounds it was at the wall, a blur of white fur. The Maharajah screamed and a sentinel raised his gun and fired. The bullet missed the monkey by a millimetre and embedded itself in the wall. The beast skittered upwards and vanished through the window.

The pain inside me was such I staggered against the wall and collapsed in a heap. My map! That foul creature had vanished with half of *my* map! It was as if half my heart had been wrenched away.

❧ Chapter Thirteen ❧

Guards rushed to the window, others poured out of the room. Too late. When I looked out of the window the monkey had disappeared, a puff of smoke melting into the midday sun. The great gardens were spread out like a jigsaw puzzle, palms, jacarandas and banyans shimmering in the heat, the trickle of the fountain. Dimly I spied a couple of dancing girls, loitering under the trees in their purdah gardens. Otherwise nothing. Or, rather, too much, with the caw of crows, the cackle of chickens, the slow munching of the sacred cows who wandered freely where they would, even monkeys swinging through the trees. Too much life here to single out one malevolent creature.

'What happened?' the Maharajah asked, his eyes bulging.

'It was some kind of animal, Your Highness,' the Dewan said.

'A monkey,' I spat. 'A disgusting little thief.'

'Find that monkey!' the Maharajah shouted at the guards, who scattered out of the door.

My father, clutching the journal in his limp hands, was close to tears. There was a feeling of jangled nerves in the room, for the odd incident had upset us all.

'We still have half the map,' I said dully, leaning on the window frame for support.

'And the journal,' my father murmured.

The Maharajah intervened. 'Borrow this thing,' he said, waving my father to the journal. 'You are a great scholar. God willing you will find answers to these mysteries.'

'This country doesn't agree with me, Kit.'

'A whole country can't disagree with you, Papa! It's a place, not a person.' I spoke with an effort, for the loss of half my map was still a physical ache.

'The heat. The food . . . and that monkey! Nothing is right.'

After the hullabaloo in the treasure vaults I had gone to my room to change into formal clothes for luncheon and then joined father in the north-facing study adjoining his bedroom. The inevitable punkah wallah was pulling his creaking fan. Dark shutters kept out the worst of the sun's glare. I couldn't really sympathise with father's woes. His rooms were pleasant and airy, the best in the lodge. Sure, like Rachel, he *was* suffering from 'Delhi belly'. But he hadn't been *chosen*, only to have it split, torn, snatched away.

'Cheer up,' I murmured. 'We have the journal. That's the main thing.' I didn't really think this was true. The journal was interesting, but the map had been special and now it was only half a thing.

'Quite right,' Father replied brightening. The journal was lying on his desk, a leather-bound book of immense age and decrepitude. It looked as though it would fall apart at one touch. I moved towards it, intending to take a look but Father was there before me. Luckily his stomach chose this moment to give another twinge:

'Don't fiddle with that, Kit,' he murmured as he made off in the direction of the bathroom.

'I won't,' I promised. Once he had gone, I carefully picked up the notebook. I think it was fate that made it fall open! The first word I saw was Shambala – the map! The very thing I was interested in. I read rapidly:

My servant Jorge grows ever more fascinated by Shambala. He is entranced by the myth of the fountain of life; the spring of crystal–clear water that gushes forth eternally in Shambala. If ye drink from this fount, they say, ye will never sicken or die. In this mountain paradise all is harmony and peace. While the world below sickens and evil blooms in men's hearts, Shambala is pure. One day, when war, plague and pestilence ravage the world, the king of Shambala will descend to save mankind.

A most pleasing story, though most clearly a story. Jorge, I fear, does not see it that way. He is obsessed with the myth of the shimmering ice city rising in the crystal mountains.

Ever since the accident that has left him disfigured, he dreams of his lost youth. I believe he seeks to regain his former beauty. This is the devil's work, I have told him. Those who aspire to the holy life should have no interest in such mortal snares. Alas, to no effect.

Earlier today when we had audience with the Great Emperor Akbar, holding court from the heights of his immense golden throne, we found also a strange, half-naked person there. This man was a pagan. An Indian magician–fakir of the most evil kind, one who claimed occult powers. I fear the Emperor was most beguiled by

his stories. To my horror I found young Jorge was
equally enthralled.

Later when I came into our chambers I found Jorge. He
blanched when he saw me, threw up his hands. I
confess, I became angry and snatched something out of
his hands. A map to Shambala. What strange writings
upon it. The scribblings of these yogis if I am not
mistaken. There is a —

'Kit!' Father's voice boomed in my ear. 'What are you doing?'

I turned round. He was red-faced, furious.

'Sorry,' I muttered, hurriedly replacing the precious journal upon the desk.

'You must wear gloves when reading ancient manuscripts. The sweat on your fingers can destroy them!'

The arrival of the servant to tell us our carriage was ready saved me from more lectures. Along with the Maharajah and the Dewan we had been invited to luncheon with the Spraggs. It was sure to be tedious I thought, as we hurried through the gardens to the road where Rachel and the others were already waiting. The six of us crammed in one tikka-gharry, and clopped by the edges of the market, thronged with people who stopped and stared when they saw the royal crests. Once

I saw a pall of oily grey smoke and heard a low hubbub, which I thought must be from a fire. It was burning bodies from the ghats – the funeral pyres by the river. Soon we pulled up outside the British Residency, a grand, colonnaded building, built in pinkish stone, surrounded by a wilting lawn. We were ushered inside by a footman in a magnificent red and white livery, wearing a turban decorated with a sort of scarlet fan.

When we arrived there were already some twenty people, including the Maharajah, the Dewan and Mr Prinsep, seated around a gleaming ebony table. Above the table, to the left of the enormous crystal chandelier, was the biggest punkah I'd yet seen. Never mind palm leaves, this one must have been made of a whole palm tree. It was operated by two liveried boys, each pulling a strand of palm. Mrs Spragg, in a fussy satin gown, presided. She was attended by her forgettable husband and her golden-haired son Edwin, dressed up in a suit just like his papa. How sweet he looked. How deceptive appearances are.

I made a slight vomiting noise at Edwin's saintly appearance to my friends. Waldo grinned back at me, then contorted his face, mimicking Edwin's prim expression.

The sight of the feast spread on the white tablecloth cheered me. I had thought Mrs Spragg might serve some rather soggy food, but she clearly had a good native cook. Dozens of silver trays heaped with fried potato patties, crispy savoury biscuits, more of the bhajis I had grown to love. Fowl, chicken, that delicious fragrant rice. Mangoes and sweetmeats. Pitchers of ice-cold lemon sherbet. My stomach was already rumbling.

No one else was going to do it, so I slipped into the empty chair next to Edwin, as the waiters filled our glasses with frosty lemon sherbet. For a while I concentrated on eating the starter, watery mulligatawny soup. Once I'd finished my bowl I could get on to some decent food.

'Father always says –' Mr Prinsep began but Mrs Spragg interrupted.

'Is that the tenth Baronet Prinsep of Prin Towers?'

'Rather,' said Mr Prinsep colouring a little. 'Well, Father has old-fashioned views about things, I'm afraid. That's why he shipped me out to the colonies. Thought I might contract an unfortunate marriage, you see. Thinks I'm too much of a romantic. I've to prove myself for three years at a proper job before he gives me my inheritance.'

Over the soup tureen I could see Miss Minchin, straining to catch their conversation. I'd never seen her so blooming. I've never been one for romance, for all the soggy sentiment that gushes around lovers. I have to admit Mr Prinsep's attentions had worked wonders on my governess. It had smoothed out her harsh lines, transformed her frowns into blushes.

Now her smile suddenly froze and I knew she had overhead Mr Prinsep's remarks.

'Looks like he's not going to be her Prinsep Charming after all,' Waldo said softly.

'That's a *terrible* joke,' I muttered.

'He'll probably marry some Indian princess, if he's out here for three whole years,' Isaac added.

'Don't you know anything?' I asked. 'Indian princesses are not allowed to meet foreigners, let alone marry them! They have to live in separate –'

I stopped in the middle of my remarks for I noticed that my governess had turned pale and was swaying slightly in her seat. Suddenly she dropped her spoon, with a clatter that turned several heads.

'Miss Minchin. Pray, what is the matter?' Edwin stood up, and leant across the table as if to assist my governess, his whole body a picture of angelic dismay.

Trust that dratted boy to call the attention of the whole table to Miss Minchin.

'Pray do not bother. It is stuffy in here . . . nothing altogether.' Miss Minchin visibly tried to pull herself together. 'Some air.'

'Here. Have this.' Edwin handed my governess his

tumbler of lemon sherbet. 'Just the thing to beat this heat.'

My governess reached across the table, her hand trembling, to take the glass. A little of the liquid slopped over the side of the rim on to the white tablecloth. It was a dark golden colour. Too dark. The cogs of my brain slowly whirred into action. Lemon sherbet. The acid yellow of freshly ripened lemons. The –

'WAIT!' I yelled.

Leaping to my feet I overturned my bowl of mulligatawny soup on to the tablecloth. I knew Edwin. I'd seen his hands flickering a blurred moment ago. For a minute I was afraid of making a fool of myself.

'DON'T TOUCH IT,' I shouted.

Rows of heads turned along the table. I glimpsed Mr Prinsep, his mouth gaping open like a goldfish, my aunt's open mouth, the Maharajah's wavering hands, Waldo trying to restrain me. Every single person in the room was watching me, Edwin and Miss Minchin. Even the waiter opposite me had frozen in the act of ladling out curry.

'THE LEMON SHERBET IS POISONED.'

There were varying degrees of disbelief on the faces around the table. Someone screamed, while the Dewan rose thunderously from his chair.

'Quiet!' I snapped and turned to Mrs Spragg's angel.

'Hold out your hand, Edwin,' I demanded.

All eyes were on the drama. The Dewan had sat back down and was watching me.

'She's demented,' the boy replied in a surly voice, but he didn't open his left hand which was clenched tightly shut around something. 'That scratch has infected her brain.'

Mrs Spragg jumped up to declare her outrage. But she was sitting too far away to intervene and I had no intention of dropping this.

'I saw Edwin put something in the sherbet,' I said slowly, in a cold voice. 'Powder from a box.' I seized the boy and tried to prise open his fingers, while the little devil wriggled under my grasp. I managed to force them open and there, clasped in his sweaty little hand, was a minuscule silver box.

'Here it is!' I said triumphantly holding up the box for everyone to see. The lid had been removed, there was white powder inside.

'That's not poison,' Edwin spat. 'I like my lemonade extra sweet. It's sugar.'

I had a horrible moment of doubt. Had I made a fuss in front of all of these people for nothing? Then I gathered my courage.

'Eat some then!' I held out the box to him. 'A spot of sugar, Edwin?'

Edwin blanched, backing away so quickly that he knocked over his chair. Down the table Mrs Spragg let out a deafening scream and her husband hurried to her aid.

'This isn't the first time Edwin's played tricks like this,' I said but my words were drowned out by the Dewan who had risen magisterially to his feet.

'ENOUGH!' he thundered. 'Memsahib Spragg, we are leaving.' He held out his hand to me for the silver box. 'We will test this powder. If we find your son has been up to mischief . . .' He paused and glared at the Spraggs. 'We will not be happy!'

The Maharajah, who I noticed cast a disappointed look at the feast, rose and the rest of the party followed, in a confused huddle. Indignation was in every inch of the Dewan's back as he marched out of the dining room, Mrs Spragg opened her mouth to protest and then changed her mind. The boy's face was as innocent as ever, but he couldn't resist snarling at me. I gave him a sunny smile in reply.

I could afford to be friendly, now I'd finally wreaked revenge on the little pest.

❧ Chapter Fourteen ❧

My friends chattered about Edwin as our horses raced back to the palace. I joined in for a bit, savouring my triumph over the appalling boy. Then my thoughts moved on. The odd incident had cleared my wits and thrown the intrigues surrounding us into sharper focus. The fragment of Father Monserrate's journal I had read about Shambala fascinated me. It was such a haunting account: a mountain paradise, serene above the turmoil of the world. Cliffs as sharp as razors, snowy glaciers and then – appearing through the mists – an ice city set in flower-flecked meadows. A place of peace, and of plenty.

I had visions of this mountain bower, shimmering in the air above me. Beckoning to me. It was the Eden where Adam and Eve romped. Before Eve was tempted by the snake and mankind began its centuries-long descent into a swamp of greed and war, and, well, *badness*. Such a place was surely a myth? Yet, yet . . . I had a feeling. My aunt and father were fascinated by the legend. There was some nugget of fact, some truth under all the swirling myths. My wounded map, safe in my inner pocket, called me. I felt the fact that it was torn as a pain inside me. Nevertheless, when I touched its crackly surface, a jolt started in my fingertips and ran along my nerves till it touched my heart. It wove a skein of enchantment that bound me like butterfly in amber. Whatever I was doing in India, this huge, heathen country, it had something to do with my map.

Have you ever had the premonition that something is waiting for you, just past that bend in the road? Not for anyone else. Just for you. It was foolish, irrational – but that was how I felt.

The scar on my cheek throbbed as I pondered. I had begun to feel less self-conscious about the mark – though I couldn't help feeling that people's eyes were drawn to it. Anyway, it was of no matter. What was important was the secrets piling up around us.

There was something my elders were not telling me. I couldn't help believing that Aunt Hilda and my father knew a lot more than I did. I tried to marshal my chaotic thoughts. To put them into categories: A, B, C :

A. The deposed Maharajah, Malharrao.
B. The monkey.

C. The two wheezing, sick Baker Brothers.

D. The blackmailed, supposedly hypnotised, Gaston Champlon.

What on earth brought them to India? Why had the gang blackmailed Champlon to kill little Sayaji? I could see, of course, that the Baker Brothers hated Champlon. I could understand Malharrao's interest in assassinating his successor. But why would those fabulously wealthy millionaires, the Baker Brothers, be interested in the fate of Baroda, this faraway part of our Indian Empire? Was it gold, diamonds, jewels? Was there something in the treasury they wanted to get their hands on? Try as I might I could not see what they wanted with this dusty, teeming place.

Unless it was *my* map.

Their monkey had snatched away half of it.

Yes, that was it. It wasn't pearls or the Star of the South. It must be my map they were after.

I shivered, despite the afternoon heat, which was so intense my clothes were damp with perspiration. The map, all these happenings, had taken such a hold on my imagination that I was exhausted. We arrived back at the palace lodge with me in a sort of daze and I trooped off to my bedroom. It was such a relief to finally be alone to try and sort out my thoughts. In my cool room, with the tick of the clock and the soothing whisper of the fountain in the gardens outside. Sighing, I took off the formal shoes I had put on for the Spraggs's lunch and collapsed on the bed.

Too soon there was a knock on the door. It was the pani-wallah, the same boy who had waited on Champlon. He bowed and indicated I should follow him.

I followed the boy through the gloomy corridors. Suddenly we heard raised voices, saw two people standing very close together. It was Miss Minchin and the Maharajah's tutor, unaware of our presence.

Mr Prinsep tried to slip his arm round Miss Minchin's waist. 'Listen.'

'No, Charles. Don't,' she hissed, pushing him away.

'I'm sorry I upset you. I –'

'Three whole years,' Miss Minchin interrupted. 'Why, I'll be an old maid by then!'

'You'll always be young to me.'

'You expect me to believe that?' Miss Minchin snapped. There was silence for a second then her voice softened into sadness. 'Why didn't you tell me?'

'I'm sorry.'

'Is that all you can say?'

'Father is no tyrant. When he finds out how I feel . . .' Prinsep's words trailed off.

'I'm not much of a match,' Miss Minchin said. She slumped against the wall, forlorn. 'Just a penniless governess.'

I cleared my throat and they jumped apart. Blushing, I hurried past, following the grinning pani-wallah. He stopped before a huge, brass decorated door. Inside I found my aunt, Father, friends, the Maharajah and the Dewan already assembled. Prinsep and Miss Minchin crept in after me. Champlon had been roused from his sick bed to join the conference. It was an impressive gathering, which could not have been held in a grander setting. Another vast room, filled from floor to ceiling with leather-bound books. Clearly the library. I settled down on a wooden bench.

'The heroine of the hour!' the Dewan rose to welcome me. 'Let us forget the bad business this afternoon and enjoy for a moment your triumph over the Spraggs.'

'Jolly good show,' the Maharajah beamed.

Only Waldo, who hates to see me 'get above' myself, was frowning at the praise.

You have to enjoy yourself when you have the chance! I forgot the death-threat letter and the monkey and gave myself over to the sheer pleasure of irritating Waldo.

Everyone smiled, relishing the memory of the Spraggs's discomfort. The moment was gone too soon, as a grim expression settled on the Dewan's face.

'Plotting,' he said, 'is the lifeblood of the palace.'

The Maharajah grinned sheepishly and a murmur went around the room.

'Normal people work and gossip, sleep and eat. We plot!'

The Dewan, though scarcely bigger than a normal boy, made an impressive figure. His bald head shone above his maroon silk kurta, as he began to pace back and forth, his eyes constantly flitting towards the young Maharajah:

'Many people want to murder our king. They disagree with the way he was chosen for his great task. They *think* they have purer royal blood or want to see their *own* sons on the throne. The palace is sick with plots and factions. I am the only one here who is one hundred per cent for the Maharajah, because, you see, I have no sons. I am unmarried and my only tie is to him.

'But you must understand something. This plot was something new.'

The Maharajah sat on the bench listening; his childish face and liquid brown eyes impassive. How calm he was. He must have lived among this atmosphere of intrigue, with the constant fear of death, ever since he came to the palace.

'Imagine the planning that went into it. Someone – who we now know was Malharrao – travelled all the

164

way to England so they could kidnap Monsieur Champlon and mesmerise him into killing our young friend.'

I glanced furtively at Champlon, searching for signs of guilt at the mention of hypnotism. But he looked remarkably smug. What an actor that man was.

'Why?' Waldo interrupted. 'Why go to all the trouble of kidnapping Champlon? There are others who could have done the job.'

Champlon, swaddled like a baby despite the heat, gave a smug smile: 'I sink eet is obvious,' he said.

'Not to me,' Waldo put in.

'Our French guest is famous,' the Dewan answered. 'He is one of the world's best marksmen.'

'Ze best,' Champlon said firmly.

'One thing I pride myself on is our soldiers,' the Dewan continued. 'Our young Maharajah is guarded day and night. It is well-nigh impossible to get to him. The plotters clearly thought they needed the best gun in the world to assassinate our king – so.'

We were all silent as we gave thanks for the fortune that had protected the Maharajah. Apart from anything else, I would not like to have seen Champlon's skull crushed under an elephant's massive leg.

'Our spies are everywhere,' the Dewan continued. 'Little happens in Baroda that we don't know about.

Champlon has given us good information about these villains – we were on the lookout.

'Last night one of our best spies brought us an interesting tale. A party of strangers had rented a bungalow about ten minutes' ride from here. They pretended to be Indians but our spy questioned the cook they had hired. He confirmed they were foreigners. A monkey with a white face went with them. Everywhere. Aha, I said to myself. Immediately I sent a party of soldiers to arrest these strangers. But when my men arrived at the bungalow they had gone. Vanished!'

Aunt Hilda let out a sudden groan.

'The place was cleaned out. Not a thing remained except for this broken thing,' he held out a bulb-shaped piece of blue and white pottery with a spout at the top. It was an ordinary Dr Nelson's inhaler, which you can buy at any English pharmacist to help with asthma. Both Baker Brothers wheezed, so it could have belonged to either of them.

'We hadn't a moment to lose. I set our guards to close the borders of Baroda.' He paused. 'I'm sorry to tell you we were too late.' After another pause he continued, 'We have information that this party left Baroda by an outlying hill path late last night. They were travelling in two carriages.'

'This is a disaster!' Aunt Hilda exclaimed.

'Quite so.' The Dewan bowed his head. 'There is one small useful fact. I have information from their cook, who overheard their preparation. We believe they are making for the roof of the world, Tibet in the Himalayas.'

I listened to the Dewan's words dully, without any surprise. I already knew the Bakers were going to the Himalayas. Was certain in my bones that the Bakers were seeking Shambala.

'We have to follow them!' Waldo declared.

'Hold on!' My father interjected quietly. 'We don't know what route they took, or what part of the Himalayas they are seeking.'

'These are deep waters,' the Dewan murmured. 'The plot against our Maharajah is tangled in mysteries. These two foreigners and their monkey have some other goal in mind.'

'I think you're right,' I cut in, addressing the Dewan. 'Their plan here has failed. These men are very practical. They've moved on to the next stage of their plot.'

'You're very sure of yourself.' The Dewan's eyes twinkled. 'How old are you, young lady?'

'That's hardly relevant.' I shrugged.

'Kit. Apologise at once!' My aunt snapped.

'I'm sorry, sir.'

The Dewan shrugged; he seemed highly amused.

'With all due respect, sir,' I went on. 'I think they were really after *the map to Shambala*. The legend of this Himalayan paradise has fascinated travellers for centuries. The Bakers believe this map will lead them there – and to something glorious . . .

'The scary thing is – they have half of this map now.'

'You are sharp, Miss Salter,' he replied. 'Shambala is believed to be in Tibet. You may be right.'

My aunt was watching us with an odd, uneasy expression. 'We will never catch them,' she said. 'We've no chance.'

She was right. We were foreigners in India. We didn't have the local knowledge to beat them to the mountains, never mind to trace my map's jagged course among the towering peaks of the Himalayas. The strangers were on the quest for Shambala – for some treasure I'm sure my aunt and father were aware of. They had a head start, half the map. They would get there before us. The only hope lay with my half of the map.

I couldn't tell the others. They would call me conceited, deluded and Lord knows what else. But I was the *only* one. The map had chosen me to lead them to Shambala. I just knew it.

My aunt rose, deep in thought. *Click-clack-click* went her shoes as she stomped around the wooden floor. She turned around and spoke to my father, in what she thought was a whisper. I overheard her hiss: 'They must know about it,' before he quelled her. So, I was right. They had *a secret*. There was some treasure in the Himalayas which they were unwilling to tell the rest of us about. I imagined something fabulous, priceless, like the great Koh-i-noor diamond, whose brilliance was said to light up the world. Father was very bad at keeping things from me. I would soon find out what all the mystery was about.

I couldn't hold my tongue. 'We must try and catch these people,' I declared. 'After all, they are kidnappers, would-be assassins, murderers.' Turning to the boy king I pleaded, 'Will you help us?'

The Maharajah made a gesture with his hands: 'Anything! For Waldo the American who saved my life – and Kit who saved my – how you say –' he tapped his head.

'Wits?' I offered.

'Yes, wits. Awful Spraggs made my head boil. Take all you need. Horses. Foods. Tents. Best guides.'

My father and aunt still looked gloomy and I understood from their faces the enormity of the challenge facing us. How would we ever find our enemies in the wildest mountains in the world?

'Do not despair,' the Dewan said softly. 'The game is

169

not over and we have the trump card.'

'What do you mean?' I asked.

'The Dalai Lama does not allow foreigners into Tibet.'

'Who is the Dalai Lama?' I asked, reddening a little, for I was ashamed of my ignorance.

'He is a monk king. He rules Tibet and allows no one inside his high mountain kingdom. Not the Chinese, not the Russians. Certainly not you Britishers, for he fears you wish to steal his country away from him.' He stopped a moment and grinned at us: 'After all, you *are* known for stealing other people's countries.'

My aunt painfully forced down a biting retort.

'No one can get inside Tibet, it is too dangerous,' the Dewan went on. 'There is no pleasant way to put this. If the guards find you they will kill you – slowly and painfully. They will roast you alive, or pull the nails out of your fingers, one by one. You will need the right guide to stand any chance. You understand me – there are only a few men in the world who can take you to this place.

'But these are only practical things. Really, the journey to Tibet and its most sacred place, Shambala, is a voyage to your soul. Only when you journey inside yourself will these holy mountains share their blessings with you.'

I stared at him. Many Indians, I noticed, could not speak plainly. They would use flowery phrases or talk in riddles, when a straightforward explanation would do. Their words created more fog than light! 'Journey inside yourself' indeed! I am a girl, not the Great Indian Railway.

'Open your mind to India,' he said, smiling.

'If I open my mind any wider my brains will drop out,' I said. The Maharajah tittered and my aunt frowned at my impertinence. But even as I spoke, my map, folded near my heart, whispered its own rebuke.

Don't mock what you don't yet understand, it murmured. *Listen and you will find a way. Go. Go. Hurry, now – because time is fleeting.*

❧ Chapter Fifteen ☙

'Is this really necessary, Aunt Hilda?' I wondered, looking at the mounds of luggage heaped on the station platform. There were mosquito nets and khaki drill tents, walking boots and mountaineering ropes, tinned meat and vegetables, dry biscuits and dates. Rifles were stacked besides glittering ammunition belts. Of course, we had brought my aunt's favourite explorer's staple, that stomach-turning concoction of lard and potted meat called pemmican. My aunt – never one to face hardship without as many home comforts as she could manage – had really outdone herself this time. There were at least five pairs of socks for each and every one of us.

'Surely all this luggage will weigh us down,' I added.

'Pish-posh,' she replied briskly. 'Better late in this life than early in the next.'

'Pardon?'

'It is an old Indian saying. It means go slowly and be

prepared. This is no picnic we're embarking on, my dear Kit. We are going to one of the most dangerous places on earth. I, for one, would like to have several pairs of woolly socks when my toes threaten to drop off with frostbite.'

She was right. I gulped down further protests.

The Maharajah had made good his promise and with incredible speed all the necessities had been assembled for our journey to the Himalayas. The royal carriages had been freshly washed, so you could actually see the Maharajah's crest – a prowling tiger. As we spoke, the steam train hooted, calling us to our epic journey – across the deserts of Rajasthan then on to Simla, in the foothills of the Himalayan mountains.

The Himalayas: the first step into the unknown.

The Maharajah had come down from the palace to bid us farewell, as had the Dewan. Part of me was sad to be leaving Baroda, for we had been showered with kindness here. I had become especially fond of Sonali, the elephant, and went to see her in the stables every day. I loved her wrinkled skin and tender eyes. I had even grown used to her attacks of wind, which were unbelievably foul smelling! Most of me, though, was thrilled to be off. But my poor afflicted father, whose stomach had been playing up ceaselessly, was very pale and I feared that Rachel was equally wan. The Minchin, in a faded frock she had buttoned up wrongly, was the most subdued. Her eyes were red and puffy and tears had left visible tracks amid the thick powder on her cheeks.

'Where's Prinsep?' Rachel whispered to me. 'Miss Minchin is terribly upset to be leaving. I wish she could stay with him.'

That would be wonderful, I thought. Every day, even during our voyage and our stay at the palace we had to take time off for 'tedious lessons'. Only lately – as love had bloomed – Miss Minchin had become rather lackadaisical in her teaching.

Without waiting for me to reply Rachel muttered something and disappeared down the platform. Where was Prinsep? Did he really care for our governess so little that he couldn't even be bothered to see us off? I looked up and down the platform, but though the station was bustling with vendors of chai and nuts and sweetmeats, there was no sign of the gangling form of the Maharajah's tutor. Suddenly the whole affair became clear to me.

Mr Prinsep was a cad!

He had been trifling with the Minchin's affections.

How dare he! Steam building up inside my head, I stamped down the platform looking for the Maharajah. It took me a few moments to find him, chatting amid the piled luggage, to my father and the Dewan.

'You must bid Mr Prinsep goodbye. For I fear he has been unable to come to see us off,' I said crossly.

The Maharajah looked at me in surprise, but the Dewan was wiser. He smiled at me, as if highly amused. 'Your kind heart does you credit. Though you do not always show it wisely,' he murmured.

'I should think those who do not bother to show loyalty to their friends are the most unwise,' I replied.

'I'm afraid it was not in Mr Prinsep's gift to accompany us here. I have sent him off on an errand.'

'Oh.'

'I realise your little governess is er . . . a bit sad.' The Dewan turned to my father. 'The Maharajah has a proposition which he wishes me to put to you before I ask her.'

'Pardon?' Father blinked. He is so clever but sometimes he fails to understand normal conversation.

'I wish to offer your Miss Minchin a position. If you agree of course.'

'A position?' Father asked. 'She isn't qualified for government –'

'She is very well qualified indeed for this post,' the Dewan interrupted. 'The Maharani, the Dowager Queen, has for a long time felt the need for a companion. She would like a genteel English lady, cultured in music and conversation, to teach her the ways of

Britishers. The Maharajah feels this would greatly aid the lady.'

Father blinked, uncertain, but my heart was singing. This was wonderful! No more Miss Minchin, no more Latin and grammar and tedious nursery tasks. She could stay in Baroda – and maybe one day, who knows, Prinsep's starchy baronet father would consent to their wedding. This was a boon from nowhere. Then I had a vision of the Minchin peering out through barred palace windows, like the dark-eyed beauty I had seen earlier that day. That awful Zenana. She would be forced to spend her life behind bars, like some creature in a zoo. Her face covered in a veil. Never able to visit the shops or stroll in the park. It would be intolerably harsh for someone who was used to her freedom. Why, she would not even be able to meet her admirer.

'She can't!' I burst out.

'I know how attached you are to your governess,' the Dewan smiled.

'I'm not,' I spluttered.

'Kit!' father objected.

'Sorry. I mean it's not that. Miss Minchin can't live in the Zenana. She would hate it. Not being able to go out by herself. Not allowed to –'

'It is hard to understand some foreign customs,' the Dewan said. 'I think you will be pleased, Kit, to learn that the Maharajah shares your poor opinion of the Zenana.'

'Yes,' the Maharajah burst in. 'I am to end the Zenana. The Maharani will be first royal lady to give up purdah. Miss Minchin will not have Zenana.'

'Oh . . . in that case the position would be fine. I mean, we are very honoured by the offer, Your Highness.'

'Shouldn't your father be the one to judge?' the Dewan asked.

'Er . . . yes, Miss Minchin can certainly come with us,' Father said absently, his eyes wandering away. I could see he hadn't been listening.

The Dewan gave me a smile of sympathy, as if he understood how difficult it was for me to manage my father. I could see he was still chuckling as he strolled down the platform to where Miss Minchin was drooping by the luggage. Isaac and Waldo were in an excited gaggle besides her and my aunt was energetically super-intending the travel arrangements. But my governess looked remote from the noise, heat and bustle. She was in a daze, floating amid her smashed dreams. I watched while the Dewan drew her aside and spoke a few words to her. Surprise chased bewilderment across her face. Then, finally, Miss Minchin understood what the Dewan was proposing. Forgetting all her manners, she threw her arms around the old man's neck. Radiant with delight.

Father was watching Miss Minchin, though I could tell he wasn't really *seeing* her.

'She's staying at the palace,' I told him.

'Er . . . is she? . . .' he muttered. 'Rather a good thing all round.'

'Heaven sent,' I agreed.

'You could stay with Miss Minchin. Keep her company, along with your friends, of course.'

I looked at him aghast. 'I don't think it's *my* company she wants!'

'No? Very well, just so,' he mumbled and strolled off, muttering to himself.

Rachel had materialised by my side and we watched my father amble away. Excitedly, I told her the news about Miss Minchin. We were free! Liberated from lessons, though I didn't expect my swottish best friend to see it that way.

At that moment someone brushed against my sleeve, it was Prinsep. He didn't bother to apologise, just flashed me a foolish smile and hurried on to the Minchin. He had plainly heard the good news.

'Isn't it wonderful?' I gushed to Rachel. 'I suppose I can take the credit for finding Miss Minchin a husband after all.'

'*Well done*,' Rachel said. Her voice was just a little sarcastic. I stared at her, dumbfounded.

'Rachel?'

'Yes?'

'It was *you*, wasn't it? *You* suggested to the Dewan that Miss Minchin could stay behind.'

'I may have had something to do with it,' Rachel murmured, mysteriously. 'Look, that coolie is running off with my bag. You there, boy!' She broke into an unladylike gallop after the man. 'Stop!'

Part Three

❧ Chapter Sixteen ❧

We travelled for three thrilling weeks after leaving the Maharajah's palace, chugging through the parched deserts of Rajasthan and up into the foothills of the highest mountains on earth. For Father, our journey was the purest misery. We were barely out of Baroda when his stomach began to gurgle. By the time we reached the Himalayas and shifted from train to swaying carriage, he was as pale as a lily, though sadly for the rest of us he didn't exactly smell like one. Poor Papa couldn't help noticing how we all tried to avoid sitting next to him. The rest of us sighed at the lovely scenery: snow-capped mountains, plunging hair-pin bends, forests clinging like cloudlets to tumbling precipices. Father spent the whole time staring at his shoes, when he wasn't stopping the carriage to vomit – or worse – by the wayside.

The only thing he was grateful for in the hills was the cool, fresh air. I breathed in lungfuls of the stuff, a relief after the stickiness of the stifling plains below. Simla was a lovely sight: a town shaped like a crescent moon, perched amid rhododendrons and oaks, on the steeply terraced hillside. I spied graceful houses and Gothic churches. The perfect place to regain our strength, before pressing onward to the mountains just visible through the mist.

I was confident that Father would recover when we rented rooms in a small boarding house. But, poor thing, he actually seemed to get worse. Admittedly, our lodgings, run by a complaining Irishwoman, were rather gruesome. Stuffed dead animals were everywhere; looming over the dinner table as you gulped down the mulligatawny soup, leering from above the mirror as you washed your face. Mummified lions, tigers, cheetahs, leopards, hares. No wonder Papa had given up and retired to his bed.

The mummy of a tortoise, its nose poking out of its shell, was placed on the wall above father's sick bed. Father and the tortoise were strangely alike. Both grey, sickly-looking and wrinkled.

'Papa, do not be too brave,' I said. 'Shall I call the doctor again?'

He groaned a refusal – but spoke no word. I wondered how much further he could carry on. Clearly he was going nowhere today. His only comfort was that he was not the only invalid. In the next room was Monsieur

Champlon, harrying the maids by ringing his bell every few minutes demanding more pillows or soda. I believe fear was behind his unreasonable behaviour. He was scared the Baker Brothers would seek him out for special punishment, for, after all, he had defied their attempts at blackmail.

But I had little attention for Champlon. Most of my worry was reserved for Father. Was it wrong to ferret secrets from a sick man? All through our journey to Simla I had longed to prise out the mystery that Father and Aunt Hilda shared, but had been unable to collar him alone. What were they looking for in the mountains? What clue did the map contain? Were Aunt Hilda and our enemies after the same treasure? Even though Father was sick, I had to be ruthless. I might not get another chance to find him alone.

'Papa,' I said placing my hand on his shoulder and speaking in my gentlest voice. 'Must you seek this treasure in Tibet?'

'Hilda has told you?' he asked, startled.

I nodded my head. Well I didn't *say* anything, so I wasn't strictly lying.

'It is more Hilda's quest than mine,' Father said. 'Though the gains could be enormous.'

I was thinking rapidly. How could I ask a question that would reveal the treasure my aunt sought and yet not reveal my ignorance?

'How big is it?'

'How should we know?' Papa said. 'What a strange question.'

'Tell me . . . please.'

At that very moment, just when I was accomplishing something, Aunt Hilda's voice boomed from downstairs.

'Kit. Hurry up.'

'One moment.'

'Get your boots down here at once – or I go without you!'

Cursing her sense of timing, I pecked at Father's brow, which was slippery with sweat, and dashed downstairs to join her. I emerged with relief into the cool mountain air, a relief after the fug of sickness in father's bedroom. Forests of fir, rhododendrons, pine, spruce and cypress surrounded Simla. This was the summer capital of the Raj – which meant that in the hot months the top British officials of the empire abandoned the sweltering plains to do their business here. I'm sure they had work to do, after all it cannot be easy running the greatest Empire in history. But Simla was also for pleasure. These officials certainly found plenty of time to stroll along the Mall, dressed in sola topis and cream linen suits, smoking cigars, dawdling and gossiping.

The Mall was broad and gracious, lined with colonnaded shops and stucco dwellings. It was singularly devoid of natives, apart from liveried rickshaw drivers, for they were forbidden on Simla's grandest road. No wonder that homesick Britons loved Simla. Indeed, the low bungalows, with their neat gardens, roses and apple trees, were like a little piece of home. 'Surrey in the Hills', the one place in India where there were more memsahibs than sahibs. Dressed in their finest calico, twirling their parasols, the ladies paraded. The 'Fishing Fleet' was out in force today. It was said if a lady couldn't 'hook' a husband in Simla, she had better give up angling.

I was just about to remark how pleasant it was in the foothills of the Himalayas when I saw something that made my heart sink. Bearing down on us was a palanquin, one of those wooden seats carried on poles. A couple of staggering native bearers carried Mrs Spragg, whose head was peering out of the muslin curtains. The revolting Edwin and his insignificant father walked alongside. I was about to suggest to Aunt Hilda that we duck down a side alley when she sighted the woman:

'Hello, Spragg,' Aunt Hilda hailed her. 'Whole lot of you run away to Simla? Quite right too! You're in hot water at the palace.'

'How dare you!' Mrs Spragg snapped, while her exhausted bearers lurched to a stop. 'Edwin has an excess of intelligence which makes him a little playful at times. It was a boyish prank, that's all.'

'The Dewan had that powder tested,' I protested. 'It was arsenic. Miss Minchin would have been very, very sick if she had drunk that sherbet.'

'Nonsense. You're making too much of it.'

'It could even have killed her.'

'High spirits,' Mrs Spragg snarled, while Edwin smirked. 'Anyway, where would Edwin get arsenic from?'

'It's quite easy to get it off flypaper if you –' Edwin began, in an I'm-just-being-helpful voice, but his mother shushed him hurriedly.

'Anyway we must be off. We're staying with the Viceroy as you know, and Lady Mayo expects us for elevenses.' Turning to me she asked, 'Where are you lodging?'

I mentioned our guest house and Mrs Spragg wrinkled her nose, as if I suddenly smelt bad. 'A native area,' she said. 'I've spoken to you before, Kathleen, about your habit of befriending *them*. It really does let down the Raj. White men have to stick together if we are to maintain our prestige. We can't let *Indians* get too close or they'll start thinking we're friends and take liberties –'

'Far better to poison the lot of them,' Aunt Hilda smiled, a little too sweetly. 'A tot of arsenic in the lemon sherbet does the job.'

This was too much for this memsahib. Pretending she hadn't heard, Mrs Spragg stuck her nose in the air and swept off, with a flurry of puffing bearers, dragging her husband and son in her wake. Aunt Hilda watched them go, grunting a little. Then she turned to me:

'Of course we're the greatest Empire in the world! But golly, narrow-minded snobs like that give us a bad name. If she wasn't swanning around pretending to run this place, Mrs Spragg would be stuck in some frightful bungalow in Esher. Just remember that!'

With that Aunt Hilda stomped off. I raced after her but was brought to an abrupt halt by a curious sight. A gaggle of ragged Indian children had gathered round an odd contraption. A loop of cord had been strung on four-foot-high sticks which had been stuck at regular intervals down the plunging side of the hill. As I watched, a tin can zoomed down the cord. Was this a local game, I wondered. Then one of the children moved and I saw Isaac's curly head. He was kneeling down, just about to send another can rattling down the hill.

'Isaac!' I called. 'What are you doing?'

He turned round and saw me. 'Inventing, of course!'

'*What* are you inventing?'

'A transport system. We'll turn these little cans into little passenger boats. Use steam propulsion and hey presto! Journeys that now take hours could take minutes!'

I stared at the little glittering cans, fascinated. Isaac did have a point, though it would take a lot of steam power to get the passenger boats back up the hill.

'I'm going to call it the Telepherage,' he said. 'Or maybe the cable horse.'

My aunt was watching the scene with some impatience. 'Wonderful idea, Isaac,' she said. 'I might even put some money into it. Now, Kit, are you coming or not?'

Without waiting for an answer she was away, turning off the Mall down a side-street and then down an even narrower one to the native area called the Lower Bazaar. The houses were closer here, huddled together. The Mall might have looked like Esher but in this pokey street, assailed by the scent of spices, we were definitely in India. We wandered down dirty, teeming alleys seething with natives, till we eventually reached a wooden house. The frontage was carved with beautiful wooden fretwork in the oriental style, though it was now shabby. A sign said:

THE CURIOUS SHOP
BASHIR ALI DEALER IN RARE GOODS

A bell clanged somewhere in the gloom as we entered. As my eyes accustomed to the darkness, I saw a golden Buddha rising from the shadows, its stomach fat as a watermelon, its smile sinister and serene. Other strange objects loomed: a Tanka – a rich Tibetan cloth painting of the wheel of life – decorated with snarling demons. A Chinese dragon carved of translucent jade with emerald eyes. A bronze statue of Kali, the Indian goddess of death, wearing a necklace of severed arms, her stomach ringed with skulls. She leered as she danced over her fallen enemy. Curling Arabic letters in gilded wood. An icon showing the Virgin Mary with a baby Jesus in her lap.

China, India, Arabia, Russia – it seemed as if the continents and the cultures of the world all met in this shop. Priceless statues thrown higgledy-piggledy with worthless pieces from the bazaar. It was like the nest of a greedy magpie, attracted by anything that glitters. I smelt adventure and mystery. The Dewan had directed us here, telling us this place dealt in much more than curiosities. He had let several hints fall about Bashir Ali: the man was an adventurer, he bought and sold everything from horseflesh, to rubies to state secrets. But though he was a trickster we could trust him with our lives. There were few people who knew more about the Himalayas than this old scoundrel.

'YOOHOO!' My aunt bellowed. 'Anyone at home?'

There was no answer, but I had the feeling that someone was watching us. Then I saw smoke curling out of a dark alcove next to the Buddha. With a start I spied an old man, smoking a hookah. He had long pigtails and a face like a pickled walnut. His eyes gleamed, red. I had the feeling that this man was measuring us, weighing what we were worth to him.

'Excuse me,' I asked the man. 'Do you know where Bashir Ali is?'

'I am he.'

'*I'm* Hilda Salter, the famous explorer,' my aunt interposed. 'This is my niece Kit.'

'Pleased to meet.' Bashir Ali nodded.

'We have come to ask for your help. I will pay you well for your time.' My aunt removed a couple of golden rupees from her purse and put them on a table at Bashir Ali's side. He didn't accept or reject the money, just inclined his head, while his face remained as expressive as a marble statue.

'We have been sent to you by the Dewan of Baroda.'

The change was instant. Bashir Ali didn't smile, but it

seemed as if stone had come to life. He had become human.

My aunt explained our mission. The man listened, not committing himself. Only when she had finished and had begged for his aid did he finally speak.

'Yes,' he said.

'Yes?' Aunt Hilda asked.

'I vill help you. You are friends of the Dewan.'

'We need a guide and a translator,' I burst out. 'Will you take us?'

Bashir Ali grinned, showing crimson gums, stained by paan, the nut that is chewed everywhere in India instead of tobacco. You constantly see men spitting into the gutters, which run red, as if flowing with blood.

'I am only old fellow. You need someone young, someone who knows the mountains like yak. There is von person for you.'

Slowly he rose from his chair. As he emerged from the shadows I could see him more clearly. He was tiny – smaller than me – and had on a yellow satin coat, richly embroidered with flowers and birds. Perching on the back of his head was a small round velvet cap. An odd costume. I did not know if it was Tibetan, Indian or Arabic, or a mix of all three.

Bashir Ali produced a quill and a bottle of ink and swiftly drew a map. A good road out of Simla, travelling up the hillsides towards the pilgrim town of Badrinath, and then onwards to a mountain hamlet called Mana. After Mana, he marked a diversion with a violet cross, near the enormous blank space on the map that was Tibet. This was the place where we would find our guide. He was a man named Yongden, a lama, a Buddhist hermit, who would take us over the dangerous border and up into the dizzying heights of Tibet. Yongden knew the trails into Tibet like no other man alive. Snowbound passes sixteen thousand feet above sea level, villages built on land that soared higher than any mountain in Europe.

The roof of the world! If we succeeded in entering Tibet we would be the first Britons to ever set foot in that legendary land.

'The way is very, very dangerous,' Bashir Ali said. 'Some would say you are fools. I do not. I see your hearts and they are pure.' He paused and smiled. 'So, perhaps, you are fools with pure hearts.'

I was already excited, picturing the travails of our coming journey, as we left Bashir Ali's shop and plunged back into the back streets of Simla. I chattered on about our success with that strange Oriental gentleman and the even odder-sounding monk, but my aunt was curiously distracted. She was not listening to me. We were just about to exit the dingy lanes on to the main street when my aunt did a very curious thing. I had seen a flash of red high up, at one of the grubby windows that over-hung the street. The vivid crimson of a soldier's uni-form, a weather-beaten white face topped by a mous-tache to rival Champlon's. Aunt Hilda stopped in her tracks, looking flustered – and maybe even a little guilty.

'You trot on home, Kit,' she said. 'I've . . . let's see . . . I need to buy some sugar.'

'We have tons of sugar!' I exclaimed. There was no grocery shop anywhere in these alleys as far as I could see. 'If you need more sugar, I'll come with you to the market.'

'Just once in your life, Kit, do as you're told. Off with you.'

A little hurt, I went. What on earth was Aunt Hilda up to? Passing a doorway with a deep arch, I ducked in. Furtively, I peered out at my aunt. She didn't go in the direction of the market at all. Instead, she turned and pushed open one of the doors into a crumbling house. A second later she had vanished.

Looking up at the window I saw the soldier's tunic again and another flash of the moustache. Had Champlon a rival for my aunt's heart? Or was she engaged in some other furtive business? My aunt was a woman born for plotting and scheming. Whatever she was up to, she certainly did not want *me* to know.

The mysteries were piling up.

⤫ Chapter Seventeen ⤫

I should have been bustling about getting ready, for we were leaving Simla this morn. Instead I was gazing absently at myself in the bathroom mirror. The tiger-scratch on my cheek bothered me. In the past few weeks the scar had turned from livid red to mottled purple. It was finally fading a little, but was of such a curious shape, like a question mark, and it drew unwelcome attention. No wonder Waldo teasingly called me 'Scarface'. Suddenly I heard a shriek fit to curdle the blood. I dropped my brush and ran helter-skelter down the stairs. The scream had seemed to come from my bedroom. I went in and stopped dead on the threshold.

'Rachel!' I said, aghast.

She was standing by my bed in her slip. For a moment I wondered if I was seeing things, for my friend had transformed into a fury. Her hair was writing, eyes flashing furiously as she brandished an antler she had broken off a stag's head. As I looked on, she shrieked again and threw the antler at the window. It crashed through the pane, sending glass scattering across the room.

'Rachel . . . what are you doing . . . exactly?' I asked, advancing cautiously into the room.

'I think I hit it,' she panted, glaring at the empty window.

I followed her glance. 'There's nothing there . . . my dear.'

My friend put her hand to her face. I noticed, with a shock, that she had a scratch on her hand.

'The little beast,' she growled.

I felt slow and fuddled for I had no idea what Rachel was talking about. She pointed dramatically at the bed. My eyes followed her trembling finger. There was a yellow envelope on the pillow. Again! This time it had been ripped open and the peacock's feather, hair and seeds had fallen out on to the cover. The answer came to me in a flash. The monkey. It must have been!

But I thought it was after *me*. I did not expect it to attack my friend. Then I realised, for truly I was awfully slow today, that we were standing in my room.

'I think I hit it,' Rachel said.

'Start from the beginning,' I said, slumping on the bed. 'Tell me what happened.'

'There's nothing to tell. I came in here to find you. I

saw that monkey dropping a letter on your bed. It ran at me and I lost my temper. You know the bowl thing.'

'Which one?'

'You know that horrible thing, made out of a rhinoceros foot.'

I nodded.

'I threw it at the monkey. Then it charged me, scratched me. Really wanted to hurt. I could've wrung its neck – but you came in and it fled. I've failed . . .' All the anger had drained out of Rachel and she sat down next to me on the bed, her breath coming in shuddering sobs.

'I suppose you would have done better,' she said, flatly.

'I'm proud of you.' I put my arm round her. 'That *thing* is vicious.'

'You know what this means,' Rachel said, quietly.

I blinked. 'What?'

'*They* are watching us.'

'At least we're on the right track.'

'How can you put it so flippantly?' Rachel turned to me, her dark eyes inches from my own. 'Don't you see what this means? The Baker Brothers are one step ahead of us. It's as though they're playing with us.' She fell silent and believing she had finished, I was about to reassure her when she burst out again. 'Kit, I know them.

Don't forget they kidnapped me.'

'How can I ever forget?'

The evil brothers had kidnapped Rachel and taken her prisoner to Egypt. She still had not told me all she had endured during that awful time.

'So, you could say we're quite well acquainted.' She gave a grim smile. 'I know how much the Bakers can hate.'

Hate. That word again, Champlon had talked about those brothers as haters, now Rachel. We were silent as we thought about this, for there is very little to say in the face of implacable hate. Then my aunt yoohooed from downstairs.

'Come on, girls. This isn't the time for primping and preening,' she bellowed, her voice booming like a steamship foghorn. 'Get your pretty faces down here at once.'

'Primping and preening indeed!' I said, insulted.

'You primp,' Rachel replied with a watery smile. 'I'll preen.'

Grinning, we threw on some clothes and raced down the stairs to where Aunt Hilda was waiting in the street outside the boarding house. Not all of us were going to Tibet, alas, for my poor papa was too unwell to proceed any further. Somehow Aunt Hilda had managed to wangle an invitation from the Viceroy himself, Lord Mayo. Father would recover his health surrounded by luxury. Frankly though, I did not envy him. Any house infested with Mrs Spragg and Edwin could not be called peaceful. Gaston Champlon had been invited to join my father at the Viceregal Lodge. But that doughty explorer was not one to miss an adventure. Though still sickly, he was ready to depart, seated on the back of the finest donkey.

We made quite a convoy as we left Simla, six of us sahibs and memsahibs, along with a retinue of sixteen small but sturdy mountain donkeys, a cook, and porters from the Sherpa hill tribes. An army going into battle. Canvas tents, stoves, boots, ice picks, crampons, food – everything but a roof and walls.

As Tibet was notoriously bandit-infested, we also carried ten Martini-Henry rifles along with five large and clumsy, but quick-loading, howdah pistols. Champlon had bought a new revolver, which I had glimpsed in its leather case. He carried it around with him at all times, like a talisman that could keep him safe from sorcery as well as attackers. I sincerely hoped that we would not have to use our weapons, but the Sherpas seemed to think they were wonderful. I caught one young boy playing with a rifle, firing it off into the tree tops as if it were a toy!

I had my own particular donkey. She was a playful young animal, with a dark brown pelt and a white splash on her muzzle, shaped exactly like a five-pointed star. I named her Tara – which means Star in the ancient Indian language of Sanskrit. Whenever something annoyed her she would flatten her ears and kick the ground, but when I fed her apples or bits of sugar she would whinny and lovingly nuzzle my hand. Riding on Tara, I felt able to cope with anything, especially as I had secretly purloined one of the howdah pistols and wore it strapped in a holster under my coat.

This part of the journey was the best. Travelling with our convoy in pleasant hills, with some of the world's highest peaks towering in the distance. I think it raised all our spirits and Champlon seemed quite restored. It took us about a week to get to the highest hill station, a pilgrim town called Badrinath. What a strange place; thronged with wailing ash-smeared men in dirty saffron robes, with matted hair flowing down their backs. They looked like the foulest tramps and the sight of them scared Rachel half to death. She was quite puzzled when I explained they were Hindu holy men, like monks or priests. After a day's rest we travelled onwards to the border and the way became harder, both physically and mentally. The boys both suffered from altitude sickness. This condition, caused by the lack of oxygen in the mountain air, drains the life out of you, leaving you dizzy and nauseous. Strangely Rachel and I were un-affected, which proves yet again that women are the stronger sex! I'm proud to say I seemed to cope, as we climbed higher and higher. My breath coming in gasps, my ankles and thighs hard as iron bands, I felt I was pushing myself to the very limit. But the Sherpas assured us, with knowing smiles, that this was nothing to trials we would have to endure in Tibet.

Indeed many of them were not willing to risk crossing into the 'roof of the world'. I do not know if they were scared of bandits, the mountain snows or even 'bad spirits', but more and more of them seemed to peel off from our party as we climbed higher and higher. When I tried to ask one Sherpa, a lad named Tensing, about the monk who Bashir Ali had recommended as a guide he turned very pale.

'He is a *najlorpa*,' he said.

'A what?'

'A sorcerer. He live three years in cave. Only human he see is hand with this on,' he gestured.

'Glove?' I guessed.

'Yes, glove. In silence every day glove put food through hole in door.'

'Gosh! That must be lonely.'

'It make you mad. Most people mad in head. Not Yongden.'

I was silent, thinking of those endless days in a dark, cold cave with only your own thoughts for company.

After a few days you would know every nook and cranny, every ledge of rock inside the cave. What it must be to spend months, years thus. Perhaps, after a time, the world inside his head had come to seem more real to Yongden, than the world outside.

'He much, much powerful. Yongden does not live in world,' the Sherpa said, echoing my thoughts. 'Please go away from him. He make play inside your head!'

What a strange land we were hoping to penetrate! As we jogged along, I recalled what I knew about Tibet. Most of that desolate country stands three miles up in the sky. It is a wind-swept plateau ringed by snowy peaks, larger than France, Germany, Spain and Italy put together. Perhaps the fact that for hundreds of years Tibet has been forbidden to foreigners makes it more mysterious and alluring. Look at any map and all you see is an enormous empty space, as if the whole country has been washed away by snow. It is more of a blank than the great Zambezi river, which my aunt's rival, Dr Livingstone, has recently explored.

I felt sure in my bones that we would make it into Tibet. We would be the first Europeans in modern history to explore this savage land.

The sun was tinting the ice on the glaciers, painting them pink, as we trudged along a steep mountain track towards Mana, the last village on the Indian side of the border. I could see it spread out before us, rocky houses with shingle roofs, surrounded by neat fields and mountain firs. All around us was the sound of rushing water from the river that snaked the mountainside. A week's trek past the village was Tibet. But before we entered that country we had to traverse a sheer wall of ice and outwit the ferocious Tibetan border guards.

My aunt called a halt to our progress and made a speech. 'The mountains have ears,' she announced. 'As you know, the Tibetans ban foreigners from their country. Our story is that we are pilgrims – I am an eccentric English convert to the Hindu religion. We have come to Mana to visit the holy site and from here our main convoy will proceed back down to the valley. Any spies suspicious of our movements will follow the main convoy and be put off our scent. Be careful, I warn you – our lives may depend on it.'

Surely we needn't have worried, I thought, as we entered Mana, for we were soon surrounded by smiling villagers with wide faces and slanting eyes. The people here in this wild borderland are a mix of Tibetan and Indian hill tribes, nomads who tend their flocks and trade with Tibet. They seemed simple, friendly folk who greeted us as if we were kings and queens, visitors from another world. Little children ran alongside our donkeys, calling out happily. Women arrived with colourful woven blankets and scarves to barter for chocolate, tea and the cheap goods which we had supplied ourselves with. I felt a little guilty as one toothless old lady, in a blue headscarf, delightedly swapped a beautiful woollen blanket with me for a pen and a string of beads. Still, the blanket would keep me warm amid the snows.

Later, as we set up our tents, the headman arrived to tell us through our Sherpa interpreter that the villagers had prepared a feast in our honour. Snowflakes had begun to fall – even though it was late August – and were melting in tiny puddles on our faces. The skies had turned a leaden grey, but by the roaring fire our hands and faces were toasty. We feasted on goat stew with rice. Later, dancers performed to the plangent cries of a stringed instrument. People, animals, huts were transformed by the flickering firelight into an unreal world, a fairytale realm where spirits and demons roamed. To the throb of a tabla drum a singer howled at the skies as the fire burnt down to glowing embers.

'My toes are freezing,' Waldo whispered to me, jerking me out of a reverie.

'Mine feel like icicles,' I hissed back

'Mine are like icebergs. Huge, solid blocks,' answered Waldo. Wasn't that just like my friend? He always had to go one better than you.

'Do we have to sit through much more of this wailing?' he went on.

'Hush,' I chided. 'They've been very kind. They could've slit our throats.'

'That would be a relief, my ears are starting to bleed.'

Another sound mixed in with the beat of the tabla and the howl of the singer. In the distance someone was shrieking and there was the sound of rushing feet.

'What's going on?' My aunt demanded standing up.

The headman rose and the singing was suspended as a young man came careening to the very edge of the fire. His turban was askew and he was out of breath. The headman and the man had a muttered conversation for several minutes, incomprehensible to us, but clearly very agitated. Then our interpreter took over.

'He finds body,' he explained. 'He is goatherd come back to village and step on body.'

'Where?' Aunt Hilda took charge.

'On path.'

We snaked after the distraught goatherd and the headman in cautious single file. He took us from the camp and up to the path that led away from the village towards the mountains of Tibet. The headman carried a flaming brand that lit up our feet and threw an intermittent light on the icy ring of peaks encircling us. The darkness, pressing in on all sides, was pregnant with the threat of prowling beasts and enemies that wished us ill.

We had been walking for about five minutes, when the goatherd came to an abrupt stop. Something was splayed out in the middle of the path. It was the body of a substantial man, his legs akimbo, his scarlet turban spooling out on to the path like a rivulet of blood. In the man's shirt front was the hilt of a silver dagger. A clean, vicious stab that must have killed him instantly. It took but one glance at the man's face to recognise him. It was Malharrao. The old Maharajah.

Rachel screamed and my aunt, stooping by the body, hissed: 'Why?'

'The Baker Brothers must have tired of him. Malharrao was no longer useful, now they've left Baroda,' I guessed. Then with quivering finger I pointed out something that lay next to the body. A dirty yellow envelope. Spilling out of it was the tip of a shimmering peacock's feather.

'Very clever,' Aunt Hilda said. 'The Baker Brothers have combined a murder and a warning to us in a single stab.'

When she straightened up, she was seething with rage. The Bakers didn't know my aunt if they thought such an act would scare her off. If anything it would only make her redouble her efforts to find Shambala and the treasure they both sought.

❧ Chapter Eighteen ❧

It was well past midnight before we retired to our tents. The funeral of Malharrao would be held at daybreak tomorrow, for it is the custom here to cremate the dead as soon as possible. I noticed, as I fell into a dull sleep on the ground besides Rachel, that the water in my bottle had turned to ice.

I woke with a start. My limbs were aching, the ground freezing under my back. I really must talk to Isaac about inventing some sort of sleeping sack. A beam of light flickered briefly through an opening in the tent and outside a twig cracked. Instantly alert, I crawled out of my tent to find Aunt Hilda and Champlon, fully dressed and about to mount their donkeys.

'Where are you going?' I asked.

'Back to your tent, Kit,' my aunt hissed.

'I want to come too!'

'Heavens. You know we must get ahead of the Baker Brothers,' she muttered. 'Can someone muzzle this child!'

'Let 'er come,' Champlon said. 'She weel wake everyone.'

'It was a big mistake to take this dratted child with us,' Aunt Hilda grumbled, but she consented to me accompanying them.

Luckily, I had gone to sleep in all my clothes to keep warm. I would not have put it beyond my aunt to have sneaked off while I was changing. Hurriedly lacing up my boots, I jumped on my Tara and trotted after them. I didn't need to ask again where we were going. This must be a mission to find Yongden, the monk, who would guide us. The murder of Malharrao would only have sharpened their resolve to act fast. I could only hope that our disappearance wouldn't lead the villagers to think we had anything to do with the dead body. In the morning, many of the Sherpas would pack and pretend to move back down to the valley. Meanwhile we would persuade Yongden to show us the secret mountain way to Tibet.

Later we would all meet again on the mountain trail – our pre-arranged rendezvous.

We had gone half a mile out of the village, up an increasingly rutted track when we had to abandon our mounts and take to our feet, for the way was simply too dangerous for donkeys. We tethered them and trudged heavy-footed up the mountain. The sky flowed over our heads, a rippling swatch of star-speckled black velvet. A pitted lump of moon lit our way. We had to proceed with great care. One blunder would have sent us hurtling down the precipice. Finally, we saw a series of caves in the rock face rising above us. Something was wrong. Badly wrong. The largest cave was scorched, grass and twigs flamed away. The opening leered at us, like an enormous black eye.

We were too late. Our enemies had been here before us.

Champlon instinctively put his hand to his holster to draw his pistol – but there was no one around, just a lone vulture which hovered above us, looking for food. Stooping a little, we entered the cave. Rocky walls enclosed us. Yongden, the hermit, had few possessions. A wooden bowl, which lay smashed in the centre of the room. A few large cushions for a bed, which had been savagely ripped. Feathers still fluttered in the air, like lost snowflakes. Religious scrolls showing a fat smiling Lord Buddha on the walls. On an altar, formed from a few pieces of wood, were copper bowls full of water and grain, lamps full of butter. These offerings to the gods were the only things which had been left untouched.

Of the hermit there was no sign.

'Blast it and ruination,' hollered my aunt, glaring at the mess. 'They've got the bloomin' monk.'

'We 'ave no chance of finding 'im in the mountains,' Champlon muttered. 'We 'ave not the –'

'We can go on without the monk,' I interrupted.

'Keep quiet, Kit,' snapped Aunt Hilda. 'Remember rule number one: children should be seen and not heard.'

With that, she turned her back on me and continued whispering to Champlon.

I wanted to hit back at my aunt with some biting retort, but a more sensible part of me realised that she was desperately worried. Why she had to take out her anxiety on me I didn't know. I wandered around the cave, trying to look proudly unconcerned. I became aware of a shaft of light, a broad golden band, coming from the altar. How strange. One of the butter lamps had flickered into life. I let out an exclamation. Where a moment before there had been empty space there was a skinny brown man. Dressed in orange robes, he was sitting cross-legged in front of the altar. He had a smooth shaven head and a soft face. It was his eyes that arrested me; pools of oily blue-black, like the liquid swirling in the very depths of a well. They weren't exactly friendly, or comforting, this person's eyes.

'Aunt Hilda!' I said.

'Seen and *not heard*,' Aunt Hilda barked, without turning her back.

The man – the monk – was watching me, impassively.

'You're not real,' I said to him.

The others turned around to see who I was talking to. Aunt Hilda screamed at the sight of the apparition.

'Welcome,' the monk said.

'Gomchen Yongden?' Aunt Hilda asked.

The monk inclined his head.

'How,' I muttered. 'I . . . I . . . looked there and –'

Yongden murmured: 'I did not wish you to see me.'

'Impossible!' Champlon barked. More to himself than the rest of us he added, uncertainly, 'It is a tricks. A cheap conjuring tricks.'

The monk shrugged.

'How do you make such tricks?' Champlon blurted.

The same smile flickered over Yongden's face and his hands danced briefly in the air. 'All this is a painted veil.'

'I stood right there,' I said, pointing to a spot a couple of feet away from Yongden.

He didn't answer, but smiled, showing us a mouth with more gaps than teeth.

'Who did this to you?' Aunt Hilda asked, changing the subject. She looked around, at the smashed and ripped things, the marks of fire on the walls. 'It's outrageous!'

Yongden shrugged.

'Who were they?'

'Ghosts,' Yongden replied.

'Ghosts?' Aunt Hilda asked uncertainly.

'Men with no souls. Ghosts.'

'What did they look like, these ghosts?' I interrupted.

'White men, white clothes. When they not find me they say, "Destroy everything".' Yongden paused a moment, reflecting. 'They strange men, some type that I not met before. When I look their eyes, I saw nothing. Something gone away from them. They were people, yes, but without a soul.'

'People without souls,' I murmured, half unconsciously. The words brought to mind one image, the Baker Brothers. Their blank eyes, blank faces. They had given me the same feeling; their eyes had nothing, *nothing*, behind them. All of us were quiet for a moment, for the thought of people without souls blew a chill into us.

I sighed, for whatever we did it seemed the Bakers were there, ahead of us. They knew what all this was about, while I was like a blind man, groping in a dark passage. Well, at least one thing was perfectly plain: they were seeking Shambala. The Bakers would not be trudging through snow and ice; facing death by exposure and avalanche, unless there was something of immense value at the end of their quest.

Abruptly Aunt Hilda snapped into a business-like mode and was asking Yongden if he would accompany us to Tibet as a guide. 'We have heard you know these mountains better than anyone,' she pleaded. She was all ready to wheedle and flatter, do anything to persuade this strange shaven-headed hermit, but he forestalled her.

'Show me your map,' he said simply, holding out his hand to me. 'I guide you.'

Aunt Hilda looked at Champlon and then she looked at me. No one had mentioned a map. A bolt of fear flashed through us all.

My hands stayed stubbornly still. I looked the monk in the eye without speaking.

He didn't speak either. He held out his hand, perfectly still.

'Kit,' Aunt Hilda said.

'No. No, I won't.'

'Kit, give him the map or I'll –'

I meant to go on refusing but that monk's eyes were burning inside me and I found my hands moving to my pocket taking out the map and handing it over. I burned with rage at myself but at the same time my hands were perfectly passive and normal.

'This is our only map,' Aunt Hilda said, as Yongden examined it. 'Not much of one. Doesn't make a lot of sense.'

'This is the map,' he said. His wrinkled hands turned over the torn parchment, so lightly his fingers hardly seemed to touch the surface. He was looking at the marking that said:

Abominable Cave
Hope and glory to those who undertake this –

and then like most of the inscriptions it ended, for the rest had been snatched away by that thieving monkey. The monk's eyes roved over the page and I felt horribly possessive. I was hurt and raging inside. He had no *right*.

It was *my* map. I was *meant* to have that map.

I held out my hand for it but Yongden shook his head. 'I keep.' He rolled it up carefully and put it in some unseen pocket in his loose saffron gown.

'But –' I began but Aunt Hilda dug me savagely in the ribs.

'You go now and I meet you before border,' Yongden said. 'At the parting of the paths, you will see a brown-grey rock. It look like bear cub. There I be.'

I was about to protest hotly at his taking my map – my map. That piece of torn parchment and I were deeply, mysteriously connected. Its delicate markings, its mountain paths and gaping ravines, flowed quicksilver in my veins. It had become my guide and mentor. Suddenly, I was struck by the conviction that this hermit, for all his shaven head, was a common thief.

I glared at him, putting all my anger into my eyes. He barely seemed to notice.

'You do us great honour, Gomchen Yongden, to accompany our journey. We offer humble thanks and salutes. When shall we meet you?' Aunt Hilda asked.

'When you are there. So will I.'

With that we took our leave, the grown-ups practically pushing me out of the cave. I was so fuming inside I could barely bring myself to put one foot in front of the other. Outside I turned on Aunt Hilda and Champlon.

'Well,' I said. 'I expect we will never see hair nor hide of Mister Yongden again.'

Aunt Hilda glared at me. 'You just don't understand, do you?'

'Understand what?'

'Frostbite. Savage border guards. Temperatures of 30 degrees below freezing. Avalanches. Glaciers. The whole kit and caboodle.'

'I know about that.'

'You read a few story books and you think you know everything,' she scoffed. 'The reality, my little dreamer, is very different. If we are to have any chance – any chance whatsoever – of getting into Tibet, that strange man is our only hope.'

Champlon agreed. ''E is our lifeline in these mountains.'

'So you see where this stands,' Aunt Hilda snapped and turning she began to tramp down the rocky mountain. 'We need him a far sight more than we need some pesky child who always thinks she is right.'

She shouted over her shoulder, as a parting shot: 'I've already told you. Talk less and *listen more*! Then you might become half-bearable.'

Why was Aunt Hilda suddenly being so nasty? She was a big bully. For a moment I wanted to pick up a piece of wood and throw it at her. But to be honest, I didn't dare. Tears spurted in my eyes. I sat down on the ground with a thump, my thoughts in a whirl. My map stolen, my stomach churning. I felt sick and hot. To cap it all Aunt Hilda was so beastly. How dare she treat me like some ninny of a girl? How dare she? *How dare she?*

For some time I sat like this, tears hot on my face. I felt very alone, because my map had so occupied my imagination it had given me stomach for this whole journey. So I sobbed, till the pain eased a little and the sun had crawled up the sky. My tears were finally spent and my sheepskin coat was covered in soot. Never mind Aunt Hilda – or, though even the thought hurt me – my map. I had to go on with the plan. We had to meet the others at the rendezvous point, or risk destroying our elaborate precautions for putting the villagers off our scent. I would play along with her plans – and see if Yongden really did meet us at 'bear-cub rock'. Sighing, I got to my feet and scrambled down the path my aunt and Champlon had taken.

But when I got to the bend in the path, my aunt and Gaston Champlon had vanished.

∞ Chapter Nineteen ∞

I hurtled down the mountain. My heart was thumping away madly, an awful sick fear welling up in my mouth. Where on earth were my aunt and Champlon? They couldn't have abandoned me on a mountain, not over a tiff. By the time I reached the place where we had left the donkeys, I was finding it difficult to breathe in the thin air and my calves had taken a pounding.

Thank goodness Tara was waiting where I had left her, tethered to a fir tree. But where were Champlon and Aunt Hilda's donkeys? We were in a ravine. To the left of us was a dizzying precipice, a sheer drop down to the valley below. To the right a craggy and impassable wall of greyish-white rocks, studded with trees and hardy grass. Up and down the mountain there was no sign of the two of them. Nothing whatsoever.

So, they thought they could give me the slip did they? Typical of my aunt. Well, I would jump on Tara and ride hard to catch them up.

'Tara! Tara!' I called striding towards my donkey.

Tara made no answering whinny. She was oddly mute, as if she didn't recognise my voice. This was all wrong. Tara always greeted me with delight, charming me so she would receive some tasty titbit.

'Tara what's wrong!' I wailed, coming up to her from behind, placing my arm round her neck. 'You silly old donkey! I had no choice. You would have fallen down the mountain!'

My dear donkey made a movement, the tiniest of shrugs. I looked into her eyes and in a rush realised everything was wrong. Her eyes were covered with a white film. Were no longer seeing. Worse, when I glanced down horror awaited me. Tara had a horizontal gash in her throat, which was dripping red. Stupidly, frozen into panic, I watched her blood drop on to the earth.

Someone had cut her throat.

I howled, throwing back my head, scaring a flock of crows which squawked in a nearby tree. I flung my arms around her neck. Hugs, tears, could do no good. My donkey, if not already dead, was very nearly there. All I received for my pains was a crimson blotch on my pale coat. Tara's life was draining away, drop by drop. Her eyes were filmed over, nearly gone.

I had no choice.

I drew my howdah pistol and looked away. The shot scared the crows. They erupted like black fire from the tree and scattered into the sky. When I could bring myself, finally, to look, Tara was no more. In her place was a pile of flesh on the rocks. Without another glance I walked away, hurrying as fast as I could.

I was unsure what to do. Should I go back and tell the monk what had happened? That thieving monk? Or should I make haste to find my friends? In the end it was quite clear. With all his sorcerer's tricks, Yongden could look after himself. My friends could not. I had to warn them. You see, Tara's murder was a clear warning. The Bakers' gang had found my donkey. In all likelihood, they had spirited my aunt and Champlon away.

Shivering in the cold, despite my furry coat, it took me a full forty-five minutes of hard tramping to reach the rendezvous point. I was obviously late, for Waldo, Isaac and Rachel were waiting with our convoy of donkeys and porters, almost stamping the ground in their impatience. As soon as I saw them, I realised something else was wrong. They were cross. I knew by the way they moved apart when they saw me, that they had been talking about me.

'The wanderer returns,' Waldo burst out, nastily. 'Please welcome our conquering heroine Dr Scarface Livingstone.'

'The Great Explorer Kit Salter,' Isaac said in a loud, theatrical voice. 'And over here, her junior assistants Isaac, Waldo and Rachel.'

I was so full of grief for my donkey and fear for my aunt I could hardly understand the meaning of my friends' words. Why had everyone chosen this horrible day to discover my faults?

'Listen to me,' I begged. 'I haven't time for this, right now.'

'You never have time for your friends,' Waldo said curtly.

'Something awful has happened.'

'Oh, that's wonderful, that is,' Waldo butted in, sarcastically. 'Something awful. You and your precious aunt go off having all the adventures while the rest of us are stuck here looking after the luggage.'

'Look here, Kit,' Rachel intervened, her brown eyes shining with anger. 'We are all in this adventure *together*. It is not decent of you to sneak off in the night without telling us. We're all taking risks here. We're all cold and tired. You have to let us into what is going on! We all sense it and feel upset. You and your aunt have secrets. We always see you huddling together. Well, if you don't want us, we will just leave, won't we, Waldo?'

Waldo nodded, while in the back of my throat I felt a terrible roar of frustration building up.

'Enough!' I screamed. 'I'm sorry if I've done wrong but I don't have time for this now! Aunt Hilda and Champlon have disappeared and Tara has been murdered.'

The porters were watching our argument silently, their slanting eyes betraying no emotion.

'Murdered?' Rachel asked stupidly. I saw shock on her face – and maybe a little regret for picking this time for silly grievances.

I walked towards them, thrusting the dark, damp patch on my sheepskin coat forward. 'See this? Know what it is? No? Tara's blood!'

Rachel screamed. Suddenly, it was all too much and I found myself dry throated. There was a tear gathering in the corner of my eye. Quickly brushing it away, I explained what had happened.

'Who could do that to a defenceless animal?' Rachel asked. 'What kind of person would murder Tara?'

The cook, Chamba, a plump and smiley man, stepped forward and began muttering about how the murderers would suffer 'bad karma'. The followers of the Buddhist religion believe that bad deeds you commit in this life haunt you in your next life. This form of luck they call *karma* – if you are very wicked you could be reborn as a slug. I don't know if I believe in next lives – and anyway, it wasn't good enough for me. I wanted revenge on the murderers who had cut Tara's throat. In this life.

'We need help from someone who knows these mountains,' Waldo interrupted. 'We've got to go back and find this hermit fellow.'

'Yongden said he would meet us up the mountain,' I interrupted, gesturing in the direction of the towering Mana peak. All my doubts about the monk resurfaced, but I put them aside. Waldo was right, we needed help. 'Something about a place where the paths part. A rock shaped like a bear cub.'

There were indrawn breaths at the name Yongden from the Sherpas. I could see them eyeing each other warily.

'Yongden is sorcerer. In good time we do not go near,' Chamba, who seemed to be their leader, said. 'In bad time he help. Follow me. I know bear rock.'

So it was agreed. I was given another donkey, though I scarcely noticed which one it was, and we moved off. I sat hunched in my saddle as we trotted upwards, scarcely taking in our dizzying ascent, towards the wall of ice – the glacier between us and Tibet. All my thoughts were inside – for my aunt and Champlon – and my poor old Tara. We could have been walking up Woodstock Road in my home town for all the notice I took of our surroundings.

At some stage the way became too perilous to ascend

sitting on our donkeys – too narrow and littered with stones – so we had to get off and walk. We had been trudging some three or four hours, concentrating on the rhythm of our feet and not letting our spirits flag, when the cook suddenly gave a shrill cry. Jerking out of my reverie I glanced in the direction the cook had been pointing. Suddenly, I realised I hadn't been looking as I walked – not really! We had left the trees and greenery of Mana village behind and were now truly in the wilderness. A boulder was lying across the path, one of a hundred or so that had fallen from the mountain. There was no tree, or flower, or patch of green in sight. Everything was a desolation of rock, snow and ice, a landscape from another planet.

This, I imagined, was what it would be like to go for a hike on the moon.

But it wasn't the landscape the cook was pointing out. It was a rock rearing over the road. It was greyish, patterned with lighter veins of white stone – a strange and monstrous eruption from the mountain. The rock was shaped exactly like a standing bear cub. It had one paw raised as if it was about to shake your hand. In this bleak place it was an oddly friendly sight. We all quickened our pace.

Part of me wanted to be right about Yongden. For him not to turn up. Of course the other, more sensible part, desperately wanted him to be at the rock rendezvous. Who else was there to turn to in our attempt to find my aunt and Champlon?

I was the first to reach the rock, and see it fully. I almost fell down the cliff in shock. Sitting on a flat ledge were three bundles of sheepskin. One of them looked up and, framed like an Eskimo in a halo of white fur, was the pugnacious face of my aunt. With her were Champlon and Yongden. They had cleared the snow away, set down an oilskin and were chatting companionably as they munched on leathery strips of dried meat. For all the world as if they were having a picnic in Hyde Park! At least my aunt and Champlon were munching. Yongden was not. I presumed that, like many Buddhists, he was a vegetarian who regarded the taking of an animal's life as a sin.

'Thank heavens,' I blurted out, completely forgetting how we'd parted. 'I thought they'd got you!'

'Who do you mean by *they*, pray tell?' Aunt Hilda asked tartly. 'Please try and be more precise.'

'The Baker Brothers.'

I held my breath and waited. Aunt Hilda's grim face was all the answer I needed.

The clammy spirit of those malevolent millionaires had hovered over us for much of the voyage. It wasn't a surprise that they were behind the desecration of

Yongden's cave. Who else could it have been? The villagers would have been far too fearful of the holy man's reputation.

'The curse,' Waldo exclaimed. 'Has it – I mean how do they look?'

It was rumoured that the curse of the mummy we had encountered in our last adventure had struck the brothers and destroyed their health. Their villainous behaviour in Egypt was said to have displeased ancient forces.

Champlon shrugged. 'They are not the pretty sight.'

'Hideous,' Aunt Hilda muttered. 'Specially one of them. His skin looks like porridge!' She shuddered. 'I suspect they are after the same thing we are . . .'

For a moment I was about to interrupt and ask exactly what Aunt Hilda was after. However, she wouldn't have told me, so I let her continue.

'We think, Champlon and I, that they mean to break into Tibet and get to the prize before us. I wouldn't put any type of skulduggery past them!'

'They 'ave some bad men around wiz zem.' Champlon agreed gloomily.

'That monkey and a gang of the most dishonest brigands they could recruit in India,' Aunt Hilda went on.

My mind had been working very slowly: 'But if they had you – why are you here?'

A smug expression spread across Champlon's face: 'It is not possible it keep Gaston Champlon prisoned,' he announced.

I refrained from pointing out that they had found it surprisingly easy in the past to keep him prisoner – and blackmail him into doing their bidding.

'You see, ze sug wiz ze monkey, 'e surprise us when we 'ave come down ze path from ze Yongden's cave. 'E took my gun, my loverly Webley. 'E bound our 'ands and took us to meet ze Baker Brothers. But zey do not reckon wiz Gaston Champlon. I always keep annuzzer pistol in my left sock. I manage to break my 'ands free, *et voilà!*' In his excitement Champlon relapsed into French.

So Champlon had fought free. Of course he was a magician with a gun. He had taken one of the Baker Brothers captive, only releasing him when their donkeys and pistol were returned.

'How did you manage to stop them? Hypnotising you, I mean?' asked Isaac. I wondered if it was suspicion I heard in his voice and glanced quickly at Champlon, who looked away guiltily.

'Ze monkey, I did not let it near me,' Champlon replied quickly.

Yongden had been listening to our talk impassively: now he stood up and said we should be on our way. But before we went on, I needed to have a private word with him. I walked right up to the monk and murmured:

'Please give it back to me.'

Standing so close to him, I could feel the tug of my map. Was it my imagination that sensed it, pulsing, pulling, in an inner pocket of the monk's loose saffron robe? The monk looked me in the eye and inclined his head.

'Please,' I begged.

'Not yet.'

There was nothing I could do. Though a bitter taste welled up from my stomach, and my hands itched to simply grab the map from him, I was powerless.

'We must get going now,' my aunt announced. 'Several days' march to the border.'

Immediately there was a wail of protest from Rachel, Isaac and Waldo.

'We haven't had lunch,' Isaac complained.

'*I* haven't even had breakfast' I snapped.

'I can't walk without lunch,' Isaac went on. 'My legs won't work.'

'Lunch?' Yongden said, as if he didn't understand the word. I had a sudden vision of his life. Eating delicious food, I sensed, would be far down on his list of priorities. 'Please eat. Then must go.'

Sadly, even Chamba was unable to conjure something

tasty out of our supplies in this frozen wasteland. I watched as he took out a flint pouch and struck a fire with rock. A few twigs of kindling blazed and then a log. It was a small, weak fire. Still it was hot. I had my first taste of what was to become our staple meal. Tsampa – a Tibetan barley grain – and dried meat. The barley tasted like wallpaper glue and chewing the dried meat felt like eating one of Aunt Hilda's boots. Even Isaac looked as if he wished he hadn't insisted on lunch. Seeing the look on our faces as we silently gulped down this fare, my aunt gruffly told us to cheer up. This was the good times, she explained, our food would get steadily worse.

Rather glumly, we finished our lunch and, shouldering our packs, got to our feet. So, we were about to try to sneak into a ferocious and hostile country under the direction of an enigmatic sorcerer monk. A man whose intentions were unclear, and who had stolen my map. Days of tramping through snow, rock and ice, some of the harshest terrain in the world, lay ahead of us.

Were we brave explorers? Or lunatics? As my feet began to plod forward – of their own accord, for the rest of me was terribly tired –I was truly not sure!

❧ Chapter Twenty ❧

Yesterday I stopped feeling my toes. Earlier today it was the turn of my fingers. My hands were protected by three pairs of gloves, layers of wool tucked into fleecy sheepskin mittens. They were wadded till they resembled two footballs. Yet they were still turning into claws of ice.

If there is anywhere colder on this earth, please, please let me never go there.

The thermometer my aunt carried had stopped working, somewhere about twenty degrees below zero. This is colder than it ever gets at home, even on those winters when the rivers freeze and we go skating on Port Meadow. Do not believe that you know what *cold* means, not till you come to a landscape like this. All I could see for miles was white. White snow, white ice, white peaks, even the sky looked bleached. The sun blazed, turning the landscape into a series of dazzling mirrors.

We were lost in a land made of ice.

Skidding on this ice, or walking into a snowdrift taller than a man, was not the greatest threat here. It was avalanches. The load of snow and rock teetering on the mountain beside us could collapse, burying us for ever. We were warned in no uncertain terms that we must be very quiet. So save for the clop of our donkeys' feet on ice and the sharper crackle of our crampons, we moved without a sound.

I was trudging along, my feet heavy as bricks in their four-spiked crampons, which we had put on to get a better grip in the slippery ice. My face was burning, as if the skin had been doused in boiling oil. I was keeping up with Yongden, who was leading a donkey piled with food, but only just. Without warning he turned and looked at me, his eyes inky shadows.

'You suffer,' he said – his voice though low, rang over the ice.

Yongden spoke so rarely that everyone stopped, our whole caravan of Sherpas and donkeys and cooks.

My eyes were watering again. We all wore goggles made from yak antlers. They were narrow strips of bones with slits cut into them, which were held in place by straps of braided sinew. The slits blocked light glaring from the snow all around. They made us look like demented bees. Nevertheless, several of us began to suffer from swollen eyes. Luckily, Isaac, our resident genius, had a brilliant idea. He had made little flaps from the see-through gauze we carried in the medical supplies, which he strung over our goggles. But it wasn't my eyes to which Yongden was referring. I could just about see. It was the rest of me that was in trouble.

'You look like a pork chop,' Waldo jeered. 'A scarface steak.'

'Broiled and ready for the luncheon table!' Isaac grinned.

'Waldo! Isaac! That's really unkind. You shouldn't make fun of people for looking odd,' Rachel scolded. Then she stopped abruptly realising she'd been rude. Even ruder than Waldo – for she hadn't meant to tease.

Oddly enough it was Rachel I was most cross with. I know I was being unreasonable but it wasn't fair. I was meant to be the strong one, the brave explorer who would weather the elements and cheerfully face all sorts of dangers. In my head at least, Rachel was the wilting violet. She was the pretty one, who only wanted to sit at home embroidering cushion covers and playing the pianoforte. She was kind and good but not exactly *tough*.

Yet she was taking this gruelling journey quite in her stride.

Ever since she had seen off the monkey at Simla, Rachel had seemed to grow stronger. She had marched uncomplainingly through the mountains. She'd learnt to brave altitude sickness. She hadn't suffered from snow blindness. She even looked ravishing in her layers of sheepskin. It wasn't fair! How the mountains conspired against me. The scorching sun skinned my face and eyes, the freezing cold crept into my bones. Just my luck that all the others managed. My aunt and Champlon both had skin like elephant hide, which could withstand any extreme. It was only me! I was the weak one! The runt of the litter.

Stop this self-pity, I told myself sternly. You have to soldier on, however much your skin boils and your eyes swell.

My aunt had turned around to see what was happening and saw the others clustered around me. 'Buck up, Kit,' she bellowed.

'I can't help it if everyone finds my face so interesting.' I flushed, my scar burning.

'Hmm,' she came closer and looked me over like a vet examining a sick cow. 'I believe you are suffering from an unusual combination of snow blindness and sunburn. Rather interesting.'

'What?' I growled.

'Do you know that Tibet is the only country in the world where you can burn and freeze at the same time? It's simultaneously icy and scorching up here, because the sun reflects off the snow. No wonder they call it the roof of the world. This can result in severe burning as well as frostbite. At the same time!'

'How fascinating!' I said, but my aunt did not notice my attempt at sarcasm.

'You have to remember,' she continued, gesturing to the icy path. 'That we are hiking at 5,600 metres above sea level. That is 800 metres above Mont Blanc, the tallest mountain in Europe.'

'I don't want a lecture on geography. My face is killing me!'

'Yes, it does look rather painful,' my aunt said, as if that was a noteworthy fact as well.

All of them were peering at me, as if I was an object of mild interest. Were they going to chit-chat about my troubles all day? Only Yongden looked at me as if I was normal. He said something to Chamba which caused the cook to scurry away to the donkeys. There he delved into a pack carried by one of them and turned round with a package clasped in his hand. Yak butter. The packet of yak butter was frozen solid, of course. It had to be heated on our Bunsen burner. I could sense my aunt's impatience at the waste of time. Finally it was about the consistency of normal butter and a coating of gloop was applied to my eyelids. It smelt unbelievably foul. Like a vat of rancid milk. Waldo wrinkled his nose, smirking at Isaac. Who smirked back.

'Well, Kit, you've held us up long enough,' my aunt boomed. 'Best foot forward now . . . If you can't keep up I'll send a couple of Sherpas back to the village with you.'

I boiled with indignation. I wasn't the one to halt our caravan. 'I'm perfectly ready,' I said coldly,

Yongden uttered a command, the convoy of donkeys and Sherpas was reassembled and we all continued on our weary march. I did not think of anything, not how I smelt like an abattoir and looked like a measle. No, I concentrated on putting one icy boot in front of the other. I could imagine, one day, feeling as if I had a face, rather than a big, red blister, above my neck. In the meantime we must get to Tibet. I had my pride. Even if it killed me, I wouldn't be the one who held us back. How dare Aunt Hilda suggest I was a laggard!

It is at times like this, when I am feeling really very low, that Rachel is kindest. Without saying a word, she slipped her arm through mine. Together we trudged on, and I found that I didn't really mind that Rachel was coping with the sun and cold while I wasn't.

'Don't worry, Kit,' she whispered. 'You'll show them.'

I looked at her mutely. Her brown eyes were glowing beneath her halo of fur.

'You're a fighter.' Her fingers pressed mine, comfortingly.

We were toiling up a particularly painful stretch of mountain, our legs aching. Suddenly, the clouds up above descended. I can give no other explanation. One moment the clouds were in the sky. The next moment they had come down to earth.

It was thick, clammy stuff. Not like the sulphurous fog of a London afternoon, but brighter, whiter. It was so dense it clothed us in a shimmering layer and I could no longer see the Sherpas up ahead. Nor the rest of our party. Rachel and I clutched each other. All I could see were her eyes, hazel lanterns shining through the mist.

'What happened?' she shrieked. 'Where is everyone?'

'I don't know.'

'I'm scared, Kit.'

We were stranded near the top of a mountain, wreathed in mist. Dusk was coming. And we had no sight of our companions. Even more terrifying than the loss of sight was the fact that we couldn't *hear* a thing. No clop of hooves. No murmuring voices. No braying mules. I wanted to scream out at the top of my voice, but was too fearful. It could be fatal if we set off an avalanche.

'Come, Rachel.' I held on to her harder. 'We must find the others.'

It was hard to walk fast though, because our view of the ground was obscured by the cloud. Carefully, testing every step, I moved forward. Not carefully enough, for at the tenth or fifteenth step I fell and nearly dragged down my trembling friend with me.

I had tripped over something. I saw it most clearly – something of ochre colour, with a craggy, pitted surface. The mist had not descended quite to the ground level and I had a horrifyingly good view.

'Get up, Kit,' Rachel hissed. 'We have to move if we're not to freeze to death here.'

The bony thing was nearly touching the tip of my nose. Its jaw opened in a grimace revealing a toothless mouth. Above it were empty eyes.

A skull. A toothless old skull. Under it, cruelly splayed at an angle to the head, was the rest of the skeleton. It looked horribly like a huge fish-bone, the spine feathering out. But no fish would have such delicate, such heart-breakingly human hands. They sat in the skeleton's lap, folded one on top of the other. The bones had been bleached by time and sun. Every scrap of flesh eaten by vultures.

My mouth opened in a scream, but with a supreme effort of will I squeezed it back.

'Stand up, Kit,' Rachel said, urgently. 'Are you all right? Have you hurt your leg?'

That was not the worst of it. My brain was unwilling to understand what my eyes were telling it. Behind the old skeleton, in a heap just off the path, were other objects. The whitened bones of a horse, another human skeleton. The thing became a blur. An awful muddle of long-dead corpses.

What had happened to this caravan? Had they been beset by bandits? I suspected it was something far simpler. The mists had come down. Men and mules frozen to death as they wandered lost in these cruel heights.

'Kit!' Rachel's panicked face loomed just above my head, her hands picking at me. 'What's wrong? Do you want me to carry you?'

Whatever happened, Rachel must not see this dreadful thing. This horror would haunt her dreams.

'No. No,' I said scrambling up and speaking cheerfully. 'I'm perfectly well. Let's find the others.'

As we set off, shrouded in cloud like walking ghosts, I prayed that we would not be stranded here on the top of the world. Till the cold ate into our bones and the mountains took our lives. To Rachel, I said not a word. Clutching each other, we moved slowly down the path.

❧ Chapter Twenty-one ❧

'Thank heavens!' my aunt exclaimed, looming towards us in the tattered remnants of the mist. 'We thought we'd lost you.'

The clouds had lifted as swiftly as they had fallen, revealing our caravan, anxiously waiting by a mound of ice. I'd expected a scolding from Aunt Hilda but instead she opened her arms and folded me in a warm embrace. I could see from the expression on her face that she'd been very worried. She clung on to me even as she began to scold me.

'Don't ever lag behind again. If you get cut off from the main party you can easily freeze to death. Foolish child.'

'What were you thinking of?' burst out Waldo, sounding as if we had done it on purpose. 'You're so reckless, Kit.'

'Oh Waldo, how lovely,' Rachel grinned. 'You were worried about Kit.'

'Don't be ridiculous,' he snapped, turning away. 'I'm just cross that she's always wasting time.'

'We're safe,' I said, trying to wriggle out of Aunt Hilda's hold. 'We're here aren't we?'

We had descended the mountain and come to a huge glacier that flowed between ranges. To our right towered icy ridges, sharp as the folds in a newly starched tablecloth. To the left was a spreading snowfield. I had always thought glaciers were a flat white, like blank sheets of paper. This one was littered with rocks and boulders, especially on the edges. Inside the glacier, the ice rose in jagged spikes and whorls, many of them higher than a man and so deadly they could cut flesh to shreds. The sky felt close, pressing down on us. We moved among shimmering blues and whites, more watery than earth-bound. My thoughts were very confused and, for a moment, I felt as if, I flailing under the sea.

'*Where* are we?' Rachel wondered.

'Brlags Pa Rmi Lam glacier,' Yongden said. 'Glacier of lost dream.'

A still, vast bowl. Bare of trees and grass, home only to the mysterious: the snow leopard, the vulture, the great beast – like a monstrous over-grown bear – Tibetans call the yeti.

A wail from one of the Sherpas, followed by a chorus

of shush and be quiet, cut into the silence. He was a quiet, squat fellow, our guide and tracker who was walking up in front, leading one of the first donkeys. I had talked to most of the Sherpas, but I realised I did not even know this man's name and had never heard him utter a word. Yongden and the man were talking, a whispered conversation that we couldn't understand. The Sherpa was alarmed, Yongden was soothing him, I thought.

I hurried over to where the two men were talking, peering over my aunt's shoulder who'd got there a moment before. Champlon stood beside her – he seemed as agitated as the Sherpa. All of us were crowding round, which was ridiculous because I didn't know what we were supposed to be looking at.

'What is it?' I asked, bewildered, because all I could see was a faint dent in the ice, slightly larger than a gold sovereign.

'It is a hoof mark,' Champlon said. 'But not yak or donkey.'

'Horse,' the Sherpa said. He was staring at the mark as if he simply could not believe it and on his blunt face was astonishment. 'A Bombay racehorse.'

'Only a fool would bring such a horse up here,' my aunt spat. 'Such horses are not adapted to the ice. It will break a leg, or die of exposure.'

'It ees cruel,' Champlon agreed.

'I'll bet you a half a crown it's those Bakers,' Waldo hissed. 'They don't care about ruining a fine horse. They'll probably just shoot it and eat it when it dies.'

The whispering around the hoof-print had become heated. Yongden raised his hand, his usual signal for silence; we quietened down like a group of well-trained schoolchildren.

'There have been many men before us. It is no matter. We will stay here,' Yongden gestured to the middle of the snow field and turning his horse began walking into the glacier.

He couldn't mean it. We were to camp on a glacier?

Silently we followed. The sun was sinking over the mountains in a Himalayan explosion of crimsons and pinks. How it had changed our ice-bound world, turning it from a blue-tinged undersea grotto to one of the most fantastic reds. The ice rose in cruel spikes, each one dripping in bloody paint. It looked magnificent and alarming. About as inviting as a bed of nails. As our donkeys clopped into the glacier my heart filled with dread. Ice all around and the Baker Brothers and their hired ruffians lurking in the darkness without.

For an instant I wished I had never come here. I wished I had listened to my father's entreaties and was back in the Maharajah's palace or safely home in Oxford, clopping through meadowsweet and willow on my loyal mare Jesse. It was but a moment of weakness. As we picked our way through the glacier and began to unpack our tents for the coldest night of our lives, I told myself that this was what adventure is all about. It wasn't all fun, frolics and digging up buried treasure; easy as helping yourself to barley sugar in a sweet shop. It was about fear. Cold. Hunger.

Most of all, it was about not knowing if you were going to survive till the morning.

❧ Chapter Twenty-two ❧

'Rachel,' I whispered.

'Go back to sleep,' she growled, shuffling in her blankets.

'I thought I heard a noise.'

Rachel opened one eye. Tangled curls and tanned skin, lit by a moonbeam slanting through an opening in the tent. 'That'll be your aunt,' she said.

'It's them. The Baker Brothers.'

On the other side of me, snuggled a little too close in our canvas tent, Aunt Hilda was snoring loudly. On our third night in the mountains we had decided to sleep in the same tent in order to conserve heat. I had grown used, now, to the presence of other bodies, even to my aunt's guttural grunts and sighs. Besides, I had exhausted myself so utterly during the last day, I could have slept in the middle of Waterloo Station.

'The Bakers are here,' I repeated.

'Oh, for heaven's sake, Kit,' Rachel snapped, but I

heard the fear in her voice. 'They couldn't find us here, in the middle of nowhere.'

'Stop pretending to yourself.'

We both went very quiet. In the pin-drop silence we heard Aunt Hilda's rhythmic snoring and then something else.

'Listen, Rachel,' I said, unnecessarily, for my friend was almost rigid with fear.

There it was again. A faint burbling noise, followed by a heavy thump. Sinister in the deep silence of the night.

Rachel sat up, the colour bleeding from her face. I was taking no chances. I grabbed my howdah pistol and un-clicked the safety catch. Rachel was gripping on to me, staring at the gun. She muttered something about where did you get that? But I shrugged her off and shook my aunt.

'Aunt,' I hissed in her ear, while thumping her shoulder. '*Wake up.*'

If anything, her snores redoubled.

'I'm going out to investigate,' I told Rachel. 'I'm not going to let them take us unaware.'

'*No*. Wake your aunt up. She'll –' Rachel grabbed my aunt and tried to shake her.

'I'll sort it out.'

'What makes you think you can sort it out?'

'I must.'

'Why *you*?' Rachel hissed. 'For heaven's sake, what's wrong with you, Kit? Why aren't you scared?'

I shrugged; Rachel's interference was making me more obstinate. I know I am sometimes foolishly reluctant to take advice, however well-meaning. And she was wrong about me not being scared. I was absolutely terrified, my heart rattling like a pair of castanets. It is just, when I'm frightened I try even harder. I ignore my fear and simply make myself do the very thing I am so scared of.

'You're not twelve-foot tall with muscles made of iron. You're just a girl. A twelve-year-old, for pity's sake.'

'My age has nothing to do with it.'

'Kit, you can't –'

Ignoring her, I hurriedly forced my frozen feet into my boots and laced them up. It was hard, for even in bed I wore my gloves and mittens and my fingers were clumsy in their layers of swaddling. Taking a deep breath I stepped outside.

'Kit!' I heard Rachel implore. 'Come back.'

My breath made clouds of vapour in the moonlight. The tents were dark patches, against the jagged white cones of the glaciers. Nothing was moving in the night; everything serene. Far above I heard the swift wing rush of a night bird. Or a raven perhaps, or vulture. Then I saw a sight so odd, it made me stop in my tracks.

A skinny man in orange robes was sitting cross-legged in the ice. In front of him was a huge hairy bear. Five or six times the size of the human, it reared over him like a giant ink-blot, a figure from a nightmare.

Yongden was nearly naked. He had taken off his sheepskin coat; his feet, legs and arms were quite bare to the elements. All he wore was a thin saffron-coloured robe.

The very sight of the monk turned my blood to ice.

Yongden's eyes were open and he was looking at the bear, which was walking towards him on its hind legs. It was massive across the chest; its paws could fell a man with a single blow. The monk was gazing straight at the creature, but I had the awful feeling that he was so deep in trance he didn't actually see it.

A horrible scream ripped out of the back of my throat and with shaking hands I raised my gun. I had to shoot, for the bear was only a few paces away. In seconds it would be upon the monk. But I hesitated. Some unseen hand was clutching me, preventing me from pulling the trigger.

From behind me a shot rang out. Startled, I turned. It was Waldo, his pistol raised, in the act of firing a second bullet. The bear raised its head to the heavens, opened its mouth and gave a mighty roar. The noise echoed, bouncing off the snow. Then the great animal turned and with a few bounds had vanished back into the night. Running to the monk, I noticed a crimson splash in the whiteness.

It looked like a bloody tear.

'Yongden. Are you all right?' I bent down, but I could have been a gnat buzzing in his ear. He was gazing past me, at Waldo.

'Why?' he asked.

'Crikey! That's a stoopid question. That bear would have eaten you with one gulp.'

Yongden shook his head. 'Bears do not attack people at night. They are frightened.'

'You shouldn't have barged in,' I snapped at Waldo, without looking at him. 'I had it under control.'

Yongden held up his hand, silencing me. 'This bear is a friend.'

The shooting had roused our whole party. Heads were popping out of dark tents, like a series of moles emerging from their mud hills. Even Aunt Hilda had finally awoken to the fact that a great drama was under way, a drama without her at the centre of it.

'I must go,' Yongden said. 'I must talk to bear.'

'You can't talk to a bear,' Waldo muttered mutinously.

'She needs my help.'

Without another word, Yongden stood up and turned away. Then, as we watched, dumbfounded, he stalked away into the night. Within seconds the darkness had swallowed him up.

Aunt Hilda stomped up to us, followed by the others disgorging from their tents, demanding to know what was going on. I explained, and for some reason she was inclined to blame me.

'You blundering child. This is a pretty kettle of codfish,' Aunt Hilda scolded. 'He'd better come back or else –'

'Or else?' I asked, staring into the darkness where Yongden had vanished. I didn't see we were in a position to issue any threats against that strange monk.

'Or else we are up the Ganges without a paddle!'

We were thinking about our predicament – stranded on the margins of the roof of the world, without guide and with dwindling supplies of food – when Waldo let out a howl. It was louder, I'm sure, than that of the bear.

'Shush, Waldo, you'll set off an avalanche,' I began. Then I saw his face.

It was twisted – a look of sheer agony on his face. Slowly he unclenched his fingers and dropped his pistol, which fell, a dark blur in the snow. For a moment I had the wild idea that Yongden had hurt him to punish him for wounding the bear. Foolish, of course, for Yongden was nowhere to be seen.

Waldo was staring at his hand. I followed his gaze. For a second I didn't understand what I was looking at. Then an awful wail ripped out of my throat.

His hands were naked.

The idiot had come out without his gloves, seizing his pistol in a blind rush. He had been a fool. We had all been warned never, ever to forget our gloves. Now he had paid for his impulsiveness. The tips of my friend's bare fingers were turning grey, glowing strangely in the moonlight. Frostbite. But it wasn't that which made me scream with disgust.

It was his little finger. When Waldo dropped his gun, the tip of his finger had remained attached to the freezing metal and snapped off, as easily as a dry twig. Looking down I could vaguely see the thing outlined against the snow, a snip of skin and bone attached to the gun.

Now he had four and a half fingers on his right hand. His shooting hand. It looked clammy, bleached, like a hunk of cod. Thank goodness, it wasn't bleeding at least, for it was far too cold out here.

Waldo was looking at his hand, blankly. His reaction was the same as mine, though far slower. He felt the pain but his brain must have frozen too, for it couldn't comprehend what was happening to him. I saw the moment of truth on his face. It hit him in a rush of terror and he mewled, a small, pathetic noise, a mouse caught in a trap.

I had to help, and fast. I rushed over to him and took his hand in my sheepskin glove while he struggled away from me. All the things I had ever learnt about frostbite came flooding back to me. Ice crystals form inside the flesh. You have to rub the affected area to restore circulation of the blood. No, that was wrong. You had to do something else, but for the moment I had clear forgotten what.

What was I meant to do? I panicked, for perhaps I was making it worse, holding his hand.

'Water. Warm water,' Isaac shouted. He was besides us and had taken in the situation in a flash. 'Wake Chamba. Fast. If he gets gangrene, we'll have to cut the rest of his fingers off.'

The fear on Waldo's face made my heart contract. He didn't scream again, just turned very pale and his cheeks trembled a little.

'Look in my pack!' Aunt Hilda ordered. 'I have some salve. I'll see Chamba doesn't make the water too hot. We can't have them burning Waldo's fingers, on top of everything else.'

I dived back into our tent for the salve. Unbelievably, Rachel was still sitting up in her blankets, her face terrified under her disordered dark curls. I filled her in on the events while I undid Aunt Hilda's pack. It was hard to see anything in the moonlight that filtered through the tent

253

opening and very hard to undo the numerous buckles on the bag. There was a jumble of things inside: letters, a strange shiny instrument whirring with cogs and levers, a compass, some spare gloves and socks. No sign of the liniment pot.

'Dratted child. What on earth are you doing?'

Aunt Hilda squatted wide-legged in the entrance to our tent. It took but a glance to see she was boiling with rage.

'You told me to look in your pack,' I exclaimed.

She crawled in to the tent, her breath coming in angry gasps as she shovelled the contents back in her bag.

'What's that anyway?' I asked pointing to the shiny instrument. 'Is it some new type of compass?'

'None of your business,' she barked. 'I meant this pack, of course.' With that she delved in another bag, the one her donkey carried, and took out a small pot of Holloway's liniment.

I grabbed it and raced outside. I didn't have time for Aunt Hilda's oddities now. There was a chaos of whinnying donkeys and milling Sherpas. Chamba had managed to fire up the Bunsen burner and melt some snow. My poor friend though, had not been able to take the pain. Isaac told me that it is when the frostbitten fingers thaw and feeling returns to your digits that it is most agonising. He had fainted away and lay cradled in Isaac's lap, while Champlon tenderly held his hand in a bowl of warm water. I smoothed back some of his blond curls, which were limp across his eyes.

'Don't worry,' Isaac whispered. 'We'll be able to save his fingers.'

'Thank God!'

'Er . . . Well, most of them, anyway.'

Most of them! It didn't seem fair. Something like this shouldn't happen to someone so young and alive as Waldo. I relieved Champlon of Waldo's hand, taking it out of the water and gently applying some of the salve. As I did my mind went back to Aunt Hilda. Why had she flared up so oddly in the tent? What was she up to? All through our voyage she'd had some murky plan of her own. I had known, in the back of my mind, she was keeping me out. It was only now, stranded here amongst the ice and snow I realised why it had been bothering me so much.

I didn't trust Aunt Hilda.

⤳ Chapter Twenty-three ⤶

I was woken up the next morning by the sounds of a commotion outside. The mats where my aunt and Rachel slept were empty. Hurriedly lacing my boots, I stuck my head outside the tent to be greeted by a scene of confusion. Donkeys neighing, Sherpas screeching, my friends and Aunt Hilda gabbling away and, most awful of all, Champlon waving his pistols as if he was about to shoot one and all.

'What's happening?' I asked Isaac, who was hopping up and down on the ice.

'Disaster,' he mumbled.

'Use your eyes, Kit,' Rachel mumbled.

It was only then that I saw what was going on. We were no longer alone in the emptiness of the glacier. Surrounding us on all sides were flitting, shadowy shapes. They resolved themselves into men on stocky ponies, dressed in a ragbag of uniforms. Some were garbed in round otter-skin hats and ancient clanking chainmail; others wore fur cloaks with conical breast-plates glinting over their chests. They were carrying spears, daggers, bows, swords and antique muskets. Though a ragged bunch, they were definitely a force to be reckoned with.

'What on –' I began.

'It's the border guards. The Tibetans,' Waldo cut in. His face was bloodless after the ordeal with his finger, his hands invisible inside his mittens. He was watching the arrival of the frontier force with an awful, grey resignation.

'What are we going to do?' I gulped, looking around wildly. I couldn't see any way out. We were hemmed in by the soldiers on all sides; trapped too by the ice and mountains.

'Nothing. We're done for,' came the dull reply.

'We can't just give up.'

The Sherpas were terrified. They had gone into a protective, murmuring huddle. I didn't know who to turn to, who was our guide and leader after the disappearance of Yongden, the monk. The Sherpas obviously felt the same way, for I could tell that there was much argument among them. Finally, Chamba the cook was almost pushed out of their group. His face was ashen but he bravely went towards the intruders. One of the men, who wore a seal-skin coat surmounted by chainmail, a shining conical breast-plate, and a flat top hat circled by a ruff of scarlet fur, dismounted and went up to Chamba.

I could not understand their talk. But the sense was clear, by the gabble of voices drifting over and ice and the harsh way the Tibetan waved his arm towards us.

'What does he say?' Aunt Hilda demanded once their talk was over and Chamba had limped his way over to us.

'We are prisoners,' Chamba replied. 'We must go with this man; he is commander of Tibetan border guards.'

'That blooming monk has left us slap-bang in the lurch,' my aunt growled. 'Listen, tell him we are a British scientific expedition.'

'He not know what that mean.'

'Confounded impertinence. My goodness, man, this is India. The property of her Imperial Highness Queen Victoria!'

'He say we in Tibets.' Chamba shrugged his shoulders, hopelessly. 'Tibet's prisoners.'

The Tibetan commander was watching these exchanges with a superior smile.

'We weel shoot our way out,' Champlon blustered. Luckily he was no longer waving his pistol around for I feared what would happen if he were to start banging off bullets. The Tibetans flintlock muskets were ancient, granted, but their bows and arrows looked lethal. There were so many of them and so few of us. Plus, I knew in my bones the Sherpas wouldn't fight.

'It not possible fight,' Chamba said, echoing my thoughts. 'Too many.'

'Yes,' Aunt Hilda agreed. 'I think this is a case for the silver tongue rather than the iron fist.' I let out a breath on hearing this. The soldiers – spread out over the glaring ice on their horses – were menacing in their stillness.

'Commander tell us pack.' Chamba's words came out in a jumbled hurry. 'He take us see governor.'

'No,' Aunt Hilda said.

'Vat?' Chamba gasped.

'We will not go anywhere. We are subjects of the Queen. This peasant has no right to order us hither and thither.'

I should have remembered that Aunt Hilda's idea of a silver tongue was different from other people's. 'Please, Aunt,' I begged. 'Let's go.' My hands were trembling

'Please, Memsahib Salter,' Chamba begged. 'Please, ve vill all die, if you refuse go.'

'I am staying right here,' Aunt Hilda declared, her bulldog chin tilting up defiantly. She had never been more splendid, more fearless – and more plain foolish – as she glared at that brute of a commander. The Tibetan was clearly trying to follow the exchanges. Now he intervened, barking at Chamba, who I could tell was trying to wriggle out of the situation.

Aunt Hilda wasn't having this. She marched up to the commander, waving her hands dismissively. 'No,' she mouthed, so even if you didn't speak English you couldn't fail to understand. 'We are staying here.'

The man lurched, as if she had struck him. On his broad, weather-beaten face was a look of utter surprise. My aunt's courage must have seemed foolish beyond belief to him. His mouth was cruel, but I caught something uncertain, from him, a breath of fear. This made him even more terrifying, for in his cowardice he might be driven to violence.

I thought he was going to spit on my aunt; instead he turned and barked out an order. Two men came hurrying forward and seized Aunt Hilda. Champlon's hand was on his pistol, but in a flash more men were on him, pinioning his arms. A soldier seized his moustache and pulled it, as if he believed it was false. Champlon and my aunt were stripped of their gloves. Before our horrified eyes, the men produced stout bamboo cords which they wrapped around my aunt's wrists and those of the Frenchman. The cords were tied to a stick, the soldiers scurrying around like worker ants. I swear we didn't understand what they intended till the last minute, when we saw the sticks tied, with more rope to the tails of two mules. Champlon bore the torture coolly but my aunt was thrashing around like a thing demented, causing more men to run to her and force her into submission.

Before our horrified and helpless eyes, Champlon and Aunt Hilda were to be made to march, half dragged along, tied to the tails of the mules. It was horribly cruel and already I could see scarlet weals standing out on their wrists. The blood was draining out of their hands, the danger of frostbite all too great.

'No,' I screamed inside, but I was too scared to open my mouth.

Waldo was watching, pale and unmoving. I felt Rachel's gloved hand creep into my arm and give me a squeeze.

'Pack tents,' Chamba yelled, spittle flying. 'Pack and go. Ve must go with the men. I no vant they kill us.'

The sun was climbing up the sky, dazzling on the cones and crests of the glacier, as we hurriedly packed our belongings. Our party of explorers, Sherpas and donkeys were a silent, wary lot as we followed Aunt Hilda and Gaston Champlon off the glacier. The border soldiers rode a careful distance from us, as if they were afraid that even the wind from our passage would contaminate them.

We were 'foreign devils' to these men. We were entering

a country stuck in the Middle Ages, ruled by the whip and the sword. The idea of treating prisoners with respect was as remote here as hansom carriages and gas lighting.

We plodded along mutely, forced to keep pace with the mules behind which Aunt Hilda and Gaston Champlon marched. A soldier walked beside each donkey, striking it with a bamboo switch, forcing the pace. Once I tried to come up to Aunt Hilda and talk to her, but the soldier turned his stick on me. I had to dodge to avoid a blow. Aunt Hilda's eyes were aglitter. We came off the glacier on to a path that wound its way around the mountain and began a slow descent. Later, sore and heartsick, we turned a corner and there before us stretched an endless plain. Tibet! You'll forgive me if the sight did not fill me with the joy I expected. It was a barren landscape, bisected by a frothing river and calm sheets of water. At that moment I couldn't understand why we had ever wanted to explore it.

Nearer to us was a frontier post, permanently in the shadow of a teetering spar of ice. Huddled together for comfort was a handful of buildings, their roofs weighted down with rocks, as if to prevent them being blown away. As we were frogmarched into the garrison, snow began to fall, blowing slantways into our faces and pulling a grey veil over Tibet. One of the houses was larger than the rest. Aunt Hilda and Gaston Champlon were untied from the mules and then we were all taken into this house and led along a dark corridor. Aunt Hilda, Rachel and I were separated from the rest of the group and shoved into a dark cell.

As we listened to our friend's footsteps plodding away, my aunt was very quiet. She rubbed her hands together to force some blood into the flesh. They were grey, as dingy and limp-looking as wrung-out dishcloths. Her wrists were deeply indented where the bamboo cord had bit into them, spots of blood standing out on the flesh. This was a hurt, subdued Aunt Hilda. Only in her eyes was there a trace of the old fire.

I took off my sheepskin gloves and gently eased them on to Aunt Hilda's poor hands. The pain must have been agonising, but she has never wanted for bravery. She bit her lip so hard she drew blood but uttered not a moan.

'A bit better?' I asked.

She nodded, not trusting herself to speak.

I silently took stock of our situation. Imprisoned in the middle of a glacial expanse by wild and heathen bandits. This was a cell, no doubt of it, bare of even mat or commode. The walls and floor were of rock, the tiny window through which freezing wind blew, was barred. There was no way out of here. No way of contacting the representatives of our Empire in Simla.

There was only one, small ray of hope. I was going to explain when Aunt Hilda did something ridiculous. She strode over to the door, which was made of thick planks of pine, and for a moment I thought she was going to batter on it with her sore hands. Instead she kicked, once, twice, raining a frenzy of blows upon the wood. It began to creak and then a splinter appeared. Outside I heard yelling and then running.

'Stop it!' I yelled.

But she would not. A wild light in her eyes, she continued to kick. It came to me that she was enjoying it, and for a moment I thought she had gone truly insane.

'Stop!' Rachel screamed and we both tried to take her arms, pull her away from the door.

A piece of wood in the middle of door slid aside, revealing a hatch. Through it slanted an angry eye. A voice called out a guttural command. She ignored it. Aunt Hilda had been driven wild by her pain and was beyond reason. She continued to kick at the door, with her steel-toed boots, the crampons doing terrible damage to the wood.

Next moment an iron cylinder slid through the door. A bullet exploded, deafening in the tiny space. Blood thrummed in my ears. The shining pellet sped through the room, ricocheting off the stone wall, sending splinters of stone spinning through the air. Rachel and I crouched instinctively but Aunt Hilda was too dazed to move, and a flying dart grazed her sheepskin-covered shoulder.

'Enough!' I screamed.

The air seemed to leave my aunt and she sagged in the corner. The hatch closed with a bang and I collapsed next to her.

'Enough, Aunt Hilda!' I screeched at her immobile form. My voice was hysterical to my own ears. 'We've got to keep our heads if we are to survive.'

As the words left my throat I spied something in the wall just to the right of my head. In the dim light I could just about discern some writing graven into the wall. I couldn't read it, for it was Tibetan. Each letter, about five inches tall, had been painstakingly whittled into the stone. As I saw them the awful conviction came to me that the letters formed a name. A name and a protest in the face of a horrible fate.

Perhaps the only thing that remained on earth of the last occupant of our cell.

↭ Chapter Twenty-four ↭

We didn't sleep much that night. The three of us crouched together in the corner of the cell. Huddled like bats, we closed our eyes and a sort of release born of deep weariness washed over us. In my blurry, anguished dreams we were trapped on endless ice. Monsters, with fur-like hair growing on their face and hands, were prodding us with giant hairpins sharp as spears. Their jabs hurt. I opened my eyes and a man with a stick was prodding me. Rachel and Aunt Hilda were stumbling blearily about and there was a sharp ache in my chest.

'Ugh ugh,' the man grunted, gesturing to the door.

He did have hair on his face. It took me a moment to realise it was a hat that covered most of his skin.

We were marched along a dark corridor to a room that was hung with embroidered parchments, rich paintings of the Buddha and Tibetan Tankas. It was so still; with shining butter lamps spluttering away, casting a golden glow on the scene. I guessed it was the garrison's shrine. Waldo, Champlon and Isaac were sitting, disconsolate, on a low bench. Waldo looked awful, his skin appeared as clammy as a beached whale. His right hand was limp inside the manacles, the missing finger-tip painfully obvious. Champlon was horribly pale and somehow twisted, askew. I had to look twice at him to understand what was wrong. They had deprived my gallant French friend of his proudest possession, his moustache. Those luxuriant, carefully trimmed and waxed fronds had been shaved clean off. Without it Champlon was naked. Anger boiled in me. The barbarians. Why had they done that to Champlon, save to humiliate him?

'Kit,' Waldo began before a guard dealt my friend a blow on the back of his head, effectively silencing him.

I wanted to lash out at these Tibetan savages, but I held both tongue and fire. I had to learn from Aunt Hilda's example what *not* to do. Losing my temper would only make our situation worse.

The commander stomped in followed by a very frightened Chamba.

Our cook cast us an imploring look, before the commander began ranting. He was carrying a bag, which I realised with a shock, was Aunt Hilda's. With a savage oath he ripped it open and emptied it on a low wooden table. The contents scattered. The brass and wood prayer wheel I had seen earlier, gloves, handkerchiefs, lacy bloomers and the vaguely familiar but strange steel instrument. The commander shouted at Chamba, who began to translate in a stuttering voice.

'The commander tell you are the spy,' Chamba said to Aunt Hilda. 'You have come here as spy for the English government.'

'Poppycock. Never heard such a bunch of piffle in my life,' Aunt Hilda declared confidently.

The commander waved his hands at the odd assortment of possessions on the table, his voice yapping and persistent as a basset hound.

'He tell you are here to steal Tibet's secrets.'

'That's nonsense,' Rachel cut in to my surprise. 'We're explorers. Here on a scientific expedition.'

'Fringies no allowed in Tibets,' Chamba translated. Fringies was the slang in this part of the world for foreigners.

'Well, we wouldn't have been in Tibet if he hadn't brought us here,' I retorted.

I was thankful that Aunt Hilda's spurt of lunacy in the cell seemed to have passed. Her eyes had lost that wild glitter and she was holding her peace remarkably well. Indeed, she looked thoughtful.

The commander had picked up that spiky steel instrument etched with numbers and containing a section of revolving bands. He was looking at it and muttering furiously to Chamba, who shook his head. I had the feeling the Tibetan was puzzled by this piece of equipment that he didn't understand, but that only made him more suspicious. The commander barked at him and, quaking, Chamba translated.

'The commander know what this is. It for finding gold. You come with your gold machine to steal Tibet's gold.'

'I will not stand for this,' Aunt Hilda replied, sternly. 'That is a perfectly harmless instrument for calculating the position of the stars. I happen to be a keen astronomer. Tell the commander that I know all the magic of the stars.'

My mind was working furiously as Chamba translated Aunt Hilda's remarks. What the commander said must be a fairytale. But on the other hand, it was clearly no star charter that Aunt Hilda had in her possession. I had seen one of these complex instruments before in my father's study. This was a theodolite, a piece of modern equipment for precisely calculating the altitude of mountains and surveying land mass.

What exactly was my aunt doing with a theodolite?

The commander had not finished. Now, his eyes almost manic with hate, he delivered his *coup de grâce*. He picked up the prayer wheel: a smooth, polished cylinder of wood, engraved with Tibetan characters which revolved with a clicking sound. I had seen Yongden flicking a similar object while chanting prayers. I knew they were as sacred to Buddhists as a cross was to us Christians.

With a flourish the commander removed the top of the prayer wheel and took a sheaf of papers from a hollow inside. This was all wrong. The papers were finely printed, bound together with a red ribbon. I could only read one word, but that word made my legs turn to jelly. It was GOLD. 'He tell you are a spy,' Chamba said. 'He tell you are a dirty, rotten, English spy.'

My aunt opened and closed her mouth but no words came out. The commander's yapping voice went on.

'The men tell him you are on Nangchpa glacier,' Chamba translated. 'They tell him he find spy there.'

Shock jolted through me. 'What men?' I blurted. Chamba asked my question, which brought forth a fresh spume of words, which the cook translated.

'These are good men. True friends of Tibet. They two Russian princes and vith them Indians, and a very clever monkey. He know they are good, because they give him much presents and tell him about you and so commander give them pass to Tibet.'

So, the Baker Brothers had set a trap for us as neat as could be. We had walked straight into it. The commander was working himself up into a crescendo of anger. Now Aunt Hilda began to protest her innocence. He didn't listen, words bubbled out, a molten flow of anger. At the end of this surge of hate he spat out an order to Chamba.

Our cook looked at us, a hunted expression in his eyes. I could see he was being ripped apart. He didn't want to translate the commander's speech but was too frightened not to. The commander struck him with the flat of his hand. A blow that Chamba took full on the cheek. Finally he dragged out the words.

'Commander say you are spies. Tomorrow you hanged.'

❧ Chapter Twenty-five ❧

Back in the cell, the three of us slumped in the corners as far away as possible from each other, as if to avoid contagion. Our prison was a tiny space, no more than seventeen square foot. We could have been back on that glacier, separated by miles of freezing ice, so carefully did we avoid each other. I was caught in my own private nightmare. What do you do on your last night on earth? You can't waste it in sleep. Besides, I was too angry with Aunt Hilda to find solace in dreams. Terrifying, empty thoughts flooded me, as did a sick fear. I looked again at the scratchings in the wall. Should I write our names so someone, some day, would guess what had happened to us?

Kit Salter   Rachel Ani

My secret should have comforted me, but it only added an edge to my desperation. I had not told Rachel or Aunt Hilda that I still possessed my howdah pistol.

The guards had taken away all the men's weapons, but they'd never searched me, obviously believing that no mere girl could be armed. Inside me a resolution was gathering, to shoot my way out. I might die in the attempt. Still it was better than being hanged, or tortured to death.

'Tell me it's not true, Aunt Hilda.'

To my own surprise I found I had spoken. My words were movements of lips and air. Talking for the sake of shutting out the cold and the fear. Rachel cast a dreary glance at me. Inside, I knew that whatever words Aunt Hilda used to deny the charge of spying, I would not believe her.

'True? Merciful heavens! Of course it's true.' Aunt Hilda looked me squarely in the face and spoke without a moment's hesitation.

'You're a spy then?'

'Obviously.'

'You led us into danger, knowing that we could be executed for spying?'

'Hellfire and demnition, child! It's a bit rich to say I led you into danger. You're harder to shake off than a limpet. I could no more get rid of you than I can get rid of the wax inside my ear!'

'But why, Aunt Hilda? Why did you stoop so low? Just for gold. I thought you were searching for Shambala. For ancient relics.'

Aunt Hilda rose, shaking herself like a bulldog coming out of a dirty lake. 'Your problem, Kit, is that you're muddled.'

'What?'

'You have cotton wool inside your head instead of brains. You're a hopeless romantic. Lost in airy-fairy clouds of make-believe.'

Rachel was watching our exchanges, as bewildered as I was, probably, to hear myself described as a romantic!

'How dare you,' I spluttered. 'I'm not a romantic. You got us into this mess and you're not even saying sorry!'

'Do you remember what I said to you on the steamer?' Aunt Hilda, as usual, never bothered to listen to things she found uncomfortable.

'Pardon?'

'I gave you some advice on the steamer to India. You weren't paying attention. That's pretty obvious. You should have been, my girl, it's the best advice you'll ever be given.'

'What was it then? These great words of wisdom.'

'Exactly that!' Aunt Hilda pounced, a satisfied look on her face. 'Words of wisdom. Don't bother with fine sentiments and noble ideas. Gold. Gold, *gold*. That's what matters, my girl, that's what makes the world go round.'

From her corner, Rachel gave Aunt Hilda a look of

utter disgust, then she buried her head in her lap, cutting herself off from any further communication with us.

'I can't really believe you think like this, Aunt Hilda,' I said slowly.

'Oh I do. I really do.' She was growling now, eyes flickering with an anger I couldn't understand. 'Have you heard of the Tibetan gold fields? Warren Hastings learned of them over a century ago. They've tantalised the British government ever since. You know about Black Hills?'

I nodded, of course I'd heard of the famous gold rush. It was a fever that had ravaged America, luring thousands to abandon home, wives, children. To forsake everything in the search for the shiny metal.

'Thok Jalung. That's a name to make the heart sing, Kit. Bigger, better, shinier than Black Hills. Nuggets as big as my fist. If I found them, I would be rich beyond your wildest dreams, my girl. I'm not talking trinkets for your jewellery box, here. I'm talking of enough wealth to fund an army. I'd be richer than the Baker Brothers. I would be able to fund any expedition I liked. Do precisely what I wanted!'

The deranged glitter had returned to my aunt's eyes. Angry red spots stood out clownishly on her cheeks. She was staring at something on the bare cell walls. I believe that it was gold, great nuggets of shining gold, she was seeing there.

'What about Shambala?' I said, quietly. Of course I like gold as much as the next person, but it was not what I was really searching for. Gold seemed to me to be a chimera. All my dreams were of riches deeper than metal, however precious. These mountains held out the promise of so much more. My missing map was still a dull ache inside me. It had teased me, calling me to some ancient mystery, only to be snatched away. I didn't believe we would ever see Yongden, or my map, again.

'Pish and tush,' my aunt scoffed. 'Schoolgirl dreams.'

'You must be after Shambala – and my map.'

'The only map I'm interested in, my girl, showed the way to the Tibetan gold fields. That map you think shows the way to paradise, actually shows the way to Thok Jalung. I met a spy captain in Simla. Did you know that?'

I remembered how Aunt Hilda had melted away from me at the Lower Bazaar in Simla. She had been so evasive that day.

'You gave me the slip in Simla, to meet your spy master?'

'The captain promised me a queen's ransom if I found those mines. An absolute mountain of gold.'

Bleakness settled like dust on me. All my dreams had ended here, in rocky cell and greedy search for gold. Then something struck me, something not quite right.

Why would the Baker Brothers risk everything for gold?

'The Baker Brothers must be after something else. They already have more than enough gold.'

Aunt Hilda sighed, and spoke very slowly, as if communicating with a nincompoop. 'Kit, learn one thing and one thing only from me. You – can – never – have – enough – gold.'

I'd had enough of this conversation. If this was to be my last night on earth, I did not want it to be spent in sordid argument over riches. The cell walls pressed in on me. The slowly ticking minutes till our gaolers came to collect us for the noose.

'That's all very well, dear Auntie,' I said, sweet as honey. 'But you can't take gold where we're going. What does the Bible say? It is easier for a camel to go through the eye of a needle than for a rich man to enter the Kingdom of God.'

If nothing else, that stopped her mouth.

❧ Chapter Twenty-six ❧

I must have fallen into sleep, despite the icicles settling in my veins and in my heart. Sometime in those despairing hours I was woken by a clatter of feet, the crash of a cell door against the wall. A burly figure in a sheepskin coat stood in the darkness without. He held a butter lamp, which lit his face from below. The flickering light turned an ordinary man into monster, with dark puddles for eyes and slanting cheekbones as cruel as knife slashes.

Through our tiny cell window I could see dark sky. Deep, black, star-speckled night in the centre of which cruised a gibbous moon, wrapped in scarlet clouds. A time for sleep, but already our executioner had arrived.

His entrance awakened the others. Rachel's face like a crumpled rose, Aunt Hilda repressing a gasp. Silently we all watched the man as he stood on the threshold and raised the butter lamp to light his way.

'Yongden?' I gasped.

'Is time,' he replied.

I had been sure we would never see the monk again, yet here he was. I did not wonder where a man who we had last seen walking barefoot into the snow, had acquired a sheepskin coat, stout boots and a butter lamp. How had he suddenly appeared in our cell? With Yongden it did not do to ask too many questions. Instead we meekly did as he bid, walking past a snoring guard in a chair, down the corridor and turning right, where there was another pine door.

'Wait,' he commanded and turned the door handle. It swung open, revealing a sleeping Champlon and Isaac. Waldo was standing up, staring at the door with huge, lunatic eyes.

'I'll die before you take me,' he muttered, clenching his fists into a ball. 'I'll kill you. Savages.'

'Shush, Waldo,' I hissed. 'It's us.'

'Kit?' His blue eyes were bleary, and he stared at me as if fearful I was an apparition.

The others had woken as Yongden stepped into their cell. Such was his mastery of us all that he didn't need to speak, just beckoned with a crooked finger. Hardly trusting myself, not knowing whether he was a phantom borne of our need for a saviour, I was the first to follow him. Aunt Hilda, Waldo and then the others falling into step behind us. We went past half a dozen soldiers, all fast asleep. Waldo removed their guns, our own Martini-Henry rifles, and they didn't stir. As we sped by on feet of air, Waldo passed the weapons out to the others. Never had I felt so fleet, so made of spirit and light. We seemed as insubstantial as wraiths to our gaolers, our passage disturbing no more than the air around them. In a flash we were outside in the cobbled courtyard where our donkeys were stamping their feet, and our Sherpas waiting for us in a mute huddle.

My breath created shimmering mushrooms of vapour in the air. It was freezing out here, with Tibet at our feet. We were ants against the majestic mountain, that jutting dazzle of ice silhouetted against the raven sky. Above it all hung the same blood-drenched moon I had glimpsed from my cell. Vultures circled above us, their harsh caws rising and falling in the wind. A dark omen? No matter. I have never been happier to feel the air on my face, to taste freedom in my mouth.

'Go,' Yongden addressed my aunt and Champlon.

'We must make haste,' Aunt Hilda agreed. 'Press onwards.'

'No.'

'What . . . c-can . . . you . . . m-m-mean?' Aunt Hilda stuttered.

'Go home. It is time.'

Aunt Hilda blinked, for a moment I thought she was going to argue, but she merely hung her head. It was

Champlon, his face naked and furious, who protested, refusing to mount his donkey and waving his gun. A bullet cut him off, cracking past his face, fizzling out in the snow. A clamour from inside the building told us the strange spell that blanketed the garrison had been lifted.

More bullets careened past us; a donkey brayed in sudden sharp pain. Ebony figures were flitting in the snow darkness; crouching, running towards us.

'Go!' urged Yongden.

There was a stampede of donkeys' hooves, of braying and thumping of Sherpas cursing and running. More and more guards had emerged from the house, inky shadows against the overwhelming darkness. Arrows, silent and deadly, mingled with bullets. Champlon, wheeling away on his steed, was taking aim, picking off the soldiers with unerring accuracy. Waldo, I saw with a pang, was raising a quavering left hand, trying to shoot.

An arrow pelted towards me. A streak of eagle feathers, a deadly tip. I ducked. Behind me someone shrieked.

Yongden, trotting by me on a fine piebald stallion, laid his hands on the flank of my donkey, calming my panicking beast. He gestured to me to follow him. Miraculously we seemed to cut a path through the mayhem; the hiss, the cries, the bullets exploding in bursts of white light.

We were among the last to escape, bringing up the

rear behind Rachel, my aunt and the mass of Sherpas. Finally came Champlon, his face set and desperate, but his pistol steady. He was holding off our attackers, cutting off their advance with deadly gunfire. On the edges of my senses I was aware of another sound, underpinning the hiss and whine of fighting. A deep ominous sledgehammer under our feet and in our ears. A rumble that froze all battle and instantaneously scattered our attackers in panic.

'Avalanche,' murmured Yongden.

He was riding fast, hooves scudding through snow. I followed, but snowflakes were whirling all around, a devilish vortex in my eyes, ears and nose. A white slab glided in front of my feet, like a magic carpet coming in to land, cutting us off from my friends. Beyond it I saw Rachel's startled eyes.

Aunt Hilda's mouth opened in an agonised yowl at the sight of the avalanche and clumsily, stupidly, she fell off her donkey. Champlon pounded off his own beast and hauled her upright. He half-dragged my aunt on to his mount, kicking it to make it run towards my friends and the veil of snow. Then he raced to Aunt Hilda's panicking donkey and began to hoist himself up. Boom – a shimmering slab of ice juddered into him, obliterating him from view. I shrieked, a scream that wrenched out my guts. It was useless. In an instant Champlon and donkey were both gone; buried under a huge white cushion.

The ridge of ice shredded; broke up into pieces, pelting hard nuggets in my face. I was sliding on something, under me my beast was braying forlornly. A sooty shadow moved in front of me. Yongden, I believed, as I clutched at hope. Yongden, keep me safe, I prayed.

Where lay earth and where sky, I no longer knew. All I was aware of was eddying light. Glaring, dazzling white that sucked and drowned, obscuring all. Dimly, I was aware that I was sliding, but where and how I couldn't say. My breath came in ragged gasps. I couldn't breathe, the pressure on my chest was suffocating me.

Darkness crashed in on me, as before there had been light. I must have blacked out for I knew no more.

When I opened my eyes all I could see was Yongden's face. He was bending over me, something hairy and ominous rearing behind him. As my eyes focused, it took the form of the nostrils and flank of his piebald stallion.

'What happened?' I rasped.

'You live,' he said sombrely.

'Rachel, Waldo! . . . and –'

'Your friends safe, they on other side of avalanche.

This was only a –' he made a coughing noise.

'Hiccup?'

'Hiccup. The mountain, she play, not very angry.'

'Play?' I repeated in amazement, remembering the thundering lava of snow, the sensation of being buried alive in ice. 'All that ice?'

'Not rock or ice,' he said, correcting me. 'Powder snow. A baby avalanches. Your friends they are on other side of avalanche. The Sherpas take them back to India. They not make mistake to come back. They go down mountain. They take care. This land is not for gold hunters. They leave this place which is not for them and go home.'

It was the longest speech I'd ever heard Yongden make. Slowly, I uncoiled my limbs and stood up. Nothing seemed to be broken, though my back ached as if it had been pelted with a thousand small pebbles. Which I suppose it had. Judging from the rosy flush of the sun crawling up on the horizon, I had been unconscious for a long time.

'My donkey?' I asked.

Yongden shook his head and I gathered she was dead. It was a curse to be my mount, I thought bitterly. Two donkeys had died, serving me.

We were in a different land now, the garrison of stocky houses with their stone-freighted roofs had disappeared. It was a precipice, an icy defile with rocky, impassable peaks rearing to either side. Far, far ahead of us ran a river, speckled with a million dancing lights. Only I wasn't sure if it was a mirage. Increasingly I wasn't certain of what was in my head and what was the world outside. What had I been warned by the young Sherpa, so long ago? 'Stay away from Yongden,' he had said. 'He plays inside your head.'

'Where are we?' I asked.

'We fell down the mountain.'

Looking up the hundreds of feet it seemed incredible that we were still alive; we should have been smashed, pulverised, nothing but a heap of bones. In my dreams I recalled something feather-like supporting me, a floating bed of snow, and it never occurred to me to disbelieve Yongden. So we must be a long, long way from the others. How would we rejoin them? A cruel thought hit me, whipping me like a lash.

'They'll look for me, Yongden. They'll put themselves into danger.'

He shook his head: 'They saw you die.'

'They saw me die?' I asked.

'They saw *us* die – you and me.'

There did not seem to be any answer to this.

'We must go,' Yongden indicated that I should climb on to the back of his mare, behind him.

'Where?'

He turned to me. I saw sorrow in his eyes, but that was only the first level of expression. Underneath were buried layers of meaning, layers of things I couldn't understand.

'Shambala,' he replied.

I mounted the horse. Yongden tapped its flank and in silence we rode off.

❧ Chapter Twenty-seven ❧

It began to snow. The flurry of tiny flakes from above rapidly swelled into a storm that seemed to suck and pull in different directions. The heavens had turned leaden; on all sides of us visibility was reduced to a couple of feet. Our pace had slowed to a crawl, for it was dangerous if our horse put one hoof wrong in this blizzard.

Yongden's back, a few inches in front of me, was painted white by the flakes, but I held on to him, a feeling which was reassuringly solid. Underneath me I could feel the steady lope of his horse, of warm, breathing flesh. Snowflakes were settling on my face in an icy mass, too cold for them to melt. I had to brush them away; lest I turned into a living snowman.

Thus we rode – I have no idea for how long. It might have been minutes or hours. All I knew was that I was living on the edge of my senses, my nerves tingling. The pain in my back, which had felt so raw, had drifted away in the snow.

'We stop here,' Yongden suddenly announced. I have no idea why. All I could see around me was the same thing, rock and mountain and a dense, white world. The stallion came to a halt, understanding Yongden, so it seemed. Yongden climbed off and delving into the small pack brought out a length of rope, which he made into a kind of simple harness.

'We climb,' Yongden said.

'Where?'

'Up.'

There was obviously no point in asking Yongden questions, he had lapsed into enigmatic mumbles. His face loomed out of the snow for an instant, like a dark moon rising. I read so many different emotions in his eyes. Pity. Compassion. Sadness.

Was he pitying me? Or was pity his normal state? I felt oddly detached from myself, from Kit Salter of the comfortable home in Park Town, Oxford. This new person was travelling through a landscape of ice with a man she barely knew. A man who spoke seldom and gave no hint of his thoughts. I felt an instant of empathy with Yongden, this monk who moved through life with no ties. He was as disconnected from everyday concerns as the shadow of an eagle flitting over a village was from the lives of those it touched. I wouldn't want to be

Yongden. I wanted to be able to love and hate, to feel life. But I admired him. To the monk, all the things that made us so passionately sad or happy were illusions, painted stage sets, while the real action went on somewhere beyond.

It was like travelling with a phantom. I would never *know* Yongden. He wasn't kind, not in the ordinary sense. If anything, he was terrifying.

I held the rope Yongden gave me in my sheepskin gloves. It was tough and fibrous. Made from fronds of a willow-like tree, it felt as though it had been soaked to strengthen it. Yongden showed me how to put on the harness and adjust it using the straps at the sides. It had a big, iron hook at the back which he attached to the rope. He didn't wear a harness himself, just carelessly tied the rope around his waist and looped a coil over his shoulder.

Yongden walked over to the stallion and stroked its muzzle. He was talking to it in a language I didn't understand. He patted it on the back and the horse whickered, nuzzling Yongden's hand. Then it turned round and slowly trotted off.

'You can't do that,' I blurted. 'Where is your horse going?'

'He is not my horse. He is his horse. He is going home.'

'How?' I indicated the falling snow, the ice all around us. 'How will he find the way?'

'He is a child of the mountains.'

Without further explanation, Yongden threw the loop of rope into the air. It floated high, uncurling itself. I wasn't altogether surprised when it landed around a jutting crag of rock. In fact I wouldn't have been surprised if he had simply walked up the mountain.

I followed him, finding footholds in the icy sides. The first few paces were easy but it rapidly became hard. It was tense, slippery work with the snow blowing in my face and the surface of the mountain sliding under my gloves and boots. The pity of it – I really needed my crampons to take firm hold in the ice, but the guards had removed them at the garrison. Once I slipped and would have fallen if the rope had not pulled tight, holding me by the harness.

'Don't look down,' Yongden warned. 'Don't look up. Look straight in front.'

Of course I did exactly the opposite of what he warned. The snow had chosen that moment to clear and I had a dizzying view down the mountain, to the gully far, far below. My stomach heaved, my insides dropping. The trotting figure of the horse was already no bigger than an ant, an ink spot against a gossamer backdrop. My hands loosened against the rope and I had a terrible sensation of falling, falling.

After that I looked neither up nor down, but concentrated on my gloved hands and the solidity of the rope. At least I hoped it was solid – when I had lurched it had creaked alarmingly. Even though I dared not risk a glance I was conscious in every fibre of my body of the mountain rearing so far above me. Kit Salter was but a tiny speck, a fleck of dust in the immensity of these ancient peaks.

Climbing thus was hard physical work, the rope of the harness cutting into my flesh, even through the layers of sheepskin wadding. My knees felt tremulous. I was aware again of a dull ache in my spine. But above it all my mind was clear, taking flight on the back of this awful adventure. This realm was free of all but birds, the warble of the mynah, the screech of the eagle. Hovering in the background the bald head and cruel beak of the flesh feeders, the vultures waiting for us to fall.

By the grace of Yongden, we didn't fall. Eventually he stopped on a ledge and I climbed up to meet him. It was a slab of rock jutting a few inches out into the air, wide and comfortable enough to sit on. When I did look down I saw that we had climbed far above the other side of the canyon. Over that shining peak I could see that river I had glimpsed before, foaming in the distance.

'We are here,' Yongden murmured.

'Where?' I asked. Even this enigmatic sorcerer could surely not refer to a dizzying perch on the edge of a precipice as 'here'. He didn't reply so I asked again, 'Where are we?'

'Your way,' he said.

I turned and saw that Yongden was pointing inwards. Behind the ledge, cutting into the face of the mountain was a cave. Too dark to see what was in the cave, but surely this was not the way to the legendary paradise.

'Here I must leave you,' Yongden said. 'You will be safe.' He was holding something out to me in his hands. Numbly I took it and saw what it was. My torn half of Father Monserrate's map.

As soon as I saw it a shock jolted through me. I snatched it greedily. 'This is mine.'

'Yes.'

I folded my map, and undoing my sheepskin coat with fumbling fingers, placed it in the inside pocket. It felt good, pulsing near my heart. A source of warmth and support, my talisman to protect against danger. Something missing inside me had healed, which gave me the courage to look Yongden square in the eye and say boldly:

'You won't leave me. Not all alone here.'

'I go,' he said calmly, his fingers working away to remove my hook from his rope.

Panic rose in my throat, an acid, lemon tang. My map was only a piece of paper, after all. 'What am I meant to do?'

'You will know.'

You can't abandon me, I wanted to wail. You can't leave me on the edge of this cliff to die of hunger and exposure. Strangely no words, no sounds at all, came out of my mouth. The heavens seemed to close in on me, sky and earth rising like another avalanche to cut off the blood coursing in my veins. Abandoned. From far away, I heard rushing wind and, skimming by, a flutter of wingbeats. A hoopoe, the wild, retreating caw of a mountain bird.

Yongden looped the end of the rope round the ledge. 'Goodbye,' he murmured. For a heartbeat he placed his hand on my cheek, as if blessing me. Then he stepped off the edge of the mountain.

Horror fluttered in my guts, but I couldn't scream. I was still too paralysed with shock. I stepped forward to see Yongden floating, almost weightless, down the mountain. Crags jutted out, vicious as axe blades, but he sailed past them. He avoided splattering his head against rock, careening into ice. Too soon, he was gone; a basalt speck far down below.

Momentarily, I thought of following him. But my rope would not have stretched so far. Anyway, I would have smashed into the rocks with the first lurch. My throat was hollow, butterflies dancing up my spine. I willed them to rest. However frightened, however bewildered, I had no choice. Yongden had left me here. He had told me I was meant to go into the cave. So I did as he bid.

I turned and stumbled into the dark, though my legs had turned to columns of liquid. It was warmer here, out of the wind and the frosted air. I removed my gloves and tucked them into my coat pocket. This nook would have made a cosy home for a snow leopard or a bear. The scattering of feathers, twigs, a dead pelt on the earthen floor suggested that some animal lived here. At the back of the cave was a shadowy area, a patch of velvet blackness against the gloom. A tunnel. Dazedly I went to it and crawled in. It was impossible to stand up in the narrow, musky space, but, carefully making myself as small as possible, I was able to progress.

After a time on my hands and knees, feeling my way through the pitch-black rocks, the passage broadened. I was able to breathe easier and it became possible to stand up. I rose and slowly began to walk, testing the way with my hands, placing one foot carefully in front of the other. There was light coming from somewhere ahead of me, a faint leavening of the darkness. I could see shadowy forms, rocks shaped like large icicles, boulders sticking out of the walls. Once a bat flitted against my face; and with a flutter of leathery wings flew away. Thus I travelled a long, long way and I felt that I was walking into the heart of the mountain.

I turned a corner and stepped into light.

It was so sudden. The sunshine seemed harsh, unearthly. It dazzled, making me blink. There was something barring my way. I could only see the silhouette of this creature, outlined in the centre of the glare. It was huge and hairy, its ears standing out from its face. I knew the stories of the monster that stalks these mountains. The yeti. I wanted to run away but there was nowhere to go. So I blundered forward blindly, so reeling with fright that I tripped over and fell forward, flat on my face. Something bent over me, an animal exhaling a warm, peaty smell.

Gently, as if I was a baby, large hands lifted me.

∾ Chapter Twenty-eight ∾

Warm breath on my face, scented with vanilla and something richer, chocolatey, underneath. Fur enclosed me. I was carried, cradled in this creature's arms, while it loped over the earth. I had the sensation we were skimming through the air, swooping like a couple of overgrown swallows. I could see nothing beyond the thing's arms and the heavens awash with opal light. Abruptly, the motion stopped and it lowered me on to the ground. I was lying on a yielding surface. A bank of leaves. I sank into the softness, looking straight up into the sky.

The hard sun dazzled my eyes after the tunnel. I realised I had found it strangely soothing down there inside the mountain. Darkness had comforted me; lifting a burden of worry and decisions from my head. Wherever I was now, here there was no escape from the light.

'Are you a yeti?' I asked.

The thing laughed. It had a beautiful, warm voice. 'No, I am not a yeti,' it said.

'What are you then?'

'I am a Guardian.'

I struggled to sit up. Above me the sun was blazing. It was different somehow, flat like a saucer, a fiercer, closer orb than I was used to. It was merciless; shadow melted away, leaving nothing but hard edges and an awful clarity.

'Am I on earth?' I asked the strange animal.

It wriggled in answer. With one sinuous movement the thing shrugged off the hairy pelt. Inside the coat that had covered her from the top of her head to the tips of her fingers and toes was a woman. With mouth and nose and, well, everything. As human as you or me. A woman, with a soft face, shiny black eyes and short brown hair, cropped as close to her head as a soldier's or a monk's. I could not say she was young or old, beautiful or not; even Tibetan, Indian or English. It puzzled me that she had carried me with such ease, for her hands were small and fine-boned, not the large, soft paws I had felt. She had, though, a very calm countenance and now she gently inclined her head.

'This is Shambala?'

'Some call it that.'

I looked around, ready for wonders. You may think

me foolish, but I expected something marvellous. Leprechauns, unicorns whiter than snow, perhaps a rainbow bridge arching into the heavens. At the very least a shimmering ice city, rising from the crystal mountains. I do not know quite what my fancies were, but I was ready for anything.

Except what I saw: a small, rather humdrum Tibetan village. The houses were built of irregular sized stones, their roofs weighted down, as we had seen in the garrison, with rocks. There were several of these clustered together, behind them was an orchard, and snaking through the village, a burbling stream. It was an oasis of green, of plants and flowers and trees, flitting with small humming birds and the thrum of bees and other insects. I spied a mynah and a hoopoe, a juniper bush in the shadow of gently waving willow. Dark-blushed cherry trees, a grove of sugar cane. It was pretty enough. Why then was there a knot of discontent inside me? Had I come so far, through snow and ice, under shadow of death for this? Peaceful and charming, and just a little bit ordinary?

Apart from the crystal peaks rising behind the meadows, ringing it in a protective barrier of ice, I could have found a dozen villages near my Oxford home a little like this. Some of the windows in the houses were cracked, the stonework irregular, even shabby.

Shabby? Could Paradise really be shabby?

'This is truly Shambala?'

Disappointment must have shown in my voice for the lady answered with a smile.

'It is what you see.' Still smiling, she asked in that same beautiful voice. 'You have something for me?'

'I don't know what you mean.'

'It is there,' she pointed at my heart. 'Our map.'

Rage bubbled up inside me. Yongden had stolen it, now this lady. But it was my talisman. My map was melded to me, had become as much a part of Kit as the scar on my face, my irregular breath and my heart which insisted on beating with such agitation.

'It's my map.'

'No, Kit, it belongs here.'

'No. It's mine.'

'Please.'

It was agonising, but her outstretched hand was a force I couldn't resist. She had taken over my own muscles, bent my will to hers, as I delved into my pocket and felt the rolled-up piece of parchment. Slowly I took it out and handed it unwillingly to the lady. 'What is your name?'

'Maya,' she answered.

'Maya,' I rolled the unfamiliar syllables around on my tongue. 'Can I have my map back, Maya?'

She shook her head. 'No. This map should have never left this place.'

'But it's useless to *you*. Just a piece of paper.' A wheedling note entered my voice. 'I never found Abominable Cave or Javelin Rock. Or *anything* on it.'

'Sometimes we do not know what we have found.'

'Pardon?'

'Look at it this way. This map brought you here. This is somewhere that doesn't want to be found.'

Everything she said was a riddle. 'What do you mean the map brought me here? Yongden brought me here.'

'The map showed him the way.'

'And this place is secret?'

'We are content not to be known.' Maya leant down and offered me her hand to stand up and I noticed that she was wearing simple cotton robes of a dark orange colour.

'Come.' She moved away, light-footed, robes swishing. I stared after her and I must confess I didn't understand. Why was I here? What made this place so special?

'Why must I follow you?' I called out.

She turned and flicked me a glance. I couldn't tell whether it was impatience or amusement in her eyes: 'Your friends are waiting for you.'

'Rachel and Waldo and Isaac!' I forgot the anger at Maya, which had been building up in me. So Yongden must have been wrong. My friends hadn't turned back for India. Joy surged through me, as I ran after her.

❧ Chapter Twenty-nine ❧

Maya led me through the village and we plunged into a screen of trees. They whispered all around us, cutting out the light, their tentacles trailing feather-light over our cheeks. Leaf mould underfoot, the wind soughing up above. I felt drawn into a place of secrets. These ancient cypress, spruce and cherry were not wood, sap and leaf, but spirits watching us. The branches parted and we were in a grassy glade. Gnarled and wily, the trees bent over the clearing, ancient prophets protecting something precious. Wild flowers exploded under their guardianship: orchids glimmering like ice crystals, blue poppies, pansies of velvety hue, oleander and lotus. Through the flowers moved indistinct shapes – butterflies on the flit, bees thrumming, dragonflies drunk on nectar. A fountain was welling up under the shadow of the largest spruce, its plashing a tinkling glissando.

'Perfect!' I sighed.

I breathed in the scents of the glade – blackberry,

chocolate, vanilla, rose and jasmine. Such a sweet smell. With every exhalation my worldly concerns flew away, dissolving in the sugar-laden air. This, finally, was an earthly paradise.

We moved deeper into the clearing and I saw figures clustered around the fountain, clothed in unearthly brilliance. They bathed in the light of the fountain, which played about them like trembling moonbeams.

I was confused, yet at the same time free. This *was* real, I was awake. But part of me wondered, was I in some way in paradise? I didn't walk so much as float over to my friends. I felt fuzzy and light-hearted.

Abruptly my feeling of enchantment was shattered. I halted, in horror.

'NO!' I howled.

'They arrived here just before you,' Maya murmured.

'These aren't my friends!'

'They are the other map-bearers.'

It wasn't Rachel, Isaac and Waldo splashing in the spring. It was the Baker Brothers. They no longer looked like ghosts. Lust fleshed them out, filling their eyes and faces with desperate longing. They scrambled to catch the water, hair and skin damp with sweat. Greed contorted their features. Lying at their feet was a heap of empty bottles. Each brother was holding another bottle into the gushing flow, disregarding the spume that flecked their white linen suits.

One of the Brothers was horribly disfigured, his skin pocked with suppurating craters that had dried out into a porridge of sores. Something had been leeching him of his blood. He was a foul, besmirched creature. A thing set apart from the rest of humanity. I recalled the rumours that he had been cursed by the spirit of Ptah Hotep. The Mummy Bite was upon him.

Chittering above the terrible Brothers was the monkey. Its yellow teeth were bared, as it stood on the arms of the pockmarked brother, holding a bottle in the very centre of the fountain. The monkey was possessed by an intense frenzy. Every fibre of its being was concentrated on the sparkling waters.

I was so close I could have reached out and touched them. I might have been a phantom, for all the notice they took of me. I didn't understand what this scene meant. Yet I knew one thing. My aunt was wrong. This – not gold – was what the Baker Brothers had been searching for.

'What are they doing?' I asked Maya, watching the threesome's naked scramble.

'Reaching for the impossible.'

'The fountain?'

'The dancing waters do not want to be captured.'

The water was indeed dancing. It was jigging, effervescing, a joyous shower of droplets, singing of life and freedom. It did not want to be trapped. Though the gurning figures were spattered in their attempts to capture the liquid, only a few drops were falling into their containers. There was something very odd about the bottles at their feet. Was it my imagination that the sparkling dew inside was escaping, flying its glass prison?

'These waters have been dreamt of through the ages by people the world over. You may know some of the names: Elixir . . . Nectar . . . Amrita . . . Manasrovar.'

'The Fountain of Life,' I breathed.

Maya's beautiful voice shushed in my ears. 'Drink of the waters and you will live for ever.'

'Live for ever?' I echoed, wonder flooding me.

'You can drink, Kit.'

The monkey moved off the brother's shoulder, swinging its bottle in triumph. Inside a few drops of water sparkled. Its eyes fell on me. Anger flared in their dull, yellow depths. It yowled, but it was too intent to be diverted. After an instant it ignored me and resumed its work, greedily trying to steal every drop of the precious waters.

'I don't know.' I stood by Maya irresolute. Half of my blood was straining towards those waters, the other half could not move. My scar began to throb and a voice whispered seductively in my head.

'*Drink, Kit, drink.*'

Maya was smiling at me.

'*You too could live for ever,*' my tempter voice murmured.

If I drank, I would become faster, stronger, better. My scar would heal. I would have no ugly wound to mark me out.

'*Drink, Scarface, drink. What are you waiting for? Scared?*' The voice was cold and high-pitched. The conviction came to me that, somehow, that monkey was inside my head.

'I will tell you a story,' Maya murmured, and her voice too seemed to be in my head, not my ears. It drowned out the other, screeching call. 'Once upon a time, many years ago, there was a Jesuit priest who travelled to the court of a great emperor. He met fakirs and sages and heard of many wonders.'

A silver butterfly, hovered, settled on my arm. I listened to Maya, not moving a muscle.

'Father Monserrate had a servant called Jorge. A man both handsome and clever. He was far more adventurous than his master and when he looked at others, he brimmed with the knowledge that he was better. Jorge knew he was *special*. A desire to become even more special possessed him. If he gained spiritual powers, he thought, he would be better than all others.

'This servant did his chores, burning with the knowledge of his specialness. He watched his dull master and marvelled that he didn't seize wisdom and power. When the chance came he snatched it. He fled his master and came to this place, for a great sorcerer had given him the map you held. Here he found part of what he sought. But he was in grave danger.

'Jorge wasn't ready.'

'We told him he wasn't ready. Be careful, we advised, some blessings are curses in disguise. The man was proud and greedy. He wouldn't listen. He only wanted to take, take and take more.'

'He drank of the fountain and then he left this place. And the water's blessing of immortality became a curse. You see, it doesn't work, not away from this place. He lived all over the world, through many centuries, but his flesh shrivelled. For years he wandered, an outcast. He couldn't find his way back to these mountains. He had lost the map, which was locked away in Baroda's treasure vaults. Recently, when he discovered the whereabouts of the map, Jorge plotted. He found these brothers; they were kindred spirits, for they too were cursed things. Together the Bakers and Jorge found the poor man who had once been a maharajah. Oh, how they schemed. They used himd and then killed him. Now Jorge stands before you a benighted thing.'

'Thing?' I said, slowly, still not comprehending. 'Which thing?'

Maya's eyes moved to the monkey.

'That would make it nearly three hundred years old,' I gasped.

Monkey-Jorge's face glistened with fountain dew. It was an outlandish tale. I looked at the creatre marvelling, not really believing. But slowly I began to see something human beneath its white fur. The shape of the nose. Those clever yellow eyes. Its devouring greed. Could any other animal beside a human *want* so terribly?

'Have you heard of Tithon?' Maya murmured.

Tithon. The name rang the faintest of bells. The Greek mortal who had asked for eternal life, but forgot to ask for eternal youth. When his wishes were granted he was condemned to torment, an infinity of endless babbling old age.

'Be careful what you wish for.'

A refrain started in my head. I don't know if it was Maya or the trees whispering, or even my own conscience. The screeching voice was back too: *'She only told you that monkey story to scare you,'* it said. *'She doesn't want you to have it. She wants to keep it for herself.'*

I looked at the Guardian for a moment, full in the face.

'Do *you* drink from these waters?'

She didn't answer the question.

'How old are you, Maya?'

Her body rippled, as if she was laughing inside. 'A hundred? Two hundred? Does it matter?'

She hadn't answered any of my questions. But I realised then, that she didn't need to. Despite the screeching voice in my head, I knew Maya was different. She wasn't like me or you. She truly was special. But I wasn't. I was just me. And you know what? I didn't care. I didn't want, at that moment, to be better, richer, cleverer, or to live for ever. I didn't even want to heal my burning scar. A momentary heat, a flash, flamed inside me. My head felt as if it was cracking open, something heavy floating away leaving only wonder and light behind. Then, finally, I understood.

Some blessings are curses in disguise.

One of the Baker Brothers turned and saw me. A pitted face and a mouth puckered in a sneer.

'You!'

The butterfly took fright and fluttered off.

'Have some. Plenty for all.'

I shook my head.

'Might help you get rid of that scar. You'll never be pretty, granted. But a mark like that'd put anyone off. Never get a husband looking like a navvy, will you?'

'I don't want the water,' I replied steadily. 'It's not for me.'

'How very quaint.' The pockmarked Brother gave a

disagreeable smile. 'And why is that?'

I struggled for the words. 'It won't work,' I said simply. 'It's against nature.'

The Brothers sneered.

'Who taught you such an idea? Your hopeless father? Your idiot aunt?'

'Poor child,' muttered the other Brother, as the monkey/Jorge gibbered on his shoulder. 'Such dull wits.'

'There will come a day, not so very far off, when you look back on these waters and you will weep over your mistake.'

'Never.'

The Baker Brother turned and spat. It was such a twisted gesture; so wrong in this beautiful place.

'It's the tragedy of youth,' he said. 'They have it all in their hands but they don't know how to use it.'

'We will not make that mistake,' said the other. 'Not this time.'

'When we see something we want, we take.'

Maya was watching our exchange, not showing by the merest flicker what she thought. Barefoot, in her orange robes, she was still as a tree. There was something about her that seemed to melt into the forest, to disappear into gnarled wood and leave us to our battle.

'In this place, I think, they believe you have to give

things up,' I said. 'Not cling on to wealth. That's what wisdom means. A kind of letting go.'

The pockmarked Brother sniggered.

'Out of the mouths of babes,' he said. 'Such pocket-book morality.'

The monkey was trying to fill its bottle. The frustration of trying to capture the dancing waters was driving the monkey – or I suppose I should call it Jorge – to lunacy. It held the bottle up to the sun, where it glinted with a thousand rainbow sparks. Empty of all but air. Jorge hurled it away. In a fit of rage, it leapt off the Brother's shoulder and waded into the spring. Its pink tongue arced, long as an adder. Greedily it began to lap at the water. It caught a drop on its curling tongue and the Brothers forgot me and turned to watch.

I was aware of the singing of the brook, the wind in the leaves, the humming of bees, and above it all a horrible, greedy gurgling and belching as the monkey's tongue lashed this way and that, desperately trying to catch the dancing waters. Time hung suspended as we all waited.

The creature before us, this gibbering *thing*, had once been a man. Born three hundred years ago, what times he must have lived through. I gazed at its wizened little face, the yellowish skin surmounted by a ruff of white hair and yes, I could see something human. The forward thrust of the jaw, the mouth. You could call those things that chittered above decaying teeth *lips*. Above all, its flaring yellow eyes, they were so canny, so clever. From the very first glimpse, they had chilled me.

Now, to my amazement, this thing was transforming from ape to man. The fur was beginning to recede from its face, its eyes to broaden and lengthen, its mouth to become a little fuller. Something human – almost handsome – was under that simian mask.

The monkey stopped and looked down at its hand. It was shedding its fur, patches of pale skin visible. A smile of vengeful glee lit up the creature's face and it threw back its head. Out of its mouth came the most chilling sound, half howl and half exclamation of pure, human joy.

'I've won,' the creature cawed. At least I think that was what it said, for it was not yet fully human.

The Baker Brothers took that as a signal. They too stepped into the waters and began to lap, as hungrily as beasts. It wasn't easy, for the dancing waters did not want to be trapped. They skittered and glinted, fleeing from their reptilian tongues. It was a truly awful sight, the naked hunger in the Brothers' eyes. It was too much for me. However evil these men, I could not stand by and watch them condemn themselves to an eternal torment.

'NO!' I shouted, stepping forward and taking one of

311

the Brothers by the shoulder. 'Don't.'

He ignored me and sticking his head deeper into the spring, guzzled. Water dripped out of his mouth and down his chin. The Brothers took no notice at all of the trees watching them. Of the indrawn breath, of the disapproving stillness, which I heard as plainly as the loudest roars. They were immune. They had what they wanted. Aunt Hilda had been wrong. There was something these men wanted even more than gold. *Immortality*. Now, they'd achieved their hearts' desire.

The skin was tautening on the cursed Baker's face, the pocks disappearing. For a moment I felt a pang, I too could be remade in a better image. My scar healed. I could be a new and pleasing Kit; all smiles and soft edges, without those quirks that made Waldo tease me. But it was an impulse that quickly vanished as I watched the grasping folly before me.

Baker gazed upon Baker. They looked at each other and saw what I did.

Two pale young men. Clothed in new flesh, the shining glory of their prime. It was as if someone had taken a knife, cut the loose skin off their faces, and then pulled it taut. Pockmarks, pimples, rough skin, imperfection of all sorts, had been flamed away. They had been pulled, stretched and reshaped into Greek gods.

The Brothers didn't smile, just looked upon each

other with a terrible, greedy intent. And the monkey, too, was fully transformed. He prowled the glade, a handsome olive-skinned man, with strong black brows and an arrogant nose.

'Come,' Maya said. 'It is time to go home.'

She melted into the trees; I followed her as if pulled by a magnet.

Before I went I could not resist turning to deliver a last, parting shot.

'It won't last,' I called to the men in the glade. 'When you leave it will turn to dust.'

I had a vision of panicked eyes.

'Piffle!' a Brother called. 'We will drink to your health in London.'

'Have no fear,' the other sneered, his plump top lip curling. 'We intend to cure you once and for all of your childish fancies.'

Their threats, meant to gash, to terrify, glanced off me. Did they not realise the waters only worked while they remained here in Shambala? For such worldly men they faced a terrible choice: to remain in this simple paradise, bereft of silks and cognac. Or to return to their luxurious world and watch, second by second, their phantom youth melt away. I followed Maya into the murmuring trees. Their branches folded about me, shutting off the noise made by Jorge and the Brothers. It felt good, here in the forest. As tendrils of leaf and vine crept into my vision, soothing me with their antique wisdom, I felt sure I had made the right choice.

I would never look back and regret what might have been. Far better to be Kit Salter, with all her flaws, than a creature whose beauty was a fleeting mask and whose very soul was condemned.

❧ Epilogue ❧

We had travelled so far and we came back empty-handed. We had found no gold, or precious relics, as Aunt Hilda so desperately wanted. Even the diamond-studded turban that the Maharajah had given Waldo had been lost in the cruel mountains. Only my father still had Father Monserrate's manuscript, precious to him, if worth little to the rest of the world. By any normal reckoning our voyage to India had been a failure. Worse than a failure, a tragedy, if you reflect on Monsieur Champlon. Poor Gaston. The proud, brave Frenchman had saved Aunt Hilda from the avalanche, only to pay with his own life. For a while we had hoped that by some miracle he would be found. Alas, thus far, we had no word at all of his fate.

And yet.

I could not call our journey to India, and my dream-like voyage to Shambala itself, a total failure. I felt I had learnt so much. Maddeningly, it is hard for me to put into words exactly what. I had been touched by the generosity of the people I met. Come through pain and fear. Most of all, in the mountains, I had learnt that sometimes to let go is as important as to take. That to not want may be better than wanting too much. Achieving your heart's desire may just show how empty your desire was.

My journey out of Shambala was even mistier in my mind than my journey into that fabled land. The Guardians had spirited me out, through the passage in the mountains, through the ice and snow, to be reunited with Aunt Hilda and the others, just inside the Indian border. I thought that days, if not weeks must have passed, but it seems my sojourn in the mountains had taken a matter of hours. Afterwards I would have thought it all a dream, except for one thing, a swirl of vivid orange cotton which I had torn from Maya's dress as we said goodbye.

I have the cloth still. I keep it in a carved Indian sandalwood box by my bedside. It is the only remembrance I have of Shambala.

As for the Bakers, the Maharajah and the abominable monkey man, Jorge, well, for many weeks we had no news. Then, Aunt Hilda was invited to a party, graced by Florence Nightingale and the Prince of Wales. The reclusive Baker Brothers were there, in the Prince's party. Aunt Hilda was stunned by the change in them. Their skin was youthful. Their ghostly aura replaced by blooming health. They were almost handsome, my aunt reported. She overheard the Prince joking about how they had been 'taking the miracle cure at Baden Baden'. The rumours of the men cursed by 'mummy bite' were triumphantly dispelled. But a clumsy waiter had spilt a little wine on one of the Brothers glove and Aunt Hilda caught a glimpse of the hand underneath.

What she saw truly appalled her. It was not a hand but a claw. Wrinkled, wizened the thing resembled a monkey's paw more than anything human.

Truly, their blessing will come to haunt them.

Aunt Hilda was devastated by the loss of Champlon. She is not one, however, to wallow in grief. Nor is she one to acknowledge failure. A few weeks after we returned to Oxford, on a particularly wet and windy afternoon, Aunt Hilda bustled into our parlour. She had, she announced, some stupendous news. The Royal Geographic Society was to award her a medal! In the following edition of their journal she was to publish an article about how she, Hilda Salter, had become the first ever explorer to penetrate into Tibet's forbidden land. Proudly, she showed us a copy of the article. The headline read:

Indomitable Explorer on the Roof of the World
Hilda Salter Reveals Secrets of the Land of the Yeti

This was picked up by *The Times*, and the *Morning Post*, both of which printed articles about her – so at least my aunt had found the one thing that mattered even more to her than gold in the Himalayas – fame! In sotto voce, Aunt Hilda confided to us that she expected a summons any day from the Queen. Yes, that is right, an audience with Queen Victoria herself!

As for my father, you will be pleased to hear he recovered from Delhi Belly and vowed never to travel again. I take it as seriously as all his promises. Which is to say, not seriously at all, for he will surely forget his pledge as soon as the words have left his mouth.

Poor Waldo, with the loss of his finger, was the one who suffered most. For many weeks it seemed he would never shoot again and sad to say, his handwriting deteriorated appallingly. Then one day Isaac appeared sporting a big grin and the most amazing news. He had made Waldo an artificial finger. My friend tried it on and it soon began to feel just like a real one. If anything, I believe it has improved his (always erratic) shooting.

I will leave you with that piece of happy news and the even happier outcome that Miss Minchin remained in Baroda, ensconced in luxury in the Maharajah's palace. I expect wedding bells any day now.

COMING IN SEPTEMBER 2010
THE NEXT KIT SALTER ADVENTURE

The Book of Bones

TURN THE PAGE FOR A SNEAK PREVIEW

❧ The Book of Bones ❧

It was a cheerless day to travel, the wind howling off Dartmoor, buffeting the coach that was taking us back to Oxford. A storm was blowing up: a few fat droplets began to splatter against the windows. The track leading off the moor past the small country villages was rough, full of potholes that jerked us about till our bones ached. I pitied Hodges, our genial coach driver, sitting on his perch high above the horses. He was exposed to the full fury of the elements. Even more, though, did I pity the four poor beasts. Already they were lathered in white froth.

Mrs Glee had decided we would travel from Merriford House back to Oxford by coach, even though the train was so much more convenient. I had tried to argue, but she had made up her mind. I suspected, frail as she was, she was frightened of train travel. Huddled between Rachel and Isaac, I recalled the old legends that told of great beasts that roamed the moor; of highwaymen who preyed on unguarded travellers. I shivered a little, thinking of these things, but I got no sympathy from my friends. Indeed the atmosphere inside the coach was as thick as a pea-souper fog. I could have choked on the dark looks, misunderstandings and ill-humour wafting around. Both Waldo and Rachel were furious with your friend, Kit Salter, and had declared they would never speak to me again. Rachel had been especially hurtful:

'You know what your problem is, Kit?' she had spat. 'Apart from being downright domineering, of course. Jealousy. Don't look so surprised. J.E.A.L.O.U.S.Y. You don't like your friends having other friends. You want to be number one, the whole time.'

The silence in the coach left me plenty of time to reflect on Rachel's words. Uncomfortably, I had to admit that there might be some small element of truth in what she was saying. But minuscule. Really very small. Truly!

As neither Waldo nor Rachel were talking to me, and Isaac was lost in his own (possibly explosive) thoughts, I turned to Mrs Glee, who was crocheting a hideous pink bonnet.

'Merriford House was lovely,' I said. 'So gloomy. I loved the way the wind from the moors blew past the towers.'

'Wasn't it lovely,' she agreed. 'I'm so happy for Miss

Minchin. Marrying a baronet's son. Usually fortune does not smile upon poor governesses.'

There was a wistful look in her grey-green eyes as she said this. I wanted to take her hand and squeeze it, to give her a little of my own courage. Life, I guessed had not been kind to Mrs Glee. You could see her disappointments in the lines on her face and the anxiety with which she greeted everything. She did try, poor thing, but she just wasn't strong enough for this world.

I had never found out about her late husband, Mr Glee. I was tempted to try a little probing.

'Is it lonely now?' I asked, gently. 'Do you miss Mr Glee very much?'

To my surprise she went rigid and arched back in her seat.

'Why?'

'Sorry?'

'Why do you ask?' Her eyes searched mine.

'I just wondered. I thought – well, I thought you must miss him sorely.'

Mrs Glee was biting her lip, 'He was a brute, Kitty, a brute.'

I didn't know what to say. She sounded so fierce.

'I'm sorry,' I murmured, lamely.

'Not a day goes by, not single day, in which I don't give thanks that I am rid of him.'

There was silence after this. The six horses pulling our coach laboured in front of us. All that could be heard was their panting and snorting and the fierce whoosh of the wind outside. I was wearing a thick navy travelling cloak above my serge dress, but I was still chilled inside and out. There were so many mysteries about our new governess. She was an angry person, I'd discovered. At the same time, everything seemed to make her fearful. Why had Mrs Glee turned down the quick and modern train? Dark shapes loomed against the sinister murk of the moor: wind-blasted trees, the occasional wretched cottage. Howling beasts and our poor horses, dodging potholes in the dusk.

Just as I was marvelling thus, the coach stopped with a jolt. Rachel was thrown against Waldo and screeched. Isaac's glasses fell off as the horses began to neigh – a high terrifying sound. Odd noises were louder in the silence of the moor: the driver Hodges shouting, the crack of a whip and then booming voices intermingling with scuffling. I peered through the window but could see only dark shapes through the smudgy glass pane.

'What's up?' I yelped, leaping into action. 'Hodges?'

'Stand back,' Waldo pushed me down.

'Highwaymen!' Isaac yelled.

'It's nothing, you booby,' Waldo snapped. 'Probably just some drunk on the track.'

Mrs Glee was the only one not caught up in the commotion. She had retreated from everything into her crocheting, ignoring the horses frenzied neighing and the lurching of the coach. Waldo was struggling now with the door handle, but quite unable to open it.

'Let me have a go.' I said. 'You have to twist it to the right.'

Sighing Mrs Glee put down her crochet, 'It won't do any good.'

'What?' We stopped and stared at her.

'I'm sorry children. The door is locked.'

Both Waldo and I were frantically tugging at the door, as it was certain now that there was something more than an ale-sodden villager out there. A sharp crack outside brought us to a stop. A second bang filled the air, followed by a moment's deep silence.

Gun shots.

'I locked the carriage door for your own safety, Kit and Waldo. I really don't want you to get hurt,' Mrs Glee murmured.

'Open it at once, you fool,' I exploded, not caring about her feelings. 'There's a highwayman out there.'

'I'm so, so sorry about this.'

'She's raving, Waldo. Smash the window pane.'

Waldo had already taken off his shoe and was thwacking hard at the glass with the wooden heel. Once. No effect. Twice the glass still held.

'Hurry,' I yelled. I couldn't bear the neighing of the horses. 'I'll smash it.'

Waldo shoved me away and thwacked with all his might. A thin crack split the pane and at the fourth blow it shattered. Waldo was about to put his head through the jagged hole when something appeared at the window. A face. It was of perfect plump roundness, framed by a fringe of red-blonde hair at top and bottom. At first glance it was friendly. But there was malice in the piggy eyes and something nasty in the way the glistening, rosebud lips were pouting.

''Allo Vera,' the man said.

Mrs Glee put her crochet on her lap and looked at the man, 'So its you.'

'Not a very friendly greeting.'

'Bert – they're just children.'

'Always liked nippers,' Bert leered. 'You know me.'

'Go easy.' Mrs Glee's hands, those wrinkled hands holding the crochet, were trembling. Her face, though, was calm.

'Orders is orders,' Bert shrugged. 'No loose ends.'

The rest of us watched this strange conversation in bewilderment, for things were happening too fast. Rachel screeched suddenly and Mrs Glee frowned.

'Quiet, please,' she said. 'For your own good, be quiet.'

'But what's happening?' Rachel gasped, 'Who are you?'

'It doesn't matter. I'm nobody.'

'Mrs Glee?!'

'I beg you to listen to Bert. It will be better for all of us, if you do.'

I had never been so bewildered in my life. Mrs Glee was clearly frightened, I could see that. But other things were wrong. She knew this thug, Bert. They were trying to kidnap us. Emily had been right. Our new governess was not who she pretended to be. There was something twisted out of shape about Mrs Glee. Never mind that now, I had to act.

'I'm sorry too,' I said, bunching my hand into a fist.

I thwacked Mrs Glee with all my might, leaving a mark on her face. At the same time Waldo seized a splinter of glass and held it to her throat.

'Call off your man,' I snapped pinioning her arms, 'or Waldo will cut your throat.'

Mrs Glee was trembling uncontrollably. 'Stop it, stop it! Please. Someone will get hurt.'

Flicking my eyes, I saw that Bert held a pistol, inches from Rachel's head. We were outflanked.

'Put the glass down Waldo,' I hissed.

'No,' Waldo barked, his hand quivering at Mrs Glee's plump throat.

'He has a gun,' I said quietly.

Waldo turned and saw Bert's derringer. In a flash it was all over. Mrs Glee stood up and handed something through the window to Bert. He took the key and unlocked the carriage door and was inside, bringing a rank stench of sweat, grease and gin with him.

'Room for one more,' he grunted, as he heaved his lumbering body into the carriage. Squashed up as we were, we had no choice. The villain sat massive on the bench. The gun lay limply in a fat paw. I saw Waldo eyeing it, but signalled him no. It wasn't worth taking a chance now, for this was a desperate game.

'The driver?' Mrs Glee asked the thug.

'Out.'

'We bringing him along?'

'Don't you worry your pretty little head about that. Your game's done.'

'Bert!'

'Shut up.' Bert closed his eyes. I could see him looking at us through his sandy lashes.

Were they talking about our coach driver, Hodges? The gentlest of men, with horses, or indeed anything on four legs. Was he even now struggling bound, in a ditch, bleeding? Or worse, surely they wouldn't have murdered him?

'You better not have hurt him,' I burst out. 'My father

will kill you if you've harmed Hodges.'

Abruptly, the carriage rumbled off, jerkily and swaying side to side. The horses whimpered and neighed accompanied by the brutal crack of the whip.

'What is this?' Waldo spat, his eyes red in a furious white face. 'Who are you? What are you doing with us?'

'Questions, questions, questions,' Bert smiled, while Mrs Glee sat whey-faced.

'If you've hoping for a ransom, forget it. Our parents aren't rich.'

Bert grinned as though this was a huge joke. 'I've had enough of you,' he murmured. 'Any of you pesky brats opens your mouf again, I'll cuff you.' In his hammy hands, a set of handcuffs had appeared, along with the pistol.

My gaze flickered over the faces of my friends, shadowy in the dark interior of the coach. Rachel, sucking her lower lip in agitation. Isaac, pale as chalk. Waldo, eyes glittering with fury. We had to wait, watch, be patient and when it came, seize our chance.

Bert seemed to read my mind. He turned to me, his eyeballs barely visible between two rolls of fat. Plump lips opened and a blob of spittle just missed my feet. Shuddering, I sank back in my seat and felt Waldo's hand gripping my arm. Stay strong, he seemed to be signalling. If we held our nerve, surely our chance to escape would come?